Rise of the Red Wolf

Book 2

The Cimbrian War

JEFF HEIN

RED WOLF BOOKS

Rise of the Red Wolf

Copyright © 2023 by Jeff Hein

Published by Red Wolf Books

Book 2 of the The Cimbrian War

Paperback ISBN: 978 -1-7375539-6-0

eBook ISBN: 978 -1-7375539-5-3

Hardback ISBN: 978-1-7375539-7-7

This book is a work of fiction. The names, characters, and incidents portrayed in it, while based on historical events and people, are the work of the author's imagination.

Cover design by Dusan Arsenic

Torque image by The Crafty Celts Available at: https://www.craftycelts.com

Formatting by 341 Enterprise

Rise of the Red Wolf

JEFF HEIN

Table of Contents

Germans and Celts
(* Fictional Characters)

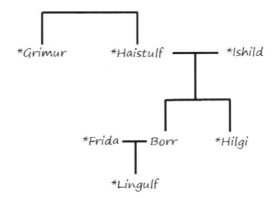

Claudicus — Hunno of the Boar Clan
Caesorix — Hunno of the Raven Clan
Lugius — Hunno of the Bear Clan
*Freki — Borr's Adopted brother
*Hrolf — Borr's friend
*Ansgar — Borr's Companion
*Gorm — Blacksmith
*Glum — Brewmaster/Frida's father
*Eldric — High priest
*Skyld — High priestess
Teutobod — Chieftain of the Teutones
*Amalric — Chieftain of the Ambrones

Marius and Caesar

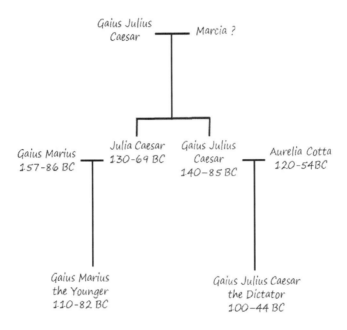

Gaius Julius Caesar ─── Marcia ?

Gaius Marius
157-86 BC

Julia Caesar
130-69 BC

Gaius Julius Caesar
140–85 BC ─── Aurelia Cotta
120-54BC

Gaius Marius
the Younger
110-82 BC

Gaius Julius Caesar
the Dictator
100–44 BC

Served under Scipio in Numantia
(* Fictional Characters)

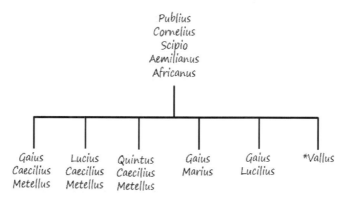

Publius Cornelius Scipio Aemilianus Africanus

- Gaius Caecilius Metellus
- Lucius Caecilius Metellus
- Quintus Caecilius Metellus
- Gaius Marius
- Gaius Lucilius
- *Vallus

HISTORICAL CHARACTERS

ROMANS

GAIUS MARIUS – (157 – 86 BC) Marius began his military career under Scipio Aemilianus at the Siege of Numantia. In 110 BC he married Julia Caesar, future aunt to Julius Caesar the dictator. Marius distinguished himself in 109 BC at the Battle of Muthul in the Jugurthine War. He is on a path that will eventually bring him into direct conflict with the Cimbri.

GAIUS LUCILIUS – (180 – 103 BC) Lucilius was the earliest known Roman satirist. He was a member of the equestrian class and served under Scipio Aemilianus at the siege of Numantia in 134 BC. He likely came into contact with Gaius Marius, Jugurtha, and other notable veterans of that war.

PUBLIUS RUTILIUS RUFUS – (158 – after 78 BC) A great-uncle of Julius Caesar the dictator. In 134 BC he served as a staff officer for Scipio Aemilianus during the Numantine War. In 109 BC he fought under Quintus Caecilius Metellus in the campaign against Jugurtha where he distinguished himself at the Battle of Muthul.

MARCUS JUNIUS SILANUS – The first of his family to be elected consul in 109 BC. He was assigned the Cimbri campaign when they reappeared in Gaul and was defeated at an unknown location in Gallia Narbonensis. In 104 BC he was put on trial for his defeat and was acquitted.

LUCIUS CASSIUS LONGINUS – (151 – 107 BC) As praetor in 111 BC he was sent to Numidia to escort Jugurtha to Rome to testify in corruption trials. Elected as senior consul in 107 BC with Gaius Marius as junior and while Marius would go to Africa to fight Jugurtha, Longinus would go north to confront the Cimbri and their allies.

QUINTUS SERVILIUS CAEPIO – As consul in 106 BC he campaigned against the Cimbrian allies in Gaul and captured the city of Tolosa, where he found the fabled treasure from the temple of Delphi, stolen during the Celtic invasion of the Balkans in 279 BC. In 105

BC, as pro-consul, Caepio was sent to combine his army with that of that year's consul Gnaeus Mallius Maximus and confront the northern tribes.

GNAEUS MALLIUS MAXIMUS – Elected to the consulship in 105 BC and sent to Transalpine Gaul to stop the Cimbri and their allies. The proconsul in the field, Quintus Servilius Caepio refused to cooperate with him due to his status as a Novus Homo, or New Man. The two armies remained on opposite sides of the Rhone River and the generals refused to speak to each other leaving them vulnerable to the overwhelming numbers of the northern alliance of tribes.

MARCUS AEMILIUS SCAURUS – (159 – 89 BC) Consul in 115 BC and then princeps senatus until his death. Considered one of the most influential politicians in the late Republic and was involved in many negotiations and delegations on behalf of the senate.

QUINTUS CAECILIUS METELLUS – Another veteran of the Numantine War, he was acquainted with many of the others who served under Scipio. As consul in 109 and 108 BC he commanded the Roman armies in Africa during the Jugurthine War. In 107 BC he turned the war over to Gaius Marius, his bitter rival.

GAIUS JULIUS CAESAR – In Rise of the Red Wolf, this Caesar is the grandfather of the Gaius Julius Caesar who became dictator of Rome, and was murdered on the Ides of March, 44 BC. Gaius Marius married this Caesar's daughter Julia, making him an uncle of the dictator. Roman naming conventions of the time meant that the entire line of males in a family often had the exact same name, confusing later historians to no end.

GAIUS MEMMIUS – Tribune of the plebs in 111 BC. His fiery speeches about ending the Jugurthine war once and for all relaunched Rome's efforts. He later accused several consuls and senators of accepting bribes from Jugurtha and attempted to bring them to trial for corruption, but he was prevented from questioning his witnesses when several senators, bribed by Jugurtha, thwarted his plans and vetoed his legislation.

LUCIUS CALPURNIUS BESTIA – Consul in 111 BC, Bestia was appointed to command the war against Jugurtha. He was energetic at first, but like so many others succumbed to Jugurtha's overtures and bribes, and returned home with a disgraceful peace in Numidia, having achieved nothing as Jugurtha continued his war against his brother Adherbal. Bestia was later brought to trial and condemned for his conduct.

SPURIUS POSTUMIUS ALBINUS – Consul in 110 BC he was sent to Africa to renew the war against Jugurtha. His effort was ineffectual, and he allowed himself to be deceived by Jugurtha's promises to surrender. Many thought that his poor performance was intentional and that Jugurtha had once again bribed his way free of a war with Rome. When the consul Spurius left Africa to attend to Rome's elections for 109 BC, he left his brother Aulus in command of the legions. Aulus quickly tried to apply pressure to Jugurtha but that resulted only in a humiliating loss, and when Spurius returned he could only bide his time until he could turn over the legions to the arriving Quintus Caecilius Metellus in the poor condition they were in.

GERMANS AND CELTS

BORR (BOIORIX) – History records the leader of the Cimbri only in 105 BC when Boiorix defeated the Romans in one of the largest defeats of their history, with a loss of more than 80,000. Nothing else is known of his origins or of him as a person. In The Cimbrian War series, his background is totally invented by the author. The story of his youth begins as a teenage boy around the time they were believed to have migrated southward from Jutland (Denmark). Boiorix translates to king of the Boii, which never made much sense to me, as the Cimbri were no friend of the Boii. He would not have been born with the title of king, so, to develope the story, I invented a name. Borr is the name of the father of Wodan the Allfather, and Borr's father Haisutlf named him for the creator god Borr. (See glossary) Borr will grow from a boy, to chieftain of the Cimbri, Borrix. (The suffix rix meant tribal leader or chieftain and is similar to the latin word for king, rex). As was common at that time his name was transformed by the Romans to suit their understanding of their world, Borrix was changed to Boiorix, the name that has stood for millennia. At least, that's my version of it.

TEUTOBOD – Leader of the Teutones tribe, he and his people left the area of Jutland around the same time as the Cimbri. They are believed to have accompanied the Cimbri throughout their journey, but it is not clear. Historians differ when and where the Teutones appeared. What is known is that they were involved in the major battles and were fated to cross swords with the Roman general Gaius Marius.

CLAUDICUS/CAESORIX/LUGIUS – Recorded as clan leaders of the Cimbri.

DIVICO – King of the Tigurini, a Celtic tribe and member of the Helvetian confederation of tribes, located in what is now southern Germany and Switzerland. He led the Tigurini during the Cimbrian War and invaded Gaul and Narbonensis as an ally of the Cimbri. He famously made the defeated legions march under the yoke after their defeat at the battle of Burdigala in 107 BC. Fifty years later he would lead a delegation to ask Julius Caesar for safe passage for his tribe through Gaul. Caesar used Divico's past defeat of Roman legions as a reason to deny that request.

The remaining characters are fictitious, and their backgrounds are explained within the book.

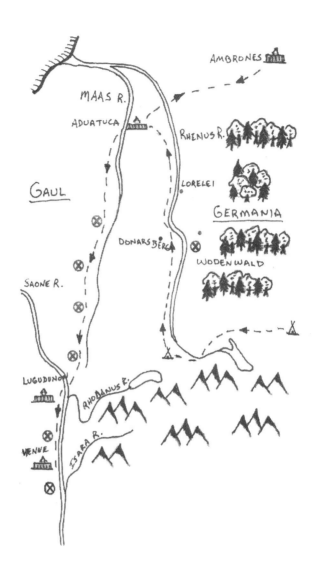

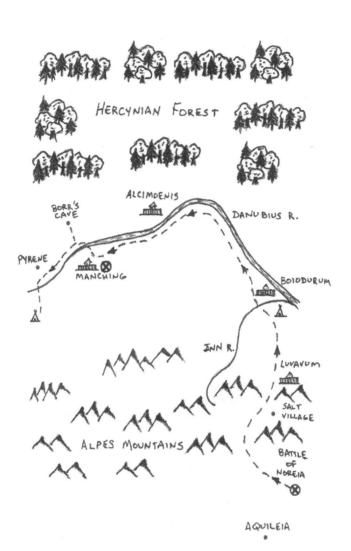

HERCYNIAN FOREST

ALCIMOENIS

BORR'S CAVE

DANUBIUS R.

PYRENE

MANCHING

BOIODURUM

INN R.

LUVAVUM

SALT VILLAGE

ALPES MOUNTAINS

BATTLE OF NOREIA

AQUILEIA

EPIGRAPH

Out of the northern mists, the Cimbri appear;

wagons and oxen, shields and spears.

Cursed by Njoror, to forever roam;

they search for a land, to call their home.

If one summer they rest, in any land;

they shall be punished, by Njoror's hand.

The Red Wolf shall rise, as king he becomes;

and defeat the red soldiers, while the tribes fight as one.

The curse will be lifted, from this great host;

when Lupa welcomes the people of the coast.

PROLOGUE

When word of the disaster at Noreia reached Rome there was great panic across the land. The mountain passes that led to the lush valleys of northern Italy were open and undefended and there were no legions in the north that could stop the invading Cimbri. The Senate recalled all veterans to the army and put together enough for two legions that immediately marched to Aquileia. They were a hodge-podge of ancient swords and shields, bronze and iron helmets of several designs, leather armor and breastplates from armies of as much as thirty years ago, but they came. They were scarred and grey bearded, but to a man they were determined to defend their homeland from the barbarian horde. Those that had been rejected from recruitment last year were called up to defend the city. Most were untrained but they could hold a shield and sword and it helped quell some of the fear to see legionaries manning the gates and walls of Rome.

The Romans did not know that the Cimbri had turned away and trekked north over the Alps, away from the Italian passes. The curse that controlled their lives could only be lifted if they were welcomed by the people of Rome, and that was not going to happen now.

Chapter One

Noricum

July 113 BC

Pillars of smoke billowed toward the heavens as the caravan turned away from the battlefield at Noreia and climbed steadily toward the soaring limestone peaks. A spiraling column of squawking, black birds reached down from the sky to mark where we had defeated the Romans and sacrificed the survivors to Wodan the Allfather in thanks for our victory. The smoldering embers of the wicker effigies were still hot and the smell of burned flesh drifted over the battlefield, mixing with that of the blood, spilled guts, and decaying flesh of the thousands of Roman dead. The ground undulated with thousands of carrion birds feasting, flapping, and hopping around from one delicious morsel to another.

The curse placed upon us by the sea god Njoror required the Romans to welcome us into their land, and their refusal prevented us from descending into the fertile valleys of northern Italy without risking our own destruction. Instead, we returned to the Dravus River valley and continued our quest. The alpine valley rose gradually as we followed the river toward its source and on the morning of the third day, we left the river behind and turned north into the mountains.

A few of the Taurisci tribesmen decided it was better to join us than fight, and they now served as guides under the watchful eyes of my own scouts. The valleys narrowed as we climbed, the steep cliffs on both sides forcing the caravan to stretch out for miles as it trudged slowly upward, ever upward. There were so many people and carts and animals that it was several days before the last of our people that remained at the battlefield began to move. By then, the vanguard was well into the mountain passes.

Freki, my childhood friend and adopted brother, now led my scouts. After passing through the foothills, I began receiving reports of the caravan being watched from the heights. There was no contact, just an occasional glimpse of movement among the rocks, or a brief reflection of sunlight from a spearhead or helmet. The Taurisci warned us of the wild mountain tribes who were fiercely independent, warlike, and trusted no one.

As darkness fell, the narrow trail prevented the caravan from setting up their usual defensive formation. Carts halted wherever they found themselves and oxen were unhitched so they could lie down. People slept on the ground and the cattle bedded down in their herds. There was some forage for the first animals that passed, but the ones that followed laid down hungry, protesting their empty bellies with a constant bellowing.

My horse carefully picked its way along the path in the twilight. Never far from my side, my companions, Hrolf and Ansgar, followed close behind, speaking softly to the people they passed along the way. Ansgar found his family and Hrolf and I returned to my cart where Frida and our three-year-old son Lingulf traveled alongside her father, Glum, the brewmaster.

Glum had started a small fire and when Hrolf and I dismounted he offered us each a horn of ale. We sat on the ground by the fire and Frida handed us dried beef and stale bread.

"How does the trail look ahead, Borr?" Glum asked, the words emerging from a mouth hidden by a bristly dark mustache. Thick dark eyebrows met in the middle and arched upwards to the hair that hung over his brow, leaving the only visible skin on his face around his eyes and nose. Glum was barrel chested, dark, and shorter than most in a tribe of tall men. His face was flat with a wide, squashed nose and slit eyes. Frizzy, wiry hair stuck in every direction from his head and constantly fluttered in the slight mountain breeze, and his thick beard reached to his belt. He was almost always jovial, and the lines beside his eyes suggested how much he loved to laugh. He brewed ale, mead, and wine and it was his passion to create new flavors and colors of the drinks and watch his patrons try to guess what he had added. His wife died when Frida was born and Glum raised her by himself, an incongruous situation as Frida was as beautiful and slight as the elves of legend, and Glum was the image of a mountain dwarf come to life. The only appearance she had inherited from him was the color of his dark chestnut hair, though hers was straight and sleek, and somehow always smelled of flowers.

I pinched off a bit of mold and bit into a particularly hard piece of bread. I chewed silently for a moment, considering the question, and winced when I bit down on a piece of grit left from the grinding stone.

"Steep," I replied with a half grin.

Frida chuckled softly beside me, rocking a sleeping Lingulf on her lap.

"Huh," Glum huffed impatiently. "I meant, are there any dangers to be wary of?"

"No more than usual," I said. "Steep hillsides on one side with rocks balanced precariously above us, precipitous drops on the other that one misplaced step can send you off into an abyss. Nervous, unpredictable animals all around. Nothing to be worried about."

"What about people? Word is passing that we are being watched," Glum persisted.

"I've heard the reports. So far as I know, they are only watching us. I've issued orders for everyone to be alert tonight." I stood and held out my hand to help Frida up. "We'll be moving again at first light," I said. "We have at least five more days to the top."

When we reached our cart, I watched as Frida kneeled and gently placed our son on a bundle of hides, then prepared our own bed on the ground. It was a clear night, and the stars were bright in the heavens. The moon just below the horizon created a glow in the eastern sky as it prepared to rise from behind the mountain peaks.

I walked to the edge of the trail and gazed into the distance, breathing deeply of the crisp, clear air. A pair of arms circled my waist from behind and I turned and slipped my arm over her as she slid around and placed her head on my chest, giving a contented sigh. I stretched my cloak around her shoulders, and we said nothing as we stood in each other's embrace for a time, feeling the warmth of our bodies in the coolness.

Lingulf stirred and Frida glanced back over her shoulder. Assured that nothing was amiss, she tightened her hold and nuzzled deeper into my chest. I rubbed my chin against the top of her head as I used to do when we played with each other, and she giggled and slapped my back lightly.

"I miss you," she whispered.

"I'm right here."

"You know what I mean. I miss us."

I said nothing. I had always struggled to speak of my love for her, even after the years we had spent together and even now that we shared a child. It was as if my heart swelled into my throat and blocked the words. If it were not for her being able to speak for both of us, we would likely never have married. Too late, I realized this was an opening, an opportunity she offered me to speak my thoughts, but I was too blind to see it. The intensity of the love we shared when we were young had cooled since she and Lingulf had been abducted and a wall had formed between us that prevented communication.

My wife and son had been kidnapped in Pannonia by enemy tribesmen. My father and I rescued them and killed the ones responsible, but not before she had been assaulted. I had failed to protect my family and the guilt always lay heavily on my shoulders.

The wall between us was formidable, built from the resentment she held for my failure to protect them, and mine from the guilt of the same failure. We still cared for each other deeply, but the divide between us deepened with time and it seemed we led different lives as I took on the responsibility of the tribal chieftain and she immersed herself into the everyday tasks of caring for Lingulf and managing every other aspect of our lives. I had avenged her sufferings upon the kidnappers, but I had never forgiven myself for failing to keep my wife and son safe, and I believed she had never forgiven me either. I couldn't express my own emotions, but I could feel her disappointment. I knew she wanted me to speak, to assure her that everything was going to be alright between us, but I couldn't form the words and instead just held her tighter, hoping that somehow, my silent strength would be enough. It was not.

She pushed away, coughing to cover the catch in her throat. She turned and reached up to wipe a tear, then hugged herself and walked to the edge of the trail, her back to me. After a moment, she sniffed and cleared her throat. I knew she was upset, for I could hear the quaver in her voice when she said, "I'm worried for our son's future. How long must we wander before we find our home?"

I knew that I had done the wrong thing once again by not talking to her, yet at the same time I was relieved that she had changed the subject. "The curse prevents us from stopping," I said bitterly. "If one summer they rest, in any land; they shall be punished by Njoror's hand," I recited my sister's words as she first spoke them to me several years ago. "Njoror has proven he can reach us no matter where we are. We have no choice but to continue moving. But I will never rest until the curse is lifted," I spoke fiercely now, "and I will do everything in my power to protect our people." To myself I added, *I will not fail them as I failed you.*

Shouts of alarm woke me in the night. When I arrived at the scene, I found that a family had narrowly escaped disaster when their cart went careening down the trail and off the side of a steep cliff. When they had stopped for the night, the oxen were unhitched, and the cart was parked on a slight incline. No one had chocked the wheels and during the night, it rolled away, narrowly missing the family's young children sleeping on the ground.

In the morning, several men climbed down to what was left of the cart and recovered whatever was still of use, but the cart was destroyed. Family and friends offered to carry the family's belongings in their carts, and we moved on.

The following night, I was awakened again by Hrolf shouting for me. "Borr! There's a disturbance back down the trail at the cattle herd."

I threw back the sleeping furs and jumped up, belting on my sword. It was too dark for the horses, so we left on foot, gathering men as we went. The herd was agitated and milling about dangerously, threatening to stampede. If they bolted, it could be disastrous. Several men circled them, speaking in low tones to calm them down.

"What happened here?" I asked the nearest man.

"We were raided," he said, pointing at a nearby spot. "Several men came out of that cleft over there and cut out a dozen or so cattle. We tried to follow, but they had men on the cliffs above who dropped boulders on us. One man has a broken arm. We were lucky no one was killed."

"Wodan's eye!" I swore. "I was afraid of something like this. We have a long way to go through these mountains. Hrolf!" I called. "Double the guards on the cattle and get some men in those rocks above. In the morning, I need to figure out how to talk with these

6

people."

I was up with the sun, talking to our Taurisci guides.

"I need to meet with the local chieftain," I told them. "Can you arrange that?"

They all looked at me blankly until one man spoke up. "I can."

"What's your name?" I asked him.

"Bran," he replied.

That evening, Bran and another man returned with a grubby look-ing warrior held between them. The man was from a local tribe and was protesting loudly at his captors. Bran cuffed him on the back of his head and said something in the man's language, then turned to me.

"We found this man watching the caravan."

"What is your name?" I asked, and Bran translated.

"What tribe are you from?"

He spat at the ground and refused to answer, until another cuff harder than the first adjusted his attitude.

"He is of the salt people," Bran said. "They are local tribes that commanded the salt trade in these mountains for generations, but they are no longer prosperous, and their people now survive by banditry."

"Who is your chieftain?

The man looked at me sullenly and did not reply. Bran punched him in the small of his back.

"Who is your chieftain?" I repeated.

"Haki."

"I have a message for him. Tell him we only wish to pass through the mountains. We are willing to pay. It is not necessary to risk lives to steal our cattle. Tell him to meet me tomorrow, here, at mid-day."

There were no raids that night and in the morning the caravan continued to move. As hoped, Haki showed up. He was late, which was no surprise. He wanted to make me wait, to show that he was not to be summoned by some stranger passing through his lands. But late in the afternoon he appeared with an entourage of thin warriors, who wore simple leather and fur clothing and carried old bronze weapons and wooden shields. It was obvious that they had not eaten well in some time.

Haki was tall next to his people and carried himself with an air of dignity that set him apart. He sat with me around a small fire, beside Hrolf, with Bran as translator. After a simple meal, I opened our discussion.

Haki listened quietly as I informed him this was not a negotiation. What I offered now was all he should expect, and in return, I wanted no further attacks. Twenty cattle, four carts full of ale and grain, a cart full of cloaks we had taken from the dead Romans, as well as twenty Roman swords and chain mail. It was a fortune to him and was little enough of a sacrifice for us. We agreed that he would guide us to his village in the morning.

Our escorts grinned at the expression of awe on our faces as we rounded a bend in the trail and the beautiful high valley suddenly opened up before us. The trail wound around a large lake, deep blue and sparkling in the mid-morning sunlight. The lake was surrounded by jagged peaks that rose steeply from the water's edge, leaving just enough room for the trail.

Following the narrow path southward along the edge of the lake, we came to a village set astride a small river spilling out of the snow-capped mountains. It frothed downward over several ledges before falling to the valley floor and emptying into the large alpine lake. The village sat on a small flat of land at the river's mouth, spreading in both directions along the lakeshore.

The buildings were in poor condition, barely standing on rotted wood foundations and moldy thatch roofs. Haki waved and called out to the villagers, assuring them it was safe to come out of the hiding spaces they had fled to when they saw us approaching. Hungry looking men and women appeared from nowhere surrounding our little group. The children looked up at us on our horses with large eyes and sunken cheeks while they clung to the skirts of their mothers.

We had arrived in mid-afternoon and already the mountains were casting a shadow that reached over the village sitting along the lake's edge. Haki gathered the villagers around as my men herded the cattle into an open area that served as the village square and the carts full of supplies pulled up behind. When he was finished explaining to his people what was happening, they swarmed my men and thanked us, grasping our hands and reaching out with sincere gratitude.

I ordered a steer cut out from the herd and several of my men butchered it while the villagers happily prepared a large cooking fire. The feast was obviously the first time in a long while any of them had filled their bellies. Our hosts emptied the carts and shouts of joy rang out when they discovered the barrels of ale and sacks of grain. In short order, they produced horn cups and wooden tankards so that everyone was able to partake in the spontaneous celebration. The sounds of children laughing and the smiles in the sunken faces softened the hearts of my strongest warriors and anyone who had questioned my decision had forgotten their doubt. Though I still ordered enough men to keep a wary eye open for trouble throughout our visit. That night, we slept around the dying embers of the cooking fire and in the gray morning twilight, Haki and I embraced and said our goodbyes. During the night, our carts had been filled with bags of salt; the only thing they had in abundance. We returned to the caravan assured there would be no further raids as we continued through the mountains.

———

Hrolf sensed I needed to be alone with my thoughts and followed me at a distance. My horse picked its way along the side trail until I came to an overlook at the top of the world. I looked out upon towering thunderheads that cast slowly moving shadows upon the land that stretched out before me. In the distance, I could see the gray streaks of a rain shower falling to earth from one of the darker clouds. From my vantage point high on the mountain, I could see for miles. A sparkling mountain stream meandered its way between the trees far below until it spilled into a larger river that disappeared behind the fold of another ridge of hills. An eagle soared on the updrafts that rose from the foothills, gliding effortlessly in the vast space before me. Looking down upon the great bird, my thoughts returned to the troubles facing my people. Though it was never far from my mind, my talk with Frida the other night reminded me of the dilemma we faced that kept us constantly moving.

Directly below I could see the front of the caravan, a thin dark column of thousands of people, carts, and livestock descending from the heights, winding around the spurs and ridges that reached out into the valley. They had walked thousands of miles over the past seven years, carrying everything they possessed with them, enduring hunger, extreme heat, and severe cold. They trudged through dark swamps, across trackless forests and vast open plains, always in search of a new home, facing rejection and even death at every turn. We had lost all in a great ocean tide that crashed into our homes and fields, leaving nothing but wreckage and grief. Now we walked with our heads high, having regained our pride and the warrior spirit that had led our people to the northern coasts so long ago. I admired them so.

Every day I deeply felt the absence of my father, who led us through those earliest days of despair. Now I was the chieftain, and I still was not sure I was the right choice. In just seven years, I had grown from a sickly fifteen-year-old boy into a warrior, clan leader, and war-chief. I was twenty-two years old and the leader of an expedition eighty thousand strong. We had been cursed by a jealous god to never rest until we were welcomed into the lands of our enemies, and I struggled to solve that riddle. Every day brought uncertainty. Why was I chosen? I was filled with doubt that I was up to the task that had been passed to me.

Though it was the Roman's betrayal that brought on their own defeat, I expected a response to the loss of their legions. Since the curse prevented us from entering Italy without their invitation, we could not stay in Noricum, and we could not turn back toward the Scordisci. Our only choice was to cross the mountains. What our future was now no one knew, but the three matrons had been busy weaving our destiny for many years and they seldom paused from setting challenges before us.

I sighed heavily as Hrolf came up beside me. He was Teuton, an allied tribe from our native Jutland. We met shortly after the great flood forced us out of our homeland. His people had helped us avoid starvation with an eel harvest that carried us through much of that first long winter and their generous gifts of clothing, tools, food, and ale kindled the fire of hope that we so desperately needed.

Hrolf was tall, like me, but that is where our likenesses ended. He contrasted my bold red hair and fair complexion with dark hair and skin bronzed from the sun. He wore his hair braided and twisted into a knot on the right side of his head above his ear in the style favored by his people and kept his beard short. His dark eyes glinted with intelligence and a quick wit, and they were set wide on a handsome face that always seemed on the verge of a smile. He was my oath-man, my friend, companion, and trusted advisor, and he oversaw the training of our young warriors when we were encamped. As a warrior, he was a fierce and terrifying opponent, and on a battlefield, he served as my second in command. We had spent so much time together over the years, he often knew what was on my mind before I voiced it.

"Rome will have heard of the loss of their legions by now," he said. "They will likely send more to avenge them."

"Mmmm," I replied, slowly coming out of my reflection. "By the time the senate argues amongst themselves about who is to blame and prepares an army, it will be too late to reach us this year. At best, they will march in the spring, and they will have to wait until the mountain passes thaw to follow us. We will be out of their reach by then. I wish to know more of the lands we are entering. Have Bran join me. I would hear what he knows."

With a half grin, Hrolf raised an arm and beckoned to someone waiting behind us. Again, he had anticipated my wish, and Bran came forward with Ansgar who had been waiting with him. We dismounted and made ourselves comfortable on the ground. Bran told me that the valley we could see stretching out in the distance was that of the Salzach River. Farther still, a column of lazy smoke marked the presence of a large fortress overlooking the river.

"That is Luvavum, the oppidum of the Ambisontes people," said Bran. "It was an important trading center for the salt mined in the Salzach area that we just passed through. Haki's ancestors worked the mines generations ago until the mines were closed by an earthquake, and they lost their only means of trade." We talked for hours as Bran informed me of the tribes, politics, and wars of the lands we were entering, and I absorbed it all.

The caravan passed Luvavum without incident, though we were watched from its ramparts, and continued down the Salzach River until we reached the En. The En in turn led to the Danubius, from where I planned to follow the great river westward toward its source. Several days past Luvavum the caravan spilled out of the foothills and spread out onto the plain where the rivers met.

Across the En River, Boiodurum sat atop granite cliffs in the center of a peninsula that was formed by the path of the two rivers. Stone quays reached out into the river at the eastern point of the peninsula to form a harbor protected from the currents of both rivers and it was filled with trade ships. It was an important site from which salt was still shipped throughout Gaul and Germania from other mines in the area. The En formed the border between Noricum and Raetia. The people that lived there were a mixture of the local tribes, with some Boii from north of the Danubius. None had any reason to think kindly toward us as we had fought with their cousins and had ravaged Noricum across the Alpes for more than a year.

On the north side of the peninsula, a series of rock shelves protruded from the surface of the Danubius. Errant ships could be caught in eddies and capsize or drop off the shelves and be broken up. The only way to pass safely in either direction was to keep to the north bank where a third river, the Ilz, joined from the north and mixed its current with the great river. It was a difficult place to navigate and required experienced rivermen.

The word spread quickly that this was the site of our winter camp and family groups spread out to find the best locations. We were now more than eighty thousand strong and the vast caravan swarmed over the land like ants. The people who lived here fled when they heard of our approach, taking their livestock and whatever they could with them and crossed the river to the safety of the oppidum, but they were forced to leave vast fields of grain that was not ready for harvest, rich meadows of winter fodder, vegetable gardens, and everything they could not take with them. It was all sitting there waiting for us to claim it. The farmsteads and small settlements on our side of the river were quickly occupied. Many spread out among the foothills and began to build the simple winter cabins they had become so used to building every year. My mounted warriors patrolled in search of any resistance but found little, save for a few stalwart Norici who stayed to defend their homes and were quickly killed or driven off.

We were watched from across the En River, but none ever came close enough to risk capture.

I sent patrols out on both sides of the En, but they were unable to gain any useful information. The local population was forted up inside the oppidum, or directly around it, and they had set up a barricade to defend the peninsula. Soon after arriving, I called a meeting of my lieutenants and discussed our situation.

"Freki, what are the dangers from the locals?" Freki was my childhood friend who had become my brother. His parents were killed in the great flood and his brother died in the plague that had killed my parents and taken a third of the tribe. Freki led my scouts, and I trusted him to gather the information that was vital to our survival.

"They remain in the city and refuse to come out or talk to us," he said. "Anyone that did not get to the city vanished into the hills or went upriver. I have sent patrols wide, and we have not discovered anything to worry about. Apparently, they don't plan to resist us, only watch from their walls, for now."

"I want you to withdraw everyone to our side of the river," I said. "Maintain mounted patrols and a screen of warriors along the river to warn us if they decide to foray from their defenses, but leave that side to them. I don't intend to fight unless necessary, but let's stay ready for anything. Give everyone two weeks to get their cabins up. By then, the grain should be ready for harvest."

Chapter Two

July 113 BC

It had been three years since Grimur lost his wife and child in the terrible plague that devastated the Cimbri. He rode out of their village in Pannonia and never looked back. He was angry beyond reason at his nephew, Borr. More than angry, Grimur hated him. Hate that filled every fiber of his being. Hate that filled the dark hole left by the death of his family.

In the deepest recesses of his mind, Grimur knew the boy had done nothing to wrong him, yet he had convinced himself that everything he suffered was due to his nephew's rise. The weakling. The boy should never have survived. Yet he was now leader of the tribe that he, Grimur, should have been. It was only right; Grimur was brother to the Cimbri chieftain Haistulf, Borr's father. It was Grimur's right to inherit the leadership of the clan, and ultimately the tribe, when Haistulf died. Not the weakling.

Borr should have died on the journey, too weak and unhealthy to survive the hardships. But he didn't, he got stronger. He became a warrior, and then a leader. He married Frida and had a child, a healthy son. Borr's happiness mirrored Grimur's for a time; until the plague came. Grimur's wife Hedda and Borr's mother Ishild nursed many through their sickness, and then when the others had either died or gotten better and they thought they had survived the worst, both of the women fell ill. Grimur watched helplessly as first his wife, and then his infant son, succumbed to the disease after a long and agonizing week of coughing and wheezing, gasping for their next breath, weeping and painful blisters, and swollen glands. Then Ishild, and finally Haistulf, died and the leadership of the clan passed to Borr, the weakling. They hadn't even considered Grimur as hunno.

The final blow was when Borr's family survived unscathed. They never even got sick. Grimur tried to drown his grief with ale and mead, birch wine, even the dried mushrooms the priests used. Anything he could find that might dull the pain. In the brief moments his mind was not numbed, he focused his grief on Borr. Finally, after a violent confrontation with his nephew, Grimur left. He wandered for weeks in the wilderness, avoiding all human contact. He grieved for his wife and son, and his tortured mind searched for an end to the pain. Many times, he considered taking his own life, but he could not bear the thought of leaving this world without exacting his revenge on the nephew who possessed everything that he had lost. When his body had finally cleansed itself of the poisons that he had poured into it, his mind began to focus. Revenge. Against the weakling, and the people who followed him. Revenge was now his only goal.

That was when he came out of the wilderness and delivered himself to the Scordisci, where he befriended a druid priest that had always resented the friendship between the Cimbri and the Scordisci. The druid had spoken out against accepting the Cimbri into their homeland and sharing the local resources with another large tribe, but he was silenced and pushed aside in favor of the northern invaders. His indignation turned to hatred that simmered just below the surface for years. He found others who agreed that the Cimbri must go, and he formed a coalition that sowed doubt amongst the Scordisci. When the plague devasted the Cimbri, the time was ripe, and he increased his rhetoric against the northern tribe. When Grimur found him, the unlikely allies formed a bond of mutual hatred. The pair influenced more of the Scordisci, using false rumors and inventing circumstances that reflected badly on the Cimbri. Finally, they had sown enough doubt that the Scordisci demanded the Cimbri leave Pannonia and began their attacks.

It was Borr who thwarted their plans when he led the Cimbri and defeated the Scordisci, demanding a truce and promising that they would leave the following spring. The two schemers lost what support they had and once again were brushed aside as the Scordisci's attention turned to the Roman invasion of their southern lands.

When the Cimbri crossed into Noricum, Grimur followed them . . . always watching, always calculating, waiting for an opportunity. He watched as they ravaged Noricum and later learned when Borr was elected chieftain of the Cimbri that fateful winter's night. When he saw Carbo's army lying in ambush, he dared to hope that Borr and the Cimbri would finally fall, but that was not to be. Again, the weakling seemed to be blessed by the gods when he turned the ambush around and killed most of the Romans.

Learning of Borr's plans, Grimur crossed the Alps ahead of them and made his way to Boiodurum, where he boldly rode up to the city gate and in the language common throughout Gaul and the Celtic lands, demanded to speak to the chieftain. His horse was haggard, and he wore tattered woolen clothing and animal skins that had seen better days. His hair was matted and dirty from living in the wild for months and he was thin, but he sat his horse straight backed and proud. Despite his unkempt appearance, Grimur's eyes held a remnant of his past position of influence as brother to the Cimbri chieftain and he stared boldly at the warrior who stepped forward.

"Who are you to demand anything of us? Dagos has more important things to do than waste his time with traveling beggars."

"He will want to speak with me," Grimur stated confidently. "There is a vast army approaching from beyond the mountains and I have information that your chieftain will want to hear."

Grimur glared at the speaker and the guard shifted uncomfortably under his intense gaze. There was something in this stranger's eyes that gave the guard pause. Intelligence, cunning, or maybe a bit of madness. The guard considered his words for a moment before deciding it might be prudent to inform his superior. Let him determine whether this stranger was telling the truth, he thought. "Very well," he said, shrugging his shoulders. "Come with me."

"My name is Grimur, senior warrior and brother to the Cimbri chieftain Haistulf, who led our people from our destroyed homeland in Jutland, many leagues to the north."

Dagos leaned forward in his high-backed chair and looked at him with renewed interest. Word had reached him some years ago about a large northern tribe that passed through the land of his neighbors, the Boii, and continued down the Danubius. "Why have you come here?" he asked.

"I have come to warn you of a dire threat to your people. Sadly, the steady hand of Haistulf no longer leads the Cimbri. He rose to Valhol several years ago during a great plague that devastated our people. His son, my nephew Borr, is now the tribe's chieftain. He was a stripling, barely old enough to grow a beard, and his inexperience allowed him to be influenced by those around him who wish to make war on the world. Under Haistulf, the Cimbri made friends with the Teutons, the Ambrones, and the Scordisci. We passed peacefully through the land of the Boii and many other tribes. Since Haistulf died and Borr replaced him, relations with the Scordisci soured and my nephew changed, becoming more and more warlike. When the Scordisci pushed them out, they ravaged Noricum killing everyone they found and stealing anything that could be carried away. When Rome sent an envoy to negotiate a peace, Borr ambushed and destroyed two legions, and now their weapons still bloody from battle, a great horde of many thousands of warriors cross the mountains just days behind me to attack your lands."

Dagos watched him suspiciously. "Why have you brought me this news? Why should I believe you?"

"I was against the invasion of Noricum, and I spoke out," Grimur lied. "I challenged Borr as the rightful heir to the leadership of the tribe, but I underestimated his influence and his supporters cast me out. I have been shadowing the tribes since, watching, and waiting. I was part of them once and I hope to one day be so again. But until the influence of Borr is broken, they are under his spell and the most I can do is warn others."

"And what is it you ask of me?" Dagos wondered aloud, taking a drink from a horn cup.

"I ask nothing. I am simply here to warn you. I urge you to gather your warriors, strengthen your defenses, and send word to the surrounding villages to prepare. I do not exaggerate the great numbers marching this way. When you have confirmed what I have been telling you, I only wish shelter for the winter, and when spring comes, I will be on my way."

Dagos sat back in his chair, resting his chin on steepled fingers. "I will consider your words. For now, you will be my guest here until I confirm your story. Do not attempt to leave." He dismissed Grimur with a wave of his hand.

Dagos sent out scouts who returned within the week, confirming Grimur's story. The chieftain brought as many of his people into the fortress that he could to wait out the winter. Grimur assured him that because of the curse, the Cimbri would move on in the spring, and the fortress could be resupplied by river. As the great caravan descended to the river plain, the last of Dagos' people streamed into the fortress, abandoning their farms and homesteads. Dagos rewarded Grimur with a silver arm ring and another audience.

"Your warning was true, and I thank you for it. But you will not be staying here through the winter. You will travel westward along the river to Alcimoennis and Manching to warn them. If these tribes move in the spring as you predict, you will advise the King of Raetia on how best to deal with them."

Grimur was elated. His plan was working better than he had hoped and promised the opportunity to destroy Borr once and for all. He walked to the palisade to watch the throng of people and animals as they milled about the river plain across from the fortress. On and on they came, tens of thousands of men, women, and children. Thousands of grim warriors with brightly painted shields and ash shafted spears. Grimur's lips pressed together, and his eyes narrowed to thin slits when he saw a man sitting on horseback on the far bank of the river staring toward the fortress, his red hair visible even at this distance.

"Borr," he snarled through clenched teeth, the muscles of his jaw quivering with tension.

There he was. The weakling. His long red hair stirring in the wind. Grimur saw him turn and stare toward the walls, and he felt as though Borr was looking directly at him. A vein bulged at his temple as the hate coursed through his body.

Watching across the river, Grimur prepared himself for the coming task he had set for himself.

Several days later, when the last of the caravan had emerged from the mountain passes Grimur rode out of the city's gate flanked by two men who would be his guides. They would introduce him to the tribes he would encounter on his way to the oppidum of Manching.

"We will pass several small villages before we come to the city of Alcimoennis in about a fortnight," the guide said, exposing the mash of half-chewed pheasant in his mouth before he forced it down. Tapping his fist on his chest, he forced a large belch and chased the meat with a large swig of ale, much of which ran down his long mustaches and dripped onto his tunic. "It is another city of the Vindelici," he paused to gulp air and force another loud belch, then continued, "and is where much of the iron is smelted in this area. It's less of a village or trading center than it is a mining and processing center. My mother's brother is the local chieftain, so I'll be able to introduce you to him." He cracked the small leg bone and sucked the marrow, then tossed the bone into the fire and watched it turn black.

"Another five days beyond Alcimoennis is the oppidum of Manching. This is the capital city of the Vindelici, and it is much larger than Alcimoennis. There are at least twenty thousand people living there."

Grimur listened absently to the guide, nodding his head occasionally. He was already forming a plan to use the Vindelici to kill Borr once and for all and claim his rightful place as chieftain of the Cimbri, and this time, nothing would stop him.

Chapter Three

Roman Field Hospital

Aquileia, July 113 BC

The beautifully serene face of Venus, the goddess of love, came into focus as Lucius's eyes fluttered and he slowly came awake. She stared down at him, gently shaking his shoulder.

"Hey, wake up soldier," she said. "It's your turn. The more urgent patients have been tended to."

Now wide awake, Lucius smiled back and sat up on the edge of his bunk, wincing at a sharp pain in his ribs that he had momentarily forgotten. She stood and walked away, smiling over her shoulder. "The medicus will take care of you."

His face fell as the ugliest man he had ever seen appeared in her place. Short and bowlegged, with a wide and toothy grimace that passed for a smile. The man pulled up a stool and started unwinding the linen wraps from Lucius' torso with surprisingly gentle fingers, revealing the deep gash along his rib. The wraps were stuck in several places, and he had to wet them to get them loose.

The wound Lucius received at the battle of Noreia was tender and red, and burned hot with infection. The edges were brown and crusty with dried blood, and a greenish pus lay wetly between them. The medicus cleaned the area and irrigated the wound by squeezing a sponge soaked in a vinegar and water solution, softening it, and washing away the contaminants, then gently dabbed it dry. With a small grunt of satisfaction, the medicus unrolled a small leather packet that held an assortment of needles, fine linen thread, and a set of small forceps. Lucius eyed the suture kit dubiously.

The medicus selected a needle and proceeded to run a fine line of stitches along the cut. Lucius sucked in a breath each time the needle pierced his skin, but otherwise endured the pain silently. When the edges of the wound were drawn together neatly and the ends of the suture snipped off, the medicus covered the wound with a mixture of butter and rose oil with a bit of honey. Then he placed a poultice of lint smeared with a plaster of tetrapharmacum, a mixture of wax, pine resin, and animal fat, onto the wound and wrapped it with strips of clean linen.

His job finished, the medicus patted an exhausted Lucius on the shoulder and handed him a cup of wine. He had boiled a small piece of mandrake root in the wine which would give Lucius some relief from the pain and allow him to sleep. Then he instructed Lucius to lie back and rest, and with a loud exhale, Lucius complied.

Before he closed his eyes, he asked the medicus, "Who was that girl?"

The man smiled knowingly and replied, "Her name is Runa. She's a local girl."

When Lucius awoke again, his ribs ached, but he felt much better. He looked around and saw that he lay on a cot inside a large white tent beside thirty or so other men. A partition swept back, and the golden-haired beauty reappeared. She saw he was awake and came over to him, smiling brightly. She poured him a cup of wine from a pitcher she carried and helped him sit up so he could drink it.

"You look much better than when I saw you last," she said.

"I feel better," Lucius replied. Then winced as he tried to sit up. "Where am I?"

"In a field hospital outside the city of Aquileia," she replied.

RISE OF THE RED WOLF

"Mmph…unnh," Lucius grunted in acknowledgment, then pain, wincing again as he moved. The memory of the battle suddenly came back to him. "How many days has it been?"

"Five days since the battle," she said. "You were carried in two days ago. That was the day I saw you. You've been sleeping since. Are you hungry?"

He hadn't thought about it until now, but suddenly he was famished and eagerly nodded his head.

"I'll be back in a moment with some soup," she promised. She returned shortly with a bowl of warm broth and a small chunk of bread and placed it on the small table next to his cot. She propped him up into a sitting position and picked up the bowl. Smiling gently, she offered him a spoonful of broth, which he slurped loudly and spilled most of it down his chin.

She giggled lightly and took a corner of his sheet to wipe his chin. He smiled sheepishly up at her.

"Let's try that again," she said.

This time he managed the full spoon. He finished the broth, then chewed the bread slowly, and washed it down with the wine. By the time he finished eating, he was exhausted again and lay back. She made him comfortable and with a parting smile from her, he was immediately asleep again.

Later that night, as Runa was making her rounds through the hospital, she was drawn to the panicked cries of a man in great distress. Rushing back into the ward, she found Lucius thrashing about on his cot in the depths of a violent nightmare. Lucius was back on the battlefield, the warrior trying to kill him while Lucius desperately swatted his shield at the barbarian's seax. Lucius woke suddenly and sat up on his cot, bathed in sweat and breathing heavily. A fresh stain of blood showed through his bandages.

"Oh no, you've torn your stitches," she said. She sat on the edge of the bed and wiped his brow. "Shhh, you've had a bad dream. It's all right," she said, her slender fingers touching his forearm.

At her gentle touch, his breathing slowed, and he regained control of his emotions. He looked at her through pained eyes, embarrassed that she should see him this way. He turned away, and in a sullen voice said, "I'm all right. It was just a dream."

She hesitated a moment, then stood with a sigh and returned to her rounds. She had seen many young men suffer this way and knew there was nothing more she could do.

––––––––––

Several weeks passed, and Lucius felt much better. The infection was gone, and the wound had changed its color from angry red to a healthy pink. The edges were puckered; it had finally stopped itching, and he could move about without the stabbing pain. The ugly medicus carefully clipped and removed the stitches, dropping them on a small tray.

"I'm not going to replace the bandages," he said. "It's healing well, and you can start your therapy tomorrow." He gently rubbed some olive oil onto the scar, then gathered his tools and left Lucius to his thoughts.

Lucius was daydreaming of Runa again and failed to notice his friend Vulca standing at the end of his bunk. "It's good to see you again," Vulca said.

Lucius blinked and came out of his reverie. Jumping to his feet, he embraced his friend. "Vulca! I haven't seen you since we got to the hospital. How are you?"

"Well," he said with his customary bluntness. He was smiling. It was an unusual expression for him, and he was not quite comfortable with it, but he was glad to see his friend. They had gone through months of intense training together and shared their first experience of battle. Vulca had dragged Lucius from the battlefield at Noreia, bound his wounds, and supported him during the march back to the hospital in Aquileia.

"Where have you been?" Lucius asked. "I haven't been allowed to leave the hospital area and I haven't seen anyone from the unit."

Vulca's face fell. "Those that had superficial wounds were treated and released immediately," he said as he raised his hand to show Lucius a scar along the side of his hand. When he tried to continue, his voice choked, and his eyes watered. "We were marched back to the battlefield to care for the dead. It was horrible. Thousands of bodies strewn about for several miles from the battlefield to the camp. The embers still smoked where they burned the prisoners alive," he shuddered. "We've been staying in a castrum several miles from the city. Lucius, we've been held under guard since the battle."

"What? Why?" Lucius exclaimed, his face registering the shock of indignation that the men who survived the battle at Noreia should be treated as criminals.

"A delegation of senators and senior military officers has been asking questions about the battle. It is led by a general named Gaius Marius, recently returned from pro-praetorship in Hispania. He is rumored to be fair, but very strict with discipline. We have not been allowed to leave the camp for weeks. There's talk of punishment because the legions broke and ran."

"Oh no," Lucius said, as the color drained from his face. They had all been warned of the punishment for cowardice. They had all sworn the sacramentum on the day they were enlisted. "Surely they can't blame the soldiers for that disaster."

"All the veterans say it was Carbo's bad decisions that led to the defeat," Vulca continued. "He fled the field and didn't stop running until he reached the Servian Wall. The word is he has been arrested and is awaiting trial while the battle is being investigated. Our fates are to be determined by those who were not there."

27

"How did you get out of the camp?" Lucius asked.

"They needed a detail to pick up supplies and I volunteered. I have to get back; they only gave me a few minutes to find you."

"It was good to see you, Vulca. Do you know if any of the others made it?"

"They posted a list of the dead and missing. Porcius and Decius were killed. Foligio is missing and most likely dead. The rest are in the camp."

"Tell them I am well," Lucius said. "I hope to join you all soon."

Vulca's expression darkened. "Be careful what you wish for," he warned ominously, and without a word of goodbye, he turned and hurried away.

———————

Several weeks passed before Lucius heard anything more. He was eating dinner with the men from his hospital tent when a centurion announced the news. "Tomorrow at dawn, all survivors of the consular legions of Carbo that were defeated by the barbarian tribes will assemble on the hospital parade ground to receive judgement. Those in the camp will march there and all wounded still assigned to the hospital and able to walk will march to the field."

It had been more than a month since the battle and there had been no official news. Now, rumors flew among the hospital tents and the men's anxiety grew with each passing hour. Many feared the harshest of punishments and worried themselves sick during the long, sleepless night.

"Alright you lazy bastards, outside now!" The centurion's gravelly voice ripped through the canvas walls of the tents. Those that could ran outside into the early morning darkness. Thick clouds blotted out any light from the stars, and the smell of rain was in the air. Lucius could not remember a night so dark and couldn't help but think it was a fitting start to a day such as this. The path to the parade field was lit by torches and the wounded men were marched to a position facing the survivors from the camp, who stood enclosed by ranks of armed legionaries. Lucius realized the others were prisoners and the soldiers were their guards. When he saw that the men from the hospital were kept separate, Lucius allowed himself a glimmer of hope. The prisoners were formed up in ranks of ten. Discipline on the field was the worst that Lucius had ever seen. Men were talking apprehensively with each other, and centurions were stalking about, commanding them to silence with a strike from their vitis. Many were visibly shaking and appeared to be on the verge of bolting from the field. They wore only the white tunic that legionaries wore as undergarments. There was no sign of the red cloak, armor, shields, or weapons by which the world recognized a Roman soldier. Lucius realized that he and the wounded men also wore only the white tunics that they had been given in the hospital and felt a moment of panic.

He jumped at the blare of the cornu trumpets that announced the approach of Gaius Marius, the man appointed by the senate who would pass judgement on the defeated legions. He wore the full regalia of a Roman general. His highly polished helmet gleamed beneath its bright red horsehair plume that stood tall and fell between his shoulders. His face was concealed behind the cheek plates that were tied beneath his chin with a leather thong, and his breastplate and greaves reflected the light from the torches that burned brightly on the rostrum. With his right hand on the pommel of his ivory handled gladius, the general climbed the three steps up to the wooden platform between the two formations.

He turned toward the wounded men and addressed them first. "You are here this morning to hear the judgement of your comrades and witness the punishment for cowardice on the battlefield. You have been granted a reprieve from this punishment as you have already suffered wounds at the hands of the enemy and thus distinguished yourselves by your bravery on the battlefield."

Lucius nearly collapsed from the wave of relief that passed over him. His knees felt weak, and he reached out for support from the men around him. Moans of grief and fear rose from the group of prisoners facing them. Several vomited with the anticipation of what was to come.

A light wind stirred his blood red cloak as Marius turned toward the doomed men. A spatter of raindrops passed over the field, foreshadowing the coming storm. He stood motionless for several long moments, his eyes sweeping over those he was about to pass judgement upon. Lucius looked with pity upon the men facing him and searched desperately for any of the faces that he knew. With a spark of recognition, he saw Vulca standing tall in the second rank, his face a stoic mask of calm among the wide eyes and sweating brows of the men who anticipated the announcement that would seal their fate.

Marius took a deep breath and continued. "Just a few weeks ago, you marched to the mountains of Noricum where your commander was tasked with stopping the barbarian horde that had descended upon an ally of Rome. His imperium dictated that, if possible, he was to convince them to leave of their own accord and without bloodshed, which to his credit, he did. However, he then acted without honor and attacked those that had already agreed to leave in the hope of destroying them. He was incompetent, and he will face trial in the coming months for his failures. Your commander failed you and you have suffered much because of him. But you stand here today to face judgement on your actions, not his.

"After thorough investigation of the battle at Noreia, it is the judgement of the Roman senate that Consul Gnaeus Papirius Carbo and his officers and legions acted with cowardice in the face of the barbarian tribes from Germania."

A growing murmur of fear rippled through the ranks, and Marius continued in a louder voice.

"The punishment for cowardice on the battlefield is death!" He shouted the last word. The accused men broke their ranks and began pushing toward the outside as the legionaries that surrounded them pushed back with their heavy shields. Marius motioned to the cornicen standing by the rostrum and the strident blare stopped the contest for a moment just as another gust of wind came with a spattering of large rain drops that stopped quickly.

"However," he shouted, raising his hands to capture their attention and regain a sense of control. "The senate has been generous. They have recognized the failure of your commander and his officers, and they will be punished accordingly. The senate has accepted that you are not at fault for this terrible loss." The mob calmed and all eyes were upon him.

"But you have violated the sacred oath that you swore to the senate and the people of Rome. For the loss of the legion standards and for throwing down your weapons and running from the battlefield, the judgement is decimation!"

The pushing and shouting began again, and this time, the guards drew blood on those in the front ranks. The unarmed prisoners quickly backed off and turned back toward Marius, slowly resigning themselves to their fate.

In a tone that suggested they should be grateful, Marius said, "You have been given a reprieve. Rather than a sentence of death for all, you will form ranks of ten and draw lots. The man in each rank of ten who loses the draw will be beaten to death by the other nine. The remaining men will be placed on rations of barley and water for a week and will be reassigned as replacements to other units. Once the punishment is complete, their crime will be forgotten, and they will be free to rebuild their life."

It was a cruel punishment that not only caused the death of many men but left an indelible imprint on every man involved. No one knew if his friends survived or where they were sent, dispersed far and wide, to the most inhospitable of lands for the duration of their service.

A slow drizzle began as the men formed back into miserable ranks of ten and drew lots. The rain became a torrent and Lucius watched as several thousand men turned on their unlucky comrades who just weeks ago, had stood by their shoulder, ready to give their lives against Rome's enemies. Like a dam bursting, the survivors released their pent-up fear and anger upon the condemned soldiers in an explosion of violence. The horror of what they were ordered to do was surpassed by the relief they felt in the knowledge that they would live. In the savage release of emotion, a madness set in. Some seemed to take joy in the beating that they would surely regret when it was finished, while others held back, revolted by the sight of their comrade's suffering. When it was done, several hundred men lay dead in the mud while the pounding rain washed their blood laced and broken bodies clean. Lucius had lost sight of Vulca in the melee and hoped that he had escaped with his life.

At dawn, a centurion entered the medical tent. "Your vacation is finally over, you lazy bastards. You will form up on the hospital parade ground, in one hour to receive your orders."

When Lucius arrived at the parade ground the bodies were gone, and the sun was shining on a new day, but the memory of yesterday's events was fresh in his mind. He doubted he would ever forget. A clerk called the names of each man, who then came up to accept his written orders.

When his name was called, Lucius stepped forward and saluted the centurion. A clerk handed him a small scroll and told him to stand beside several other legionaries that had also been separated. After yesterday's events, Lucius was nervously standing in the small group at the front of the formation and anxiously wondered what was happening.

When everyone had been called, the centurion brought the formation to attention and signaled a cornicen to blow the trumpet call that announced a general officer. As the notes echoed across the parade ground, Gaius Marius returned to the rostrum where he had issued judgement the previous morning.

"This is the last time you will be reminded of the disaster that occurred at the battle of Noreia. Today, you begin your lives and your careers again. Judgements have been made and punishments issued. For you, the matter is closed. Your officers are either dead or being investigated for their role and will be treated accordingly. Despite the terrible events of that day and days since, despite the failures of your leaders and the dishonorable actions of many of your comrades, there were some who acted with exceptional bravery and honor. The men you see before you distinguished themselves on the battlefield in individual combat with the savages from Germania who call themselves Cimbri. I am pleased to recognize them today with the presentation of the armilla for valor. Centurion," he said, indicating it was time to present the award.

The centurion cleared his throat and in a clear voice read the citation, "The silver armilla is awarded to the following legionaries for bravery on the battlefield at the battle of Noreia in the kingdom of Noricum, friend and ally of the Roman Republic, in the six hundred and forty-first year since the founding of Rome, also known as the year of the consulship of Caprarius and Carbo. They conducted themselves with honor and courage and did not quit the field until they were unable to continue to fight due to the wounds they had suffered themselves."

As the tribune called out their names, Marius stood before each of the men and handed him a pair of serpent shaped silver arm rings, clasped their forearm in his, and said a few personal words. When he came to Lucius, he stopped and smiled, then turned to the centurion and nodded.

"The gold armilla is awarded to legionary Lucius Aurelius for bravery on the battlefield at the battle of Noreia in the kingdom of Noricum, in the six hundred and forty-first year since the founding of Rome, also known as the year of the consulship of Caprarius and Carbo. Lucius Aurelius conducted himself with extraordinary courage and honor when, without thought to his own safety and at risk to his own life, placed himself between a fellow legionary and a pursuing enemy warrior, killing the warrior and suffering a grievous wound. Though he suffered from his own wounds Lucius Aurelius treated other wounded legionaries and assisted them back to safety, over several days and many miles, back to the field hospital at Aquileia."

Marius turned back to Lucius, who felt like he was about to faint at the recognition. His thoughts were screaming in his head. *That's not what happened! The German threw himself at me as Titus ran past. I stumbled as I backed away in panic and the warrior ran upon my spearpoints. He killed himself.*

Lucius felt the general gripping his forearm and realized he was holding out a pair of gold armilla. Lucius nearly dropped the arm rings as he reached out and took them from the general. "Stand tall man," Marius grinned and leaned in. "You are an example to the men here. I'm proud of you. They needed to see not everyone was a coward that day. Well done."

Turning back to the formation, Marius lifted Lucius's arm and waved as the formation dutifully broke into roars of applause.

Lucius was shocked. This was the last thing he had expected, and he looked dumbfounded standing there next to the barrel chested general.

By the time he got back to his bunk, his mind had finally cleared, and he unrolled the small scroll. He was being released from the hospital and sent home for several months to fully recuperate, after which he was to report to his new assignment in Rome.

"Come on ladies," the centurion bellowed from outside the tent. "I know you're all big heroes now, but I am leaving in ten minutes. If you are not here, your armilla won't save you from a caning. Let's go!" As Lucius hurriedly stuffed his few possessions into a burlap sack, his mind drifted back just a few short months ago when he met the friends that had become so close, and to that fateful day in the mountains when those friends had been torn apart. He hoped that his future held more than the grief and guilt that he was feeling now.

Chapter Four

Rome

July 113 BC

Rome fairly buzzed with talk of the barbarian horde that was poised to invade Italy. News of the disastrous defeat at Noreia had flown back to the city and spread rapidly. The fear was palpable. The Senate immediately called an emergency meeting to decide what should be done, but as usual, the senators were busier pointing fingers and making accusations than discussing a response.

The senate house was filled with senators wearing the snowy white togas draped over their left shoulder, the purple stripe along one edge indicating their exalted position. Some were gesticulating wildly with their right hands while tightly clutching the folds of their toga praetexta with their left, so it did not fall to the ground. The fat ones with bright red faces and spittle flying off their bulbous lips as they shouted at their peers were the most embarrassing. Yet, perhaps the worst were the pale timid ones who trembled in their distinctive red shoes, their cowardice clearly showing as they learned of the Cimbri threat. Confusion, fear, and anger ruled the day.

They were either seeking to weasel out of their part in the disaster at Noricum just a week ago or positioning themselves to blame their rivals publicly so they could take political advantage of the staggering defeat of Carbo. No politician could ever let a crisis pass when there was something to be gained for themselves and none would ever take accountability for their own actions. To expect them to take swift action to address a real problem was simply too much to ask. If they ever actually solved a problem, they wouldn't have anything to promise to fix when they campaigned in the next election.

After the battle at Noreia, Vallus had returned to Rome to check his properties and financial investments. When he arrived, Felix welcomed him enthusiastically as he unlocked the iron gate to Vallus' modest home. Felix had served under Vallus in Numantia, and not long after Vallus had been wounded and sent home, Felix had lost his right arm below the elbow to an Iberian falcata and been medically discharged. Vallus had recognized him one day as he passed down the street shortly after dawn on his way to the baths. Felix was sleeping in a doorway when the shop owner arrived and began yelling at him to leave. An empty wine jug rolled off the curb and broke as he scrambled away from the kicks. The front of his tunic was stained with blood, or maybe it was wine, and fresh vomit was stuck to the cloth. His eyes were vacant and sunken, his chin was stubbled, and his hair was unkempt.

"Get out of here!" the shop owner yelled, kicking him in the ass a last time.

Vallus put out a hand that stayed the shop owner.

"Do you know this man?" the merchant asked, and when Vallus nodded, he jabbed a finger at Vallus' chest. "This is the last time I'm telling him not to sleep here. If I see him here again, I'll kill him, and the street cleaners can throw his body in the Flavus."

"Show some respect," Vallus said savagely. The shop owner stepped back from the sudden rage that erupted from Vallus. "This man is a veteran of the Numantine war. Can't you see his scars? Look at his tattoo. He lost his arm while you sat on your arse getting fat and rich and now, he's cast away like so much dung. Get to your business, this man will no longer be a problem for you."

The merchant sniffed in indignation and turned away, disappearing into his shop.

Vallus squatted to look into Felix's eyes. "Do you remember me?" he asked.

After a long moment, slowly, recognition crept into the man's eyes which then filled with tears, and he nodded his head, looking down in shame.

"Come my friend," Vallus told him. He supported Felix as they walked the remainder of the way to the baths and paid for a pair of slaves to bathe and barber his former colleague. Another was sent to purchase a new tunic. Vallus brought him home, where they spent weeks talking, exercising, and eating, putting healthy weight back on his thin frame. In time, Vallus raised him from the depths of his depression and Felix never looked back. He suffered from phantom pains from his missing arm and many sleepless nights when his dreams of the war came back with intensity, but gradually, ever so slowly, he got better. They rekindled the friendship that had begun in a terrible war, yet seldom talked of their experiences. They didn't have to. They knew, and they were simply comfortable in each other's company.

In time, Vallus left again, and he employed Felix to care for his home during his long absences. Felix had lived there ever since, a trusted friend and confidant who will ever be grateful for the second chance that his former commander provided.

Vallus had collected a fair amount of silver during his latest travels and after making a deposit in the Temple of Saturn where the priests safeguarded the fortunes of wealthy Romans and receiving an updated report of his savings he returned to his home and re-dressed into his beggar's clothes before heading out into the streets.

He entered a smoky tavern and walked directly to a table against a wall in the back of the room. The owner demanded payment in advance from the man who looked like a beggar, doubting he had the means to pay. Vallus had the coin ready when the owner approached and by keeping his gaze on the table, he kept his face in shadow, sliding a copper coin into view. The tavern keep snatched it up and squinted at the old man suspiciously, then shrugged his shoulders and turned away. Over his shoulder he called, "One cup of wine and a handful of bread."

"Don't mind him none," said a busty middle-aged woman who came up behind Vallus and set down a heavy clay cup. "He'sss ornery as a wild boar and sssmellsss like one too," she said, hissing her s's. She leaned over his shoulder to fill his wine cup, ensuring her heavy breasts brushed his arm. "You jussst call me if you need anything darlin'," she said, flashing him a smile that was missing a front tooth, the reason for the sibilant sound of her words, "Name'sss Sssabina." She produced a small chunk of bread from a filthy apron pocket and dropped it on the table.

Vallus hunched protectively over his food and said nothing, and the woman soon walked away in search of better prospects. He pinched a spot of mold off the bread and took a bite, then took a drink of the disgusting liquid the barmaid had brought, grimacing as it burned its way down his throat.

It's going to take me a week to recover from this meal, he thought. He showed no outward interest in the conversation taking place a few tables away, but he was listening intently to the hushed words of a group of men who worked for an important senator. These men were often present during the private discussions of their master but were so insignificant in his eyes, they were ignored as if they weren't even there. One was a bodyguard, one a scribe, and two were attendants.

Like most of Rome, and even broader Italy, they were discussing the barbarian threat. Their rapid-fire questions, and angrily hissed replies belied their concern.

*What is the Senate going to do? I heard they were raising two more legions.
…memories of the Gauls invasion… This is a disaster! Not since Brennus
have the barbarians threatened to attack Rome. What about Hannibal? My
grandfather fought Hannibal and we defeated him easily enough. Easily? Are
you mad? We lost more soldiers to Hannibal in one battle than any other war.
Do you think they are coming here? Why wouldn't they? We're pretty much
defenseless, all our legions are elsewhere making the generals and senators rich.
This threatens them too, they'll do something.*

Conversations like this were taking place in every home, every tavern and on every street corner. Rome was in a panic.

When Vallus returned home, he sat late into the night talking with Felix. His friend had become accomplished at gathering information and was full of news from the city. Most of it wasn't anything he could sell, but interesting nonetheless, and it filled in a few blanks in the picture he was painting of the current situation.

Vallus knew, of course, that the Cimbri had turned away from Italy and had no intention of invading but told no one. He didn't wish it to be known that he traveled with them from time to time. If anyone learned that it could be disastrous for him, and he didn't trust anyone with that knowledge, not even his close friend.

"Something's on your mind Felix," Vallus said the next morning. "Let's have it."

"I . . ." Felix began, unsure of how to open the subject, then decided to just plunge in. "I am in love," he said, blushing, his knee jumping rapidly as he bounced one foot up and down.

Vallus stopped chewing on the chunk of salted bread he had just lathered with a thick layer of butter. Like so many soldiers who had served in the north, he had developed a liking for the golden, creamy substance spread on fresh bread. Most of his fellow citizens wouldn't touch the stuff and thought of it as barbarian food, though they used it to treat wounds and to soften the skin. The northern tribes used it generously in their diet, eating it daily if they were able.

"Love?" he asked, his eyebrows lifted in surprise.

"Yes," Felix said softly. Then went on dreamily, "She is a vision, Vallus. Dark hair, dark skin, an exotic beauty." Then his voice dripped with anguish, "I want to marry her, but she is a slave. Her mother was captured in Macedonia and sold into slavery, and Sofija was born into the household of a retired Roman legionary. That's her name, Sofija. Even her name is beautiful," he said wistfully.

Vallus smiled at his friend, "Go on. How did you meet her?"

"I was at the market one day when I heard her voice through the babble. It was like the song of a meadowlark amidst a murder of crows. Soft, yet it cut through the harsh noise. She laughed as she haggled with a fruit vendor and the joy in her laughter drew glances from all the men nearby. She was aware of their attention yet acknowledged no one, but when she turned to walk away with a basket brimming with oranges our eyes met. She looked down with a shy smile breaking the momentary connection and disappeared into the crowd. I was stricken by her beauty, and I knew instantly that I loved her. I tried to follow her so that I might speak with her, but the crowd parted before her and closed behind as a wake behind the most graceful swimmer. I reluctantly gave up, vowing that I would find her and make her the mother of my children."

"And?" Vallus asked, intrigued by his friend's story.

"I returned to the market every day for several weeks and I began to think that I had lost her before I had any chance to speak with her, when I heard the hypnotic sound of that voice again. She was complementing a flower merchant on the beauty of his collection when I stepped up beside her and plucked a narcissus, tossing a copper to the merchant. I turned to her, and we locked eyes. I could see that she recognized me, and for a moment she looked as if she might run away when instead she offered me a dazzling smile. I was dumbstruck but offered her the flower. I stammered out that the flowers were a poor reflection of her beauty, and I asked if she would stay and speak with me, which she did. We've been seeing each other every day since."

"You really are smitten," Vallus smiled. "But why do I detect a sadness behind your joy?"

His eyes fell and when he looked back up at Vallus there was a sadness in them. "She is a slave," he said plaintively. "We cannot marry, and I can't afford to buy her freedom. It's hopeless."

"Who is her master?" Vallus asked.

"She attends the young sister of a powerful man. Gaius Julius Caesar. The son of another Gaius Julius Caesar, who is the son of another. The Julii is a patrician family that stretches back to the earliest days of the Republic, and the Caesares for generations. They both have many ancestors of consular and magistrate rank. He is a senator and a respected military officer.

"But enough of all that," Felix said, anxious to change the subject. "I must be content with the way things are. Please tell me of your adventures. Tell me where you have been this time, what strange things have you seen?"

Vallus sipped his wine, his quick mind considering the information he had just gained and how it might be of use to him. The two continued to while away the day with idle talk, and before long the sun's long shadows creeped into the streets. Finally, Vallus stretched and yawned, "ahhhuhhh! It is time I got myself ready for tonight's activities," he said.

"You will find your formal toga hanging in your bed chamber, freshly cleaned and whitened," said Felix.

"You are ever efficient my friend, thank you."

"It is little enough for the man who gave me back my life."

Gaius Lucilius had invited a few dozen former officers who served under Scipio Aemilianus in Numantia, to his villa. Lucilius hosted these reunions for his fellow veterans every few years to maintain the relationships they had formed during the Numantine war. In Rome, relationships were more valuable than gold. Lucilius was gaining a reputation for his works of satire, many of which spoke of his own experiences in the war.

This year a surprise guest was attracting a great deal of attention. Jugurtha, a prince of Numidia in northern Africa and ally of Rome, was in the city. Jugurtha had commanded Numidia's auxiliary cavalry that were attached to Scipio in Numantia. He was a born politician with a natural ability to make friends. People loved him. He was tall and athletic, handsome to both women and men, and at ease in all company, from kings and consuls to the lowliest soldiers and peasants. His charm was irresistible, and he was in his element tonight.

The three princes of Numidia had been at each other's throats since the death of their father, King Micipsa. Five years ago, Jugurtha had his brother Hiempsal assassinated, and then attacked Adherbal who appealed to Rome for protection. Rome's protection consisted of sending a delegation under former consul Lucius Opimius to meet with Jugurtha. Opimius was promptly bribed to return to Rome with assurances that the conflict was settled. Jugurtha kept his head down long enough to let things cool down, and now, he was plotting a new attempt at making himself sole king of Numidia and he had come to Rome to garner support within the Roman political and upper classes.

As Jugurtha scanned the room, his eyes fell upon Gaius Marius reclining on a dining sofa, absent mindedly popping grapes into his mouth and staring into space, thinking about what he had learned in his recent investigation of the defeat of Carbo's legions in Noricum. As he was obviously preoccupied, no one bothered to approach the former praetor, except Jugurtha.

"Hello old friend," the Numidian prince greeted Marius warmly.

RISE OF THE RED WOLF

Marius snapped out of his reverie and stared at the prince through half-lidded eyes. "Jugurtha. It's good to see you," he lied. "How are your brothers? Oh, forgive me, how is your brother?"

Ever in control, Jugurtha let the gibe slide smoothly past and complemented Marius on his recent return from Spain, showing that he kept up with the news.

"I hear your trip to Hispania was more profitable than when we served there under Scipio."

"You hear too much, and you talk too much," Marius growled.

Jugurtha smiled back, his perfect teeth and dark eyes masking his thoughts. He knew that he walked a razor thin edge, balancing his own ambition with those of Rome, and if war between Numidia and Rome were to break out, he knew that Marius might be the man he faced. That was something that concerned him.

"What do you want Jugurtha?"

The prince spread his hands and smiled again, knowing that he was getting to Marius. "I want nothing Gaius. I came to enjoy the good company of my fellow veterans, that is all."

"Hmmph," Marius grunted. He was a simple and straightforward man, and he did not appreciate the intrigues and maneuvers of politics. He was astute, and intelligent, a brilliant military strategist. No man that was not could rise to the levels of power and success that he had. But he had no stomach for the guile and deceit that came with that power.

He turned his back on Jugurtha and greeted his old friend Publius Rutilius Rufus, dismissing the prince. Jugurtha rose smoothly, playing off the snub and continued his circuit of the room. It was obvious he wasn't going to get anything directly from the man. Marius watched him surreptitiously, taking his measure and wondering if they would be meeting across a battlefield sometime soon.

"I don't trust that man, Publius. He's got half of the senate in his pocket."

Rufus snorted. "Half? The ones he hasn't bribed follow him around like puppies hoping to get their ears scratched."

"That's why he's here now. He's drumming up support for his next move. He's gauging his popularity with the senate, testing how they will respond if he takes up the sword against his brother again. He won't act unless he's confident of where Rome will stand. He will not stop until he rules all of Numidia, but he doesn't want to face us on the battlefield if he can avoid it."

"The 'Old Man' liked him," Rufus said, referring to their former commander Scipio Aemilianus.

"Jugurtha has talents, there is no doubt of that," Marius acknowledged. "He's a capable commander and his troops adore him. But he's a clever bastard, too clever, always sneaking around and setting up deals. Scipio liked him, but how much did he know about the real Jugurtha?" Marius watched the prince making the rounds, talking with old friends and allies, shaking hands, bending his head to whisper a joke, then laughing raucously at the punch line.

Rufus wisely changed the subject. "Have you given any more thought to the problems facing the army?"

"Ah, yes, I have," Marius replied, eager to talk about something other than politics. The two often discussed their observations about the military, identifying issues, picking them apart and coming up with solutions. It was a game they enjoyed, and they both excelled at the intellectual challenge.

"I've noted quite a few actually," Marius began. He sat up and became more animated, as he warmed to the subject. "I'm forming an argument to change the requirements of military service. The senate has always required recruits to own property, except in times of crisis when they have temporarily lifted those restrictions and allowed common citizens, and even slaves and criminals to serve."

"That's happened fairly often," Rufus agreed. "When the Gauls attacked Rome, when Hannibal invaded Italy, the slave wars, I'm sure there were more."

"In the past, when we raised legions, the men served for the period of a campaign. Now they sign up for a six-year stint, and if they choose, they can re-enlist and stay until they retire at twenty years."

"If they don't die in battle first, or from illness," Rufus put in. "Or are injured badly enough to get them kicked out."

"Those rules worked fine when our battles were in Italy. But now our armies are flung across the world. Every time we levy troops they are away from their farms for years," Marius went on. "If they are gone too long, or don't return, or if they are injured badly, the farms often must be sold. The land speculators step in and buy up the small farms cheaply to create large estates, then run them with slaves. This leaves the veterans with no choice but to move to the cities. The streets are filled with bitter and broken men that were once landowners and are now forced to beg for enough alms to buy a loaf of bread and jug of wine."

"It's driving up the population of unemployed men who turn to theft and murder to survive," Rufus said. "Some even sell themselves into slavery and go back to work the lands they once owned. Urchins run rampant on the streets. I can tell you have a solution to propose, don't keep me in suspense," he encouraged.

"The answer is simple. End the requirement for property. It has been in place for centuries and was originally thought that men who owned property would fight to protect it. It also meant they had at least some money to buy their own arms and armor. The treasury now provides their equipment, they don't need to buy it. But now, what reason do they have to fight? They come home to live in poverty and squalor. Sure, the crippled get a small pension, maybe they get a small share of the booty from a successful campaign that they squander on wine and women in a year or two, or if they live long enough to retire, they are given a small farm on some godforsaken hillside or marsh in a country far away, only to die from old age in ten years."

Rufus rubbed his chin, thinking. "You'd have an uphill fight to pass that proposal. Most of those speculators that profit from this system are in the senate, and those that aren't have at least one senator deep in their pockets. It would take a great deal of support to pass it. The Gracchi brothers proposed similar changes and they were both murdered for it."

"Well, some of what the Gracchi proposed has taken hold," Marius pointed out. "The state is now paying for arms and armor. The tribunes have more power. Even Scipio sided with the plebes on some of these things."

"That may have gotten him killed as well," Rufus said sourly.

Marius popped another grape into his mouth. "The time is ripe for change, and for the men who see it there is opportunity here."

Rufus grinned slyly. "What are you suggesting?"

"I'm not suggesting anything yet," Marius told him, offering his own wolfish smile and toasting his friend with a newly filled wine cup. "But the time to act is approaching. We must be ready."

The conversation around them mostly revolved around the northern threat from the Cimbri, clearly Numidia was not the priority at the moment, but Jugurtha continued to press for information about Rome's attitudes and intentions toward him. By the end of the evening, Jugurtha had determined that Rome had little interest in Numidia at this time, which is what he had hoped to learn. With luck, he would return home and finish off his brother before anyone in Rome could interfere, and once he was king, he was confident Rome would accept him as the sole ruler and be happy to move on to deal with the barbarians. Jugurtha knew the key was to keep the grain flowing from his country to Rome's warehouses, and his gold flowing into the pockets of its most powerful men.

As a cavalry officer under Scipio, Vallus always received an invitation to these reunions. He seldom was in the city when they occurred, but this time he took the opportunity to attend. The sedentary life of a farmer did not appeal to him, so he sold the farm he had been granted for his service and became a traveler. He was not a spy, he gave away no great secrets, but he had become wealthy by trading information for silver. He listened, and watched, and he carried news far and wide, which he freely gave to anyone who provided a warm fire, a good meal, and a few pieces of silver.

Vallus had the ability to make friends and gain trust easily, and he had learned that alcohol loosened tongues. He always remained sober at this type of function but took advantage of those who did not. There was no shortage of men who liked to hear themselves talk and the effects of wine only enhanced that fact. As he moved through the room, he took note of the more well-known attendees and positioned himself where he could overhear without appearing to do so.

By the end of the evening, he had garnered much useful information and wandered home through the empty streets, satisfied that the evening had been fruitful, and more than ready to leave the cobbled streets and marbled halls of Rome for the hardpacked trails and mud and wattle huts of the north.

A month later Jugurtha took ship to Numidia. As soon as his feet were on dry ground, he declared war against his brother Adherbal, reassured that Rome's attention was elsewhere.

Adherbal, who was not aggressive or warlike and had hoped to settle their differences peacefully, had finally accepted his adopted brother's intentions and had used Jugurtha's absence to gather an army. The two armies met outside the trading city of Cirta where Jugurtha's men stole into his brother's camp in the dark of night and routed Adherbal's army. Adherbal fled to the city where a number of Romans who lived in the town were manning the walls. The Romans, aware of Jugurtha's intentions and sympathetic to Adherbal, opened the gates and repulsed his pursuers.

At this, Jugurtha besieged the town, storming it with mantlets, towers, and every kind of war machine available to him, demanding they turn his brother over. Jugurtha was anxious to defeat his brother and consolidate his power before Adherbal could get word back to Rome of his actions.

However, Cirta being near the coast allowed Adherbal to get messengers through to the Senate. Still stinging from Carbo's loss to the Cimbri and preoccupied with the invasion from the north they felt was imminent, the senate sent three young senators without experience or influence to negotiate a truce between the Numidian princes.

Jugurtha, wishing to keep up his façade of innocence and cooperation agreed to a meeting. The three ambassadors met with the prince under a canopy outside the gates of the city, where Adherbal, too frightened to leave the city remained within the safety of its walls.

"It is the wish and the will of the senate and the people of Rome that the princes of Numidia should lay down their arms, and settle their disputes by arbitration rather than by the sword; since to act thus would be to the honor of both the Romans and themselves."

Jugurtha was quick to speak. "Nothing holds greater weight than the authority of the senate, and there is nothing I respect more. It has always been my endeavor to deserve the esteem of all men of worth. Have I not shown this by gaining the favor of Publius Scipio, a man of the highest eminence, through my own merit? Was I not adopted by Micipsa through my own good qualities rather than the want of heirs to the throne?"

The three young senators had grown up on the stories and legends of Scipio's defeat of Carthage and Numantia. They knew Jugurtha's reputation and were susceptible to his smooth lies.

"But as honorable as my conduct has been, I could not bear to endure the injustices of my brothers. Micipsa had willed that Numidia be equally divided between his three sons. Hiempsal, Adherbal, and myself. Yet Adherbal wished the Numidian throne all to himself. Shortly after my father's death, Adherbal assassinated Hiempsal in the dark of night, to eliminate a rival to the throne."

The three delegates could not know that it was Jugurtha that had murdered Hiempsal.

"And now, Adherbal has formed designs against my own life. While I was gone to Rome, he raised an army and intended to remove his last rival. But having discovered this I called upon the loyalty of the good people of Numidia and defended myself. Now, when I have all but defeated him, it cannot be just nor reasonable for Rome to withhold from me the common right of all nations. In any case, I will soon send ambassadors to Rome to explain the whole of these proceedings."

The ambassadors were satisfied that Jugurtha spoke true. And in the absence of Adherbal, had no other course. They returned to Rome, and as soon as Jugurtha was assured they had departed Africa, he renewed his efforts.

Chapter Five

Near Boiodurum

September 113 BC

The first fiery colors were bright upon the beech, oak, and hornbeam, and the birch and aspen glittered on the steep slopes like a vast golden treasure, their quaking leaves shimmering in the sunlight of a cool autumn morning. The change of the seasons was upon us, and everyone felt the sense of urgency that came at this time of year. The sights, smells, and sounds of the preparations for winter filled the valley.

The sound of axes and falling trees filled the air as ox teams dragged firewood to a huge pile on the edge of camp to be used through the winter. More teams of men cut the hardwood and dug the charcoal pits for Gorm's forges as he and his smiths built their chimney forges, smelted some of the iron ore we had captured in Noreia, and made repairs to the carts, tools, weapons, and other equipment.

A small army of women and children stooped in the grain fields, cutting the grain stalks with curved hand sickles, where it would lie for several days to dry. Groups of threshers bashed the dried seed heads onto a cloak laid on the ground to loosen the seeds and chaff. When they had a few pounds in the cloth, they picked it up and bounced the grain into the air, allowing the slight breeze to whisk away the light chaff, leaving pounds of clean grain on the cloak which was then stored in clay jars.

The entire valley was a hum of energy as the people prepared for winter, guarded by our warriors, who kept a close watch on the nearby oppidum and surrounding area.

Vallus had told me once that the Romans thought us poor and that we ate raw flesh. That was a myth. Though there were lean times, we seldom went hungry, and now we had wagons full of gold, silver, and iron, weapons and armor, and much more. We had never been richer.

When the leaves turned brown and fell from the trees, it was time for the calves that were born in the spring to begin their training as oxen. This was the responsibility of the adolescent boys, and they took it seriously. Each boy was assigned a team to train to the yoke. First, the calves would be weaned, then castrated, making them steers. The boys would groom them, talk to them, and just spend time with the animals to make them accustomed to human companionship, as up to now they had spent all their time with the herd. As they progressed, they would be hitched to their partner with a light yoke to get them used to the feel of the yoke itself and to begin learning to work together as a team. The boys used voice commands and a crop to teach the young steers to go forward, back up, turn right or left, and stop by tapping them lightly on the shoulders. They began by pulling sleds loaded with wood or small carts and gradually pulled larger and heavier loads. This training would continue for several years and when they were ready to begin their life of service as oxen, a competition was held.

I walked to the field where the four-year-old steers would compete, accompanied as usual by Hrolf and Ansgar. Most of the boys were around fourteen, lanky and tall, and boasting to each other about their teams. When they saw us approach, they ceased their banter and stood tall next to their team.

"A fine bunch of animals I see here today," I said, walking up to the first team, their young master grinning at the praise. I reached out and scratched both animals' necks as they stretched their chins out for me. I could not help but laugh at their reaction to the attention as they both turned their heads and nuzzled into me.

We walked further down the line, speaking to each of the teams in turn until I came to one boy that was taller than the rest. "He's a big one. Reminds me of someone," Hrolf said, glancing at Ansgar and comparing the hulking man at his side to the boy he and I had competed with years ago in the last spring games we had held back in Pannonia. Ansgar had won the champion's competition over Hrolf and earned the privilege of marrying the spring bride. His shaggy blonde hair was cut shoulder length and he wore a long, blonde mustache. He was a huge man, thickly muscled, and covered with battle scars. He was known to friends and family as a gentle giant who seldom uttered harsh words or acted without cause. He was fiercely loyal and completely dependable, but he was a simple man. He did what he was told, and he did it well. He did not have imagination or initiative, but in battle, he was terrifying. When combat was near, he became agitated and anxious, and nothing calmed him until the last enemy lay on the field. He had stood in the front of our lines and led the charge at Noreia against the Romans, naked, wielding a huge battle axe and when the shield walls clashed, he went berserk, laying waste to anything he could reach. Once, a Roman officer tried to rally his men to surround the giant, but Ansgar killed the officer and then half of the remaining legionaries before the rest ran from him. They were probably still running.

"What's your name?" I asked the boy.

"Gunnar, lord," he replied with respect, but without fear. I was surprised at the title.

"And your father?"

"Hugas, lord. He was killed by the Scordisci. My mother died in the plague, and now I live with my uncle's family. We were Boii. My family joined you on the march, lord."

"Why do you call me lord?" I asked.

"It is the custom of my people to call our kings and nobles lord, lord."

"I am not a noble, and I certainly am no king," I said too harshly, embarrassed by the notion. Our people chose clan leaders who were approved by an assembly of elders. The honor tended to pass from father to son. My father and grandfather had been hunno of the wolf clan before me, and there was respect and privilege, but there was no right to the leadership of the clan. If there was no son, or he was not worthy, a new hunno would be chosen. That is why I had not expected to become hunno, as I had been a sickly, unproven young man. After nearly drowning in a raging river, I coughed up the sickness that had clouded my lungs for so long. I was somehow cured, and I immediately began healing. With my father's example, and the tutoring from my friend Vallus, I learned what it meant to become a leader and when my father died in the plague that struck our people in Pannonia, I was chosen to lead the clan, and later the entire tribe.

"Yes, lord," the boy stammered. "I mean, yes, I understand."

I stared at him a moment longer, embarrassed at my outburst, and moved on. We reviewed the rest of the teams and moved to the edge of the field where we would watch the competition.

"The boy's words bothered you," Hrolf said.

"I'm not a king. I was chosen by the elders."

"You were chosen by the gods," he reminded me. "I heard the thunder; I saw the lightning. Donar chose you to lead our people; everyone knows that."

"I'm not a king," I said flatly, making it clear the conversation was over.

Some tribes did have kings. The Boii was one of them. They were

Celts, or Gauls, as the Romans called them, and they called us Germans. But our people were Celts too in ancient times, as were the Scordisci and many other tribes we had come across. The elders remind us that centuries ago, we fought as one under the tribal chieftain Brennus when he invaded Graecia and sacked the ancient temple of Delphi before we traveled north to settle on the coasts of Jutland. It made me wonder if we all came from the same roots in the distant past. We all called ourselves by tribal names, but did all the tribes carry the same blood? We had similar traditions and gods. Could we really be the same people? It was a question for another day. The sound of the horn that announced the beginning of the competition brought me back to the moment.

A sturdy wooden sled sat to one end of the track, loaded with several large boulders that provided the weight to test the oxen's strength. After each round, more stones would be added until the strongest team won. But it was not only a test of strength. They had to pull as a team. If they did not pull together, they could not win, and if the trainer had not done his job well, they would fail. It was not only a lesson to the oxen, but to the boys who trained them. They would one day be warriors in our ranks, and they learned while individuals could have great strength, the real strength was in the tribe all pulling together at the same time for the same purpose.

I looked up as the first team maneuvered to the sled and the heavy chain was hooked to their yoke. The horn sounded a short blast, and the boy shouted a command. The oxen's hooves dug into the ground and their haunches quivered with the effort until the sled began to move, slowly at first, then gaining speed. The spent beasts slowed to a stop and a marker was placed. When they were unhooked from the sled, a team of four oxen moved the sled back into position.

The competition went on for a while as the sleds became heavier and heavier, until it was down to the last five teams.

Gunnar guided his team onto the track. They were tall, a rich brown and were thick in the chest and haunches, and lean in the belly. One had horns that turned downward and the other outward. They were magnificent animals, and it was obvious that he had trained them well.

The horn sounded and Gunnar shouted. The oxen pulled, the crowd cheered, and the sled moved farther than all the other markers. A grinning Gunnar waved at the crowd when the judge declared him the winner.

Nudging Hrolf, I said, "I want Gunnar as a retainer. Teach him everything he needs to know."

Hrolf frowned, "Are you sure? He's just a boy."

"Make him a man," I said. "I want him ready by the time we move on."

There was no harvest celebration for the people who were barricaded behind the walls of Boiodurum. Whatever supplies they had secured before we arrived were likely dwindling, and they were facing a winter of hunger and cold while our bellies were full and our fires warm.

Our encampment stretched for miles along the east side of the En River. The combined tribes now numbered well over eighty thousand with more than twenty thousand warriors. Tribes were normally broken down into clans and spread out over a large area as the land could only support so many people living in one place at the same time. But our herds and the spoils of our conquest allowed us to gather. The hills were denuded of trees for building and for firewood, but we would be moving on in the spring, so it was of little concern to us.

In the midst of the celebration of Samhain as our people feasted before the onset of winter, Hrolf and I threaded the maze of open fires. People shouted drunken greetings and invited us to their fires, and we stopped at many along the way. Eventually, we reached the river's edge and stared across the water at the palisade. Torches flickered in the darkness and reflected off the helmets and spearheads of the sentries at the top of the wall. I could imagine the tightness in their bellies as they watched with hungry eyes.

"We should attack them," Hrolf gestured toward the fortress with his cup of ale.

I remained silent for a few moments. "We will cross when the river recedes in the spring, and we will see then what fortune brings. I see no need to lose good men on an assault on those walls." I said, recalling the strength of the walls of Posonium.

"Besides, what is there to gain? We have already taken their fields, their livestock and the goods they left behind. They might have some gold and silver behind those walls, but is it worth the loss? Better to move on in the spring, I think."

In the days before we left Jutland, our cattle symbolized the tribe's wealth and were vital to our survival, as they are still. They provide the meat that sustains us as our main source of food, but they also provide milk, cheese, and butter.

Culling the smaller and weaker cattle each fall kept the herd healthy and ensured the best animals for breeding. The meat would be smoked, salted, and dried for the winter and the remaining herd required less fodder.

The entire tribe was kept busy from dawn to dusk during the fall slaughter to ensure there was no waste. It was an efficient process and people were assigned according to their abilities and skills. The warriors killed the animals and dressed them out. Children caught as much of the blood as they could in pots and cauldrons and chilled it in a nearby stream. It would be mixed with wild herbs and ground grain or oats to create a thick pudding, especially popular with the elders who had lost their teeth. The youngest separated the kidneys, liver, and stomach into buckets. The heart and tongue would be cleaned and roasted over an open flame and eaten fresh, and the tails were skinned and cut crosswise to make a delicious soup paired with wild onions, herbs, and various wild roots. More children cleaned the intestines, which would be stuffed with the finely chopped kidneys, liver, fat, and smaller bits of flesh that were cleaned from the bones and hide and made into sausages that were salted and then smoked. Once dried, the sausages would last for months. Tripe was a particular delicacy made from the interior lining of the stomach.

Several men stood by to skin the animal immediately after it was killed and dressed out. Each animal was quartered on the hide to keep the meat clean, and then carried to the makeshift tables where the women further butchered the meat into smaller pieces for salting and smoking. The strips of beef were soaked in a salt brine for a day, then hung from willow racks above small fires to allow the smoke to waft over them, curing, and drying the meat. When prepared this way, the meat could be stored for months in clay jars and wooden kegs and barrels.

Tanners took the heavy wet hides aside where they scraped what little meat and fat remained from the hide, then processed it into the leather that would be used for shoes, belts, hats, clothing, leather armor, tents, and the rawhide strips that would provide thongs used to tie up hair, lace shoes, wrap a sword handle, fasten a spearhead to its shaft, or hold a man's leggings tight to his legs.

Their horns were thrown into a pile and would later be turned into drinking cups, signal horns, fasteners, spoons, jewelry, and more.

After the slaughter, the women and children gathered wild onions, roots, mushrooms, and herbs as well as whatever late season berries they could find. Fishermen fished the local rivers, bringing home sturgeon, asp, perch, and pike to add to the smoking fires while the rest of the men headed to the forest to hunt deer, boar, and fowl.

The snows on the northern slopes of the Alpes were deeper than any of the lands we had traveled. The trails had to be tramped down daily or they would become too deep to walk through. There were trails between cabins, to the firewood pile, the water source, the food storage, and the cesspits. The battle of the shit-pits I chuckled to myself, remembering how the people resisted the idea.

I remembered the cesspit back in Borremose. Someone had dug it many years before and the chamber pots were emptied into it daily. It was dug outside the walls to keep the smell at a distance. Slaves came about every morning to collect the foul brews in a handcart and wheel them out to the cesspit, where the wooden pots were emptied, rinsed out, and returned to the longhouses.

On the march, we could have been followed by the trail of dung alone and when halted, the stink became overwhelming within a day, especially at the height of summer. Vallus told us that when the Romans marched, more men were incapacitated from sickness than from combat injuries, and we certainly had experienced that reality in the first years of our journey. In the beginning, people just squatted wherever and whenever they chose, creating an infuriating maze of piles that attracted hordes of buzzing flies all round. The people were despondent from the trauma of the great flood and their forced exodus from our homeland, and they were careless of how they lived. Vallus suggested to my father that when the caravan paused, people should move outside the camp by fifty paces before digging a small hole and covering it up when done. This would at least prevent everyone from stepping in the foul mess.

My friend Vallus, who had served in the Roman army, had convinced my father of the importance of maintaining a clean camp and taught us how to deal with the vast amount of human waste created by a compact group of tens of thousands of people. Not to mention the hundreds of thousands of small animals, fowl, and cattle that accompanied us.

When we halted to set up our winter camps, my father ordered pits dug at several locations around the camp and chamber pots be made for every family. By locating them at a distance from living quarters, and consolidating where people disposed of their waste, we cut illness in half.

On the march, there were thousands of carts pulled by oxen, plus great herds of cattle and other animals that walked within the caravan. Those who traveled at the rear faced the prospect of walking all day over the dung covered ground. To lessen this problem, the herds were separated from the carts and traveled between columns whenever possible, and during our winter halts, they were pastured at a distance from the camp.

These changes made an immediate difference, and they quickly became habits.

I was in deep thought, standing outside our cabin and absently watching the snowflakes floating down upon each other. The countless specks of white, occasionally swirling in a slight breath of air, created a veil that gave the illusion of solitude in the midst of so many souls. I was reminded of the downy seeds of the cottonwood trees floating on a spring zephyr and the billowing clouds of brown leaves that fell from the hardwoods in autumn. I marveled at the many wonders of this world as it cycled through its seasons year after year.

The muffled sounds of my three-year-old son Lingulf arguing with his exasperated mother reached my ears through the cloaked doorway. I smiled as I pictured his defiant stance and the indignant look on his face, upset that she dared to interrupt his play to eat dinner.

The snowstorm was a reminder of that day just a year ago, high in the mountains of Noricum, when Donar announced his approval of my rise to chieftain with thunder and lightning in the dead of winter. I was taking advantage of the rare silence the storm brought to ponder our future. At first, my thoughts returned to the beginning of our journey and the terror that I felt when the great flood devastated our homeland, leaving my people broken and hopeless. My father had provided the strength and wisdom that guided us through that first year when we were forced from our homes. Through his leadership, we traveled many leagues southward until reuniting with the Scordisci, a Celtic tribe living on the plains of Pannonia. Our two tribes had once been part of an ancient expedition that invaded the land of the Hellenes and sacked the shrine of Delphi, plundering the treasures hidden at that holy site, before the Cimbri had migrated northward.

We joined with the Scordisci against an invading Roman army and in return we were welcomed into their lands, rebuilding our homes and our future, until we were struck down by a plague that killed a third of our tribe and made enemies of our two peoples. After a war with the Scordisci, we left Pannonia behind and followed the Dravus River into the mountains of Noricum, where we encountered the Taurisci, a tribe that unknown to us was allied with Rome. After losing so many to the plague and our troubles with the Scordisci, our people were in a killing mood, and they scourged the lands of the Taurisci.

It was in Noricum, in a storm such as this, that my blind sister Hilgi revealed we were cursed by Njoror to roam the world, always searching, never staying in one place more than a winter or risk the wrath of the sea god. The curse could only be broken if Rome invited us into their lands, so when the consul Gnaeus Papirius Carbo arrived with Rome's demands that we leave Noricum, I requested land in exchange for military service, but we were refused and betrayed. After an agreement that we would leave peaceably, Carbo laid an ambush, thinking he would destroy us and gain fame for himself. He failed and we killed twenty thousand Roman soldiers and their auxiliaries. The standards of those legions now stood outside my cabin, a symbol of our victory over the red soldiers.

How was I to convince Rome to grant us land? Surely, they would never consider allowing an enemy into their midst, and after that significant defeat, we had become their mortal enemy.

But the curse of Njoror was also a prophecy that suggested we must fight the Romans, and it named me as the Red Wolf who would defeat the red soldiers while the tribes fought as one.

It foretold that I would lead our people in the quest for a new homeland, and so I was elected chieftain of all the Cimbri, as my father was before me. My unlikely rise from a sickly boy to tribal chieftain meant that our people now looked to me for leadership, something that I still questioned the wisdom of at times.

The curse presented a second quandary. It could only be lifted when the people of Rome welcomed us into their lands. The Roman generals I had seen and spoken to were arrogant, filled so full of pride and disdain for anything not Roman that they seemed incapable of negotiating.

We could appeal a second time to their mercies, but I was sure they would just refuse us again, as they had no need for our skills and now that we had defeated them in battle, we were considered their enemy. We could invade Italy and take the lands we desired, but then we faced destruction as Rome must invite us into their lands to lift the curse. We could turn away again and continue our search. Maybe we could find new lands elsewhere that suited our needs. We had done it once with the Scordisci, why not again? But then, if we stayed anywhere else more than a winter, we faced the wrath of Njoror, who has demonstrated his ability to reach us anywhere. I did not have an answer. What I did have for the moment was time. Winter was beginning, and I had months of inactivity to decide. Realizing that I would not solve our problems today, I turned and entered the cabin, reveling in my son's delight as he saw me come through the door and ran to me, squealing with his arms raised to be picked up.

Chapter Six

Rome

112 BC

Several months later, Adherbal got another message to the senate pleading for their military intervention. Jugurtha had assassinated Hiempsal and now had besieged Adherbal and his loyal citizens along with a number of Roman citizens within the walls of Cirta. He needed help.

"Five months we have been besieged. My army has been defeated. Your ambassadors have been ignored. What then is left, except your arms, that can make an impression upon him?" Adherbal pleaded.

When this letter was received there was talk of sending an army to Africa, but Jugurtha had spread his money wide and there were many senators who believed his lies, or were paid to. Enough to prevent any decree against him being passed. Besides, they were still preoccupied with the northern threat from the Germanic tribes. The senate, growing tired of the incessant fighting of the brothers of Numidia, decided to send another delegation. This one led by the princeps senatus Marcus Aemilius Scaurus.

The following spring, Scaurus arrived in Utica, the provincial capital of Roman Africa. His mission was to negotiate a peace between Jugurtha and his brother Adherbal. This war between brothers had gone on long enough and Rome feared that it would affect the grain supplies that flowed to their warehouses from Numidia. If there were any disruption, it could prove disastrous.

Scaurus was the same man who had negotiated with the Cimbri in Noricum two years earlier. His negotiations had not been successful then, mostly because there was no single leader of the Cimbri and there were many differing voices on what to do. The failed negotiations resulted in a Roman army marching to confront the Cimbri, only to be annihilated when consul Gnaeus Papirius Carbo betrayed the tribes and ambushed them as they turned north and away from Rome's Taurisci allies.

Scaurus summoned Jugurtha to Utica. When the prince learned that a delegation of powerful men that he knew and respected was waiting for him, he made an even stronger attempt to take the city, hoping to be in control of the entire kingdom of Numidia before meeting them. But this attempt failed as well, and so, fearing the displeasure of the senate, he left the city surrounded and rode to meet Scaurus.

"The senate requires that you withdraw your army back beyond the borders that you agreed to three years ago," Scaurus began.

"Senator," the word flowed over Jugurtha's tongue. "I am but righting a wrong that was thrust upon me by my brother. I believe he will soon be ready to admit his treachery, confess to the murder of Hiempsal, and surrender his army. I understand that the senate has received messages requesting your help, but I assure you nothing of what he says is true. This is a matter for Numidia to settle. There is no need for the senate to concern itself." Jugurtha lied smoothly.

Scaurus knew he was lying, and Jugurtha knew that Scaurus knew he was lying. But they continued the game, nonetheless. He continued as if Jugurtha had not spoken. "Numidia is a rich country that plays a significant role in the food supply for Rome, and Rome has pledged its protection to Numidia. But this infighting is unacceptable. Rome really does not care who is in charge, we just want stability, and this endless quarreling is bad for business."

"You can assure the senate that I understand, and that this will soon be over. They have no reason to fear; the grain will flow, trade will flourish, and there will be peace."

"I am also aware that there are Roman merchants and other citizens within the walls of Cirta. We expect you to grant them safe passage to Utica as they wish. There shall be no Roman lives exchanged in your . . . disagreement."

"I will ensure it is done," promised Jugurtha.

When Scaurus returned to Rome, he reported that the matter would soon be settled between the brothers, and that Jugurtha would ensure the supply of grain. The next evening, a messenger arrived at his door. The slave who answered the door said nothing when the messenger handed him a heavy sack. The slave bolted the door and the messenger disappeared into the street. Scaurus smiled slightly when he heard the metallic clink as the slave set the sack on the senator's writing table.

———————————

When Adherbal learned that the senate delegation had left and Jugurtha's troops still surrounded the city, he knew he had been defeated. He had no choice; his people were starving. He surrendered the city, under the terms that no one would be killed, and Jugurtha agreed. But the prince had no intention of letting his brother go free. He wanted this over once and for all. Adherbal was seized and tortured horribly, suffering an agonizing death. In the confusion, one of Jugurtha's commanders misunderstood the prince's intentions and ordered his troops into the city. In the chaos, the Roman citizens were all killed. Furious, Jugurtha in turn killed his commander, but it was too late, the damage was done.

Chapter Seven

Noricum, Salzach River Valley

Spring 112 BC

I led a small scouting party back into the mountains, wandering high above the En River through the naked, gray-brown larch and dark green spruce trees, avoiding the deep snowdrifts that still remained and the limestone boulders strewn about. Picking our way carefully along the steep slopes, we paused often to take in the spectacular views. I was tired of being isolated in a cramped and smoky house and needed no excuse to get away to clear my head. I was thoroughly enjoying the warm spring day.

A pair of my men spotted a roe buck and tracked it down into the valley. I could just make them out in the distance, watering their horses at the river's edge, when my stallion's head suddenly jerked up, ears cupped to a distant sound. I instantly knew something was wrong, but my ears took longer to hear the noise. A deep resounding boom echoed between the hillsides, and the horses shied and whinnied. In the distance a slowly growing rumble filled the air, enveloping us in a blanket of sound. The awareness of what had happened dawned when a wall of water cascaded into the river valley from a gorge high above.

An early thaw had caused a huge amount of meltwater to back up behind a large ice dam high in the mountains. Heavy spring rains brought more water that filled the high valley, creating enormous pressure until the thawing ice began to crack, and with a thunderous crash the water surged forth. The crystal-clear glacial melt turned to a roiling muddy brown mess that contained chunks of ice, uprooted trees, and swept up small boulders in its headlong race down from the heights.

"Get to higher ground!" I shouted to my men, who needed no such instruction and were already scrambling. I turned in time to see the pair of hunters racing back toward the safety of the hillside when the water caught them. They were swept away in an instant and not seen again.

The rest of us frantically climbed above the waterline and turned to watch helplessly. When the surge finally passed, the river crested and returned to its former size, but the entire valley was made nearly impassable with debris. We hurried after the rushing water as best we could, concerned for the safety of our people, whose encampment lay at the mouth of this river. The towering wall of water had emerged from the narrow canyon above our camp and swept everything before it, destroying homes, farmsteads, animals, and everything else in its path. The sentries posted about the encampment blew a warning on their horns, but there had been too little time for people to react.

Those homes built on high ground and out of the water's direct path were safe, but anything close to the river was vulnerable. The vast herds of cattle were pastured near the river where the spring grass was thickest and thousands upon thousands disappeared in the surprise flood. Nearly all the new spring calves who had been frolicking in the river plain were gone. It was a disaster reminiscent of the cataclysm that caused us to leave our homes in Jutland. Several hundred souls were lost to the irresistible wave, swept away into the larger rivers, and drowned. Dozens of homes destroyed, carts and supplies gone. It was a solemn reminder that the sea god still cursed our people.

A month later, the fresh, clean smell of new grass and spruce tips was in the air. We had mourned our dead from the flash flood and the time to move on neared. Once again, the sound of axes chopping and trees crashing to the forest floor echoed off the hillsides. Teams of men felled trees by the hundreds. Wide strips of the partially thawed earth were churned into a deep greasy mud by the teams of oxen that hauled the trees to the riverbank, where another group of workers cut them to size and split them into planks. Dozens of carpenters were supervising the building of new carts to replace the ones we had lost and the flat bottom river barges that the many thousands of our people, animals, and carts would use to cross the river. Once again, Gorm had demonstrated his skill at organizing large projects with many moving parts and the entire operation was running efficiently. He seemed to be everywhere, shouting encouragement, issuing instructions, making corrections and occasionally using his great physical size to make his point to someone who wasn't moving fast enough or working hard enough. The blacksmith was a powerful man, and few cared to match strength with him.

We stood together observing his men put the finishing touches on one of the barges when I heard my name called. I turned in surprise to find Vallus, Tala, and Anik walking toward me with wide smiles.

"My friends! It is so good to see you."

Each came forward and embraced me. Tala engulfed me with his huge arms and with the deep rumble that was his laugh, gave me a heavy swat between the shoulder blades. I was no longer the boy I was when we first met in Posonium, and I stood taller than most, but the giant still towered above me. Tala was a Nubian warrior who, together with his Indian friend Anik, were adventurers who traveled as mercenaries when they could find an employer, and performers when they could not.

Vallus, an old friend of my father's, had been a Roman soldier as a young man and seen the fall of both Carthage and Numantia. When he was gravely injured in the Numantine war, he was medically retired and since then he spent his days walking the trails and roads of the world. He was a trader in information and was always

71

welcome beside a fire as all looked forward to hearing the news from beyond their own small world.

Now he was nearly sixty years old, and though he still had the muscular legs of a legionary, a result of walking thousands upon thousands of miles, he was showing his age. Since I was a child, I thought him old. He seemed almost immortal to me, but he had aged much in the year since I had seen him last.

He could tell by my face what I was thinking. "What's the matter Borr, never seen an old man before?" he chuckled through a toothless grin. I smiled warmly, genuinely glad to see my old friend, and with a welcoming arm around his shoulders, we walked back to my cabin. Frida was outside hanging up the clothes she had just finished washing at the nearby stream and exclaimed with joy when she saw us approaching. Lingulf held back, staring at the strangers who he did not remember. He could not take his eyes off the black giant and when Tala squatted to his level, Lingulf hid behind his mother's skirt.

I don't know if it was Tala's deep voice, brilliant smile, or the mysterious closed fist that he held out toward the boy that convinced him to come forward. When he did, Tala turned his fist over and opened it to reveal several small yellowish-brown objects. Slowly, Tala picked one up and put it in his mouth, smiling broadly and rubbing his belly with the other hand.

"Mmmmmm," he said, and raised his open palm toward the child, offering him a piece. Lingulf stepped cautiously forward and gingerly took one of the bits and placed it in his mouth. His eyes immediately grew large as the crystal dissolved in his mouth.

"It's sweet like honey, Mama," he said excitedly. "It's hard like a rock, but melts in my mouth."

We all stood there, smiling at the exchange between the small boy and the giant warrior.

Tala stood and shrugged when I looked at him expectantly. "Anik got some from an Indian trader at one of the ports we stopped at. It's called sugar."

Frida greeted each of them with a hug and kiss on the cheek and invited them to sit while she prepared some food. Vallus had left us last year in the spring before we met Carbo and wanted to hear the tale of our battle and everything that had transpired since. We sat for hours as I recounted my meetings with the treacherous Roman general and our defeat of his two legions. He was fascinated by the description of the beautiful hidden valley of the salt people and appalled when I recounted the hundreds dead from the flash flood.

During his travels, Vallus avoided the mountain passes because the wild mountain tribes did not recognize his neutrality and would have robbed and killed him for his meager possessions and the meat his ox would provide. When he heard we had gone over the mountains, he returned to Posonium on the Danubius River, where he found Tala and Anik again. Together they paid for space on a trader's barge, traveling west on the Danubius until they came to our camp. Vallus tipped his head toward Gorm's boat works and asked what our plans were for the summer.

"Providing we don't have any further disasters I hope to cross the river as soon as possible and continue westward. The curse requires us to continue moving, so we have little choice," I said.

Vallus said, "If you'll have us, we hoped to travel with you. I have not traveled in Gaul on the north side of the Alpes and would like to see it before I die. These mountains are truly something to behold."

"I will be happy to have you and your counsel," I said. Then, nodding toward Tala and Anik, I continued, "And both of you by my side in battle."

Later that night, Vallus brought me up to date on the news from Rome. It was nearly a year since the battle at Noreia and they were still waiting for the attack they were sure would come from the north.

"The edge on that blade is dulling," he said. "The legions you defeated were punished and disbanded. Carbo was prosecuted and committed suicide. And time has a way of fading even such a terrible memory. Their attention is shifting toward Africa, where Jugurtha is making noises."

"Who is Jugurtha?" I asked.

"A prince of Numidia, a kingdom in the north of Africa. If you remember, I told you that I fought in the war against Carthage, that is on the same coast across the Mare Nostrum from Italy."

"I remember now," I said. "How is Rome involved there?"

"Numidia is a large grain supplier for Rome. They have also been a military ally for many years. In the Numantine war where I was wounded, that was in Hispania to the west," he explained, "Jugurtha commanded an auxiliary unit of Numidian cavalry. They are some of the best horsemen to be found. Anyway, when King Micipsa died about five years ago, the kingdom was supposed to be split three ways. Between his two sons, Adherbal and Hiempsal, and his nephew and adopted son, Jugurtha. It didn't take long for Jugurtha, an experienced warrior prince, to assassinate Hiempsal and then attack Adherbal. Adherbal appealed to Rome and things have been at a stalemate since, but now Jugurtha appears to be making another attempt at getting rid of Adherbal and claiming the throne for himself. There have been several attempts to intervene, with little success. Jugurtha has bribed the peace delegations and much of the senate to look the other way. He's as slippery as an eel and cunning as a fox. He is a competent military commander and very persuasive in politics."

I considered what Vallus said, then replied. "So, Rome has forgotten about us for the moment?"

"There are still those that fret you will come back and attack into Italy, and there are some who would seek you out for retribution, but it seems most have moved on to other concerns. They are still fighting with the Scordisci in Macedonia. The new consul Marcus Livius Drusus is heading there now, and this business with Jugurtha has the potential to pull them into war in Africa. Since you have seemingly disappeared back to the north, their attention is elsewhere."

We all toasted to friendship and laughed and cried long into the night, recounting tales of bravery and defeated enemies and lamenting loved ones who were no longer with us.

The following day, I sent a party across the river to seek out the local tribes and negotiate our passage if possible. I watched as the last of them disappeared into the forest to continue their reconnaissance.

They were gone for several days when I was alerted of their return. "Something isn't right," I said to Hrolf and Freki, who had followed me to the riverbank and looked into the distance.

Only one was visible. His horse seemed agitated and moved about in a small area without any seeming direction from its rider, who sat his mount stiffly. Freki took a dozen riders across the river to investigate and as they approached, they could see that the man had been tied to a framework which kept him upright on his mount as if he was riding it. His throat was slit, and his chin rested on his chest, which was covered with dried blood. The horse was staked to the ground with a length of rope that allowed it to move about in a small circle, and two burlap sacks hung across its withers caked with blackened blood. The entire area was swarming with black flies attracted by the blood and were tormenting the horse. As they approached, the stench threatened to cause them to lose their breakfast. One of the men sent to investigate sliced the bottom of a bag and the heads of the rest of the scouts tumbled to the ground.

The message was clear. We were not welcome in Raetia.

Mid-June 112 BC

I led my horse from the first barge that touched the sandy shallows of the En River, followed by Hrolf and Ansgar, Tala and Anik, and a dozen of my retainers. After an undignified scramble up the muddy bank, I mounted the stallion to watch as hundreds more rafts, barges, and boats just behind mine delivered ten thousand warriors out of Noricum and into Raetia, home of the Vindelici. The river was the border between the two Celtic lands, and was a significant obstacle, but we had grown competent in crossing rivers of every size.

Gorm and his crews had made many crafts that could be poled across the wide river, and the first wave was an impressive sight as they landed on the far shore.

The polemen were near exhaustion by the time they got to the far side. Gorm made the correction when they returned and fresh warriors poled the next wave over so that the polemen were fresh for the return trip. The crafts made many trips that day.

My men had been well briefed and were moving as soon as they touched dry land. The mounted warriors immediately fanned out and established a screen to warn us of any threat. Warriors on foot moved behind them and took up defensive positions in a semi-circle around the landing site. No one opposed us and as I looked toward the oppidum, I could see heads above the palisade, watching our invasion of their land. I smiled grimly as I imagined what they were thinking.

Frantic shouts from the river alerted me to a crisis. The current had pushed two rafts into each other and the oxen, already on edge from standing on the moving flatboats, were knocked off balance. In an effort to find solid footing, they made matters worse by shifting their great weight, jostling the barges and causing water to slosh over the sides. Each team was hitched to a treasure cart and the great weight of the gold and beasts made the rafts ride low in the water. When the water sloshed around their feet, the oxen panicked. They were not far from the bank when suddenly one of the oxen in the first craft decided it had had enough and bolted for dry land. When it tried to push its way to the front, the boat became overloaded and nosed down into the river. Immediately, the deck was washed with water and spun around in the current. In an instant, it flipped over, dumping everything into the river. Several men drowned before they could swim ashore or be pulled onto another barge. The oxen still hitched to the treasure carts were dragged to the bottom while the capsized barge careened off several others, threatening to sink them in turn. A worse disaster was avoided when two men who had been crossing with their families managed to get a purchase with their poles and push the capsized barge out into the river where it was swept downstream. The men on the second barge calmed their beasts and made it to shore through it all, though I don't think they took a breath until they were safely on land. It took the remainder of the day and half the next to get everyone across, but there were no further incidents.

I took two thousand warriors to investigate Boiodurum. They approached from the west, pushing aside the crude obstacle that crossed the peninsula. There were no guards and we walked unopposed to within sight of the city gates. For the last few days, I had noted that there was less and less smoke rising from inside the fortress and my suspicion that they had abandoned it was confirmed when we walked through the open gate. The ground was littered with belongings that had been dropped in their hasty evacuation that had begun when they had seen us preparing to cross the river.

We followed the trail of personal things toward a gate that was open on the far side of the fortress. Hrolf and I stood at the top of the stairs that led to the river harbor and watched as the last of the river boats struggled against the current and past the rock shelves, pushing their way west. A group of men on the boat watched us, flinging curses at us as they disappeared behind the trees at the river's edge.

Chapter Eight

Rome

"This is an outrage!"

"This calls for war!"

The senate was in an uproar. They had just learned that the Numidians had executed the Roman merchants, and Jugurtha's silky tongue was not going to save him this time. Even the senators that had received bribes for protecting his interests in the senate were cursing him now.

Gaius Marius decided to attend the emergency meeting and was secretly enjoying the show of mock indignation. Most of the men in this room had taken bribes or accepted gifts from Jugurtha. The thought that they cared about the deaths of Roman citizens was preposterous. They cared little for the lives of their own subjects. What they cared about was the appearance of weakness that this situation presented, and any perceived weakness threatened their positions of influence. They were suddenly faced with the reality that the Roman public demanded action and if decisive action was not taken, the least of their worries would be political losses.

Jugurtha himself maneuvered outside the awareness of the average citizen. They only knew him as a hero of the Numantine war, the handsome prince from the exotic continent of Africa that commanded the Numidian cavalry that served Scipio. Most had no idea where Numidia was, but they knew that it supplied Rome with the grain that kept the masses from starving. The thought of that supply being cut off during a war was frightening. But they also wanted vengeance. How dare these African upstarts openly murder Roman citizens?

On their way to this morning's session, the senators walked through the gathering crowds. Soon the crowds would turn into angry mobs demanding something be done. Names would be called out as having been corrupted by Jugurtha's influence. Accusations would be made. A blow would be thrown. The whole situation could turn bloody in an instant. The senators knew what had to be done.

Both consuls for the current year had already left for their assigned duties, as had pro-consuls and pro-praetors who might have taken up arms against Jugurtha. Besides, it was already mid-summer. By the time legions were raised, equipped, trained, and prepared for transport to Africa, the stormy season would have arrived, and no one wanted to send an army into the unpredictable weather that ruled the Mare Nostrum from October to April.

Under the law passed ten years ago, the senate selected the consular provinces before the consuls themselves were elected. The senate declared war on Numidia. One of the two consuls elected for the coming year would be responsible for bringing Jugurtha to justice. In the meantime, a fresh army would be raised, and money set aside for the campaign. As soon as the weather allowed in the spring, the army would embark.

Chapter Nine

Along the Danubius

Summer 112 BC

"Damn these infernal bugs!" I smacked my forearm with a loud slap, crushing the insect and smearing a large spot of blood and sweat. "Why is it they never seem to bother you?"

"Clean living, I suppose," Hrolf chortled. "Maybe you have angered one god or another and they are punishing you."

"If that were true, he's punishing everyone but you."

Clouds of insects swarmed about the horses and cattle, who shook their heads constantly, flicking their ears and swishing their tails in a futile attempt to chase away the biting flies.

I was still stinging from the loss of our scouts and the fact that I was unable to speak with the Raetians. I wanted information and I was getting none. I did not like moving blind.

Our path had taken us into the swamps that fringed the Danubius River, and it had been a miserable week as the heavy carts slogged through the shallow water, muck, fallen branches and underwater hummocks. Carts got stuck constantly and required another oxen team, even two sometimes to pull them out. In the worst places, teams of men were assigned to cut small trees and create a rough roadway of timbers.

When night fell, there was little high ground to take advantage of.

Most had to sleep in the cramped carts with their belongings and the animals were forced to bed down in the shallow water or stand all night. Those without carts had little choice but to sit with their back against a tree, their buttocks and legs and feet submerged. Many suffered from skin rashes and chafed until they bled in the crotch, knees, and armpits. Leather boots rotted and fell apart and many were now barefoot. Everyone was covered in muddy, wet clothes that never fully dried, and their feet and toes were puckered and pale.

At last, the trees began to thin, and we slowly climbed out of the wetlands to emerge into bright sunlight and a wide plain. The caravan needed no instruction to spread out and make camp and by nightfall a great many had left the swamp behind them. It took several more days for the rest to join us and I ordered a halt to allow everyone to rest and recover before we moved on.

The traveling was much easier now that we had left the swamps and biting insects behind us. We skirted the southern foothills and spread across the river valley until we came to the Isar River, which fed into the Danubius. There was a gravel bottomed ford that allowed us to cross with little delay and we continued into the vast plain ahead.

The beauty of this land was striking. The Danubius flowed through a wide valley that lay between the snow-capped peaks looming to our south and the smaller, forested mountains north of the river. The southern edge of the Hercynian Forest began across the great river from us and extended northward for untold leagues. Staring at the dark trees, I thought of the weeks we had spent crossing that trackless forest on our journey south what seemed like a lifetime ago. So much had happened in just seven years. Our home was destroyed by the great flood at the hand of Njoror, the sea god, and we had suffered much on our journey. I had lost my parents and my friend Skalla along with a third of the tribe to a mysterious plague that we later found was set upon us by Njoror, just when we believed we had found a new home. Njoror's curse was later revealed to me by my sister, Hilgi. Blinded by the plague, she became a dreamer and was now cared for by the mysterious priestesses who, along with the white-robed priests, kept our religion alive. When we met with the Romans in Noricum, I requested land that would allow us to end our quest, but we were denied and betrayed by a treacherous Roman general who attempted to ambush our caravan. But we found them out before they could do so and instead defeated them in a one-sided battle that left two of their vaunted legions lying dead on the battlefield.

The road before us was wide and hard packed as it wound through the vast fields south of the Danubius. The caravan, too large to be contained by the width of the road, tramped through the fields of unharvested wheat and other crops.

A column of smoke attracted Freki's scouts where they found an old man cooking oat cakes beside a small fire. He had stayed behind when the other villagers had fled. "I'm too old to run," he said, gumming an oatcake into a mush and swallowing. "Besides, what have I to fear of death?" he asked with a shrug. "I have nothing, and I have lived a long life. I do not fear death. When it comes, I will welcome it." When I questioned him, he told me nothing that I didn't already know, so I ordered them to take him back to where they found him and leave him be.

The land we traveled now was tamed. Small steadings of well-built circular houses and communal buildings appeared over each rise. Modest roads connected the villages. The fields were cultivated, and large paddocks surrounded by fences of stone and timbers had enclosed swine and cattle and sheep and goats a short time ago, but they were all empty now. We saw no people as the caravan swept through the small farming settlements whose occupants had fled ahead of the horde of fierce warriors that strode boldly at our front.

"It wasn't deserted a few days ago," Hrolf pointed out. "The word is spreading of our approach. I think we should proceed with great caution. They've likely pulled back and gathered their forces. We know we are not welcome here. Boiodurum refused to talk with us, and our scouts were killed. We have received no ambassadors. We have to assume they're hostile."

"Wouldn't you be?" asked Freki.

"We'll halt here for two weeks," I said. "I want any settlements you come across searched but left standing. Take anything useful. I want the fields harvested if they are ready. If there is any livestock, add them to our herds."

"And if we encounter anyone?" Hrolf asked.

"Send your patrols out strong. Take what we need. If we are attacked, we will defend ourselves, but I want no unnecessary killing. So far, they seem to wish to avoid conflict. Let's keep it that way if we can. We are just moving through their land, and I have no wish to start a war."

The oppidum of Alcimoennis sat upon a high limestone cliff across the Danubius from us, on a peninsula formed where the Alcimona River joined with the greater watercourse. The fortress was unassailable on three sides due to the cliffs and on the fourth a defensive ditch and wall crossed the peninsula, blocking the only approach. It looked much like Boiodurum except for the numerous columns of acrid black smoke rising from the iron smelting furnaces. The smell of rotten eggs and burning charcoal hung in the air. The entire valley was pockmarked with shallow pits where iron ore was dug, and the surrounding fields and hillsides had been stripped of trees to fuel the furnaces.

The walls of the fortress itself consisted of upright timbers sunk into the earth separated by a space equal to a man's outstretched arms. Stacked limestone blocks filled the space between the timbers to the height of three men, behind which was a thick earthen rampart. The fortress appeared invincible, and they obviously had no wish to trade or talk, so I kept the column moving westward.

The caravan stretched more than a mile from side to side and when

I looked behind me, the train of people, animals, and carts disappeared into the distance. I sat my horse on a hillock for a time, watching the multitude pass below me.

A rooster stood tall and crowed, flapping its wings pretentiously from his perch on a fallen log as his brood of hens cackled loudly, running randomly amongst the feet and hooves, stopping to scratch and peck for bugs. A large black hen found a fat grub and a second one immediately snatched it out of her beak and swiftly ran away, pursued by the protesting victim and several more fowl seeking to steal the morsel for themselves.

A sounder of swine happily rooted in a turnip field, plowing the vegetables up with their snouts. Long tendrils of drool flapped about as they chomped loudly, crushing the fibrous roots to a pulp in their powerful jaws. Several piglets squealed and scattered when a fat sow spun around and snapped at the litter of newly weaned piglets that chased after her, still trying to suckle at her low hanging teats. Cattle lowed, ducks and geese quacked and honked, goats and sheep bleated.

Tens of thousands of people walked beside the lumbering carts that creaked and rocked back and forth over the uneven terrain, their axles straining and shrilly crying out from the heavy load they were carrying. Here and there a cart was broken down and a team of Gorm's wagon tenders surrounded them, making repairs. The sights, sounds, and smells of the march had become familiar, even comforting, and as we passed that formidable bastion across the river, I could not help but feel pride in the horde that tramped through this river valley while those who hid behind those walls watched impotently.

I wondered where all the people had gone and, more importantly, where were their warriors.

"We should have made contact with someone by now," Hrolf said. He was concerned that we hadn't seen any warriors except the occasional scout since we left Boiodurum. "I would have expected at least some raids along the column or something. Nothing has happened. We've been burning villages, taking livestock and anything left behind and they don't respond."

"It is strange." I was puzzled. We had traveled many miles and passed several fortresses without encountering any resistance. "Each of those fortresses should be able to muster several thousand warriors," I said. "Where are they?"

A day later, one of my scouts galloped into camp as twilight fell. I had called an assembly of leaders to discuss our progress and we had just finished a supper of hard bread and beef stew prepared by Frida.

"A large army...a day's ride west," he reported breathlessly.

"How many?" I asked.

"Thousands lord, too many to count," he said excitedly. I frowned in distaste at the appellation but ignored it for now. Apparently, the use of it was spreading. He misread my expression and added, "Maybe twenty thousand?" trying to be helpful.

Claodicus whistled softly. He was tall. A handsome man and fearsome warrior that led the boar clan.

"Twenty thousand!" exclaimed Lugius, hunno of the Bear Clan. He was of my father's generation and the eldest of our clan leaders.

"Cavalry?" I asked.

"Five hundred at most," replied the young scout.

"What are they doing?" prompted Freki. "How are they positioned? What's the terrain like? Come on man, spit it out."

The young man was nervous, but he was a good scout, and he knew his business. "They are assembled on the river plain in our line of march. They're dressed and armed for war and appear to be waiting for us. Their left flank is anchored on the wetlands by the river and their right is against a cliff."

"Good," I said. "At least we know where they are. I was wondering when they would show themselves."

"Twenty thousand warriors," Caesorix repeated. "They must be consolidating their forces. We will be closely matched in numbers. We might have twenty-five thousand able to fight." Caesorix was hunno of the raven clan and had opposed my rise to chieftain but had since become one of my most loyal supporters.

Hrolf nodded his head in agreement and raised an eyebrow at me in question.

I didn't reply. I turned and stared into the fire for a moment to think. What could we do? They were directly in our path. I had been expecting a fight since our scouts were murdered. But since we left Boiodurum, we had seen no warriors, only scouts that monitored our progress and always kept at a distance. We had passed two fortresses and many villages and farmsteads. Those people must have withdrawn as we advanced and were now formed up against us.

"We will move in the morning as usual. Tomorrow evening, keep a screen on our flanks and rear and move the bulk of your warriors forward in the line of march," I said. "Prepare for battle the day after tomorrow," I said, dismissing the gathering as Freki approached. "Hrolf," I beckoned with a tip of my head. "Would you wait, please?"

When everyone else had left I nodded at Freki to speak.

"I sent the messenger back when we sighted the army and continued past them to see what lay beyond. There is a large city on our side of the Danubius. It sits on low ground beside a tributary that leads to the river. It has formidable walls, but we won't have to cross any water or climb cliffs to get to it." We talked well into the night and when we parted I had settled on a plan of battle.

Chapter Ten

The Vindelici anxiously watched the horizon as the sounds of war drums reached them. Their first sight of our army was a wide line of ox-drawn carts cresting the rise before them. The hide of a young calf was stretched and dried between the staves of a dozen carts to create a huge drum. A deep rumble carried across the field as priests enthusiastically beat them with the leg bones of the calf that provided the leather for the drumhead. Boys who were too young for battle carried their own drums of various sizes and their sounds added to the din.

Our battle song echoed off the nearby hills as my warriors assembled before the Vindelici. With practiced speed, the clans formed into their hundreds, their headmen, or hunnos, at the front of each wedge. My companions and I trotted across their front to the center of the line. A great cheer arose as we passed and followed us like a wave through the gathered warriors. I was flanked by Hrolf, Ansgar, Tala, and Anik. Gunnar carried my standard, a long pole with a red painted wolf's skull affixed to the top and a long red linen streamer that caught the wind and flowed out behind. My wolf-warrior Skol, who I had raised from a pup stood at my side, his lips pulled back, baring his teeth and snarling toward the enemy.

Each hunno had a standard at the head of their clans; a black raven's wing fastened to the top of a tall pole for the raven clan, a bronze boar for the boar clan, and so on. Some were cast or shaped from metal, some carved from wood, some were pennants of linen in various shapes and colors with painted symbols on them. All represented a hundred or more warriors who followed them into battle. And there were many of them.

Behind us, beyond the crest of the hill, were the thousands of carts that carried our families and everything we owned. The carts formed a fortified encampment that encircled our livestock, and its defense was under the command of my trusted friend Gorm the blacksmith.

We looked every bit the fierce north men that the more civilized Gauls had clashed with in the past. Long hair was knotted on the right temple or hung unbound. Nearly every man wore a beard. Many wore only trousers or went completely naked. Some wore the mail coats captured from the Romans, but most could not as they were so much larger than the soldiers who died wearing them. There were many Roman swords in our ranks, but most still carried spears, axes, or the longer swords favored by our people for generations.

At my signal, the drums went silent. I stepped forward, accompanied by Hrolf and Ansgar. The Vindelici chieftain met me at the center of the field, two fierce looking warriors a step behind him.

He was resplendent in a polished mail coat that glowed in the morning light and a conical bronze helmet topped with a black horsetail plume. A thick torque of twisted gold encircled his neck, and his sword belt and scabbard were laced with gold wire and decorated with colorful enamel panels. The long tails of his blonde mustache hung below his chin and quivered in the slight breeze.

"Who are you?" he challenged me.

"Borr," I replied. "Chieftain of the Cimbri and leader of the allied tribes you see before you."

"I am Reginus, king of the Vindelici," he said thumping his chest. "These are my lands you invade. My people you threaten. My crops you have stolen. You were warned not to come here, yet here you are. My scouts have been watching you since you entered my kingdom at Boiodurum. We have withdrawn our forces from each city, each village, as you advanced, to gather here to meet you in battle."

He turned round, proudly sweeping his arms to emphasize the size of his force.

"We are prepared to destroy you, here and now," he continued. "But I am a generous king. I offer you a choice. You will go north across the river, and back into the swamps that spawned you, or you will be slaughtered. Your women will become playthings for my warriors, and your children will be sold into slavery. All that you own will become mine, and you will be forgotten. Like a flock of birds that flies overhead, you will leave no mark of your passing."

I had wished to avoid conflict. I only wanted to move on, to take what we needed to survive, and to avoid another disaster brought on by the curse. We were not conquerors. The one thing we could not take was their land. But the Vindelici had formed for battle, and that could not be ignored. I understood, of course; I expected it. When a great mass of people passes through land ruled by another, there must be conflict. We took what we needed to survive, which meant that the Vindelici would go hungry. No king could allow that.

I stared at him until he looked away. He was afraid. His seeming confidence was bravado. He shifted his weight and looked back at me, awaiting a reply. Our armies were close in number, and his men were defending their homes and families. But ours had been fighting for survival for years. We had fought the Boii, the Scordisci, the Romans, and I knew each of my men was worth two or three of theirs. We were the wolves of the north. Battle hardened, honed to a fine edge by the challenges to our survival that we had faced over the years. This was his gamble. He was betting everything that we would just go away. But we would not. Not this time.

"I tried to talk with you before we crossed into your lands," I replied. "You killed my scouts and avoided me. If you had bothered to meet me, you could have avoided this. I've been north of the river. I don't wish to go back."

Reginus opened his mouth to say something, and I cut him off. "I will give you a choice. We don't wish to stay in your lands, but I will not leave an army at my back. You may surrender your arms to us, pay tribute in food and gold, and you may live, or you may fight us here and die and we will take those things anyway. Which do you choose?"

He drew himself up. "We will never surrender to you, northern scum," he said, pointing with his chin to the ranks of warriors behind me.

I was looking past the chieftain's shoulder and for a fleeting moment thought I saw a familiar face in the ranks that faced us. It disappeared in the rippling line just as quickly as it had appeared and at Reginus' last words I looked calmly back at him. "So, you choose to die then?"

His hand went to his sword hilt at the insult, but when Ansgar took a step forward he decided against drawing it and instead turned on his heel and stalked back to his lines.

I was becoming more confident, and I allowed my arrogance to show. I was young, and I was still uncertain of my path, but I had seen battle many times. I had led my people to victory over the vaunted Roman legions at Noreia. I no longer doubted my ability to fight an enemy. In fact, I looked forward to it. I had come far since I was the weakling son of Haistulf, Hunno of the Wolf Clan, and at twenty-three, I was still young enough to feel the need to prove it.

I returned to my warriors smiling and raised my arms above my head. The drums renewed and the barritus began. They held the top of their shields before their mouths to resonate the sound of their voices as a low, guttural roar emanated over the battlefield. It is strange what passes through a man's mind before battle. Time seems to slow, and the senses sharpen. Standing there across the field from a formidable enemy, the sound of the war drums and the barritus faded in my consciousness as I was distracted for a moment by a bee crawling slowly around the top of a bright yellow flower several paces in front of me in the meadow. The flower bobbed back and forth from the motion of the bee as it crawled inside a blossom and backed out to repeat his task again and again, gathering the sweet nectar, oblivious to the pending battle. Its task complete, it lifted off, translucent wings propelling it toward the enemy lines. I watched the black speck as it flew directly at Reginus until I could no longer see it. Suddenly he jerked and slapped the side of his neck, reacting to the bee stinging him. It was an omen. A good one.

Warriors all boast of their eagerness for battle, giving the impression that they have no fear of death. Bards sing their songs and recite stirring poems of the slaughter of past battles and the bravery of this warrior or that, but so much of it is nonsense. When a man is faced with the possibility of his own death, he begins to question the wisdom of charging into the blades of an enemy shield wall. They question if their cause is worth the risk. Some allow the men beside them to step past them in the ranks, gradually slipping backward into the mass, especially in the last rush forward. This is not cowardice, but simply the natural fear each of us holds of a crippling wound or death. It is a natural act of self-preservation. Sometimes, the fear of being seen as a coward is enough to overcome this.

For many, the false courage provided by ale was enough. For others, the promise of Valhol through honorable death on the battlefield helped. However it was achieved, conquering that fear was the real bravery.

The Vindelici warriors stood a hundred paces to our front. Many wore iron chest plates and tall helmets crested with figures of animals and birds, most wore only simple trousers tied at the ankle, and some wore nothing at all. Their noblemen wore mail coats, and most carried long swords and spears. They displayed an assortment of oval and round shields painted in bright colors and designs. There were at least twenty thousand, probably more, but as our warriors continued to pour onto the battlefield their lines

93

visibly wavered as doubt crept into their minds.

Their leaders shouted at them, haranguing them to respond to our battle song, and they did, hammering their shields with swords, axes, and spear hafts in their own battle song. Warriors up and down both lines were loosening up, shaking their heads, bouncing up and down, shaking their weapons, hefting their iron bound shields, and working up the battle courage that was needed to face an enemy that must kill you to survive.

I looked left and saw Caesorix at the front of his men watching me, then looked to my right at Claodicus and Lugius beyond him, then nodded to Hrolf. He raised the ox horn to his lips and blew a long note to signal the advance, and with a sweep of my arm, I stepped forward. With each step, spears and swords and axes clashed against shields, and a great shout arose. Crash, crash, "Hoosh!" Crash, crash, "Hoosh!"

Maintaining the kind of battlefield discipline that the Romans displayed was impossible with warriors who were accustomed to fighting as individuals. But I had learned that I could control my warriors up to the point of joining battle, and that would have to be enough. Our steps settled into a pace that matched the rhythm of the drums, and the ground seemed to tremble with each step as the barritus grew louder. When we had advanced halfway across the field, the carnyx came alive with a strident blare. The drums pounded faster, and our pace quickened. This was the signal for the wedges to begin their charge and with a roar they burst forward, finally unleashing their pent-up battle rage in an unstoppable assault. Twenty paces before the two sides crashed together, the rear ranks seemed to stutter a few steps as they loosed their javelins over the heads of the leaders.

The Vindelici spears darkened the sky just before the impact and we raised shields to receive them. Men fell, and those behind stumbled on them. Skol raced ahead and just before our lines met, he leaped at a man in the front rank. I saw the warrior brace himself, but he was thrown back by the impact of the hurtling beast. Men tried to skewer the flash of fur and teeth, but Skol leaped over the fallen warrior and into the second rank, creating a break in the shield wall as men scrambled to avoid his snapping jaws.

A spear lodged itself in my shield, the point finding its way between two willow boards and penetrating through to the inside just missing my arm. It dislodged as I drove my shield into the man directly in front of me and I followed Skol through the opening, screaming my challenge. Hrolf was to my right protecting me with his shield as he widened the opening, and the giant Ansgar followed him. His large battle axe cleaved an elaborate helmet in two and buried itself in the man's torso, blood and brains erupting in a shower of gore. Tala was to my left, his huge sword stacking the dead as the Vindelici warriors pushed forward to close the gap. Anik protected the Nubian's flank. He was the fastest swordsman I had ever seen, and he parried spears and swords alike with a fury of flashing blades.

As the points of each wedge made contact, the flanks rushed forward, crashing into the opposing line with an immense force. More warriors followed us through the breach as Skol created chaos in the enemy ranks. I stabbed my sword at the man pushing against my shield, but the crush pressed us as close as lovers and I had no room to move my arm. My sword was trapped between the bodies and all I could do was saw it back and forth and try to reach an unprotected spot. A spear grazed my arm, and I heard a scream behind me as it found a target. The sudden pain caused me to lose my grip on my long sword and it fell to the ground. I pulled my seax and stabbed the short blade between the shields. This time it struck mail and I leaned into the thrust. I felt a sudden give as it pierced the rings and then ripped into the soft belly of the man in front of me. His face contorted in pain, and he opened his mouth in a silent scream, but only his ale stinking breath escaped. A stream of bright red blood ran down his chin as I heaved up on the blade, cutting him to his breastbone.

A horn blast sounded to my right, announcing the enemy cavalry as they charged forward, attempting to turn our right flank. For a moment I feared they would succeed, but Hrolf had prepared the units on our flanks well and they were ready. They planted the butt spikes of their spears into the ground and leaned the blades outward from behind their shields. Horses will hesitate when faced with a solid shield wall bristling with spears, and that is what they did as they pounded toward our lines. Confusion reigned as the lead mounts slowed and tried to veer off and those behind crashed into them.

Seeing the Vindelici commit their horsemen, Freki charged from his hidden position striking the rear of the Gallic cavalry. Clods of earth flew toward the sky as they pounded forward, spears leveled at the enemy. I risked a glance above my shield and watched as the point of Freki's spear pierced his opponent's back, bulging out the front of his mail coat as the man arched away from the pain. In the same moment, my brother let go of the spear and pulled his sword, swinging it back into the neck of another warrior whose blood splashed red in the sunlight. The screams of man and horse filled the air as they were trapped between Freki's horsemen and my heavy spearmen, who now charged into the chaos. The thick hafted spears drove into the bellies of the confused and terrified horses and the riders were pulled to the ground. The spearmen drew their swords, and it became a slaughter.

The Vindelici infantry facing us were stubbornly holding their ground. We had broken through their center but because the two armies were so close in number, we were spread thin and didn't have the depth to exploit the breach. My retainers and I had pushed forward through the gap and formed a pocket, and now we were surrounded on three sides by enemy warriors. Suddenly, we were in danger of being separated from our lines. I shouted for them to lock shields and step back. There were just too many enemies in front of us. Our small group was being constricted by the weight of the ranks pushing hard against us, and Reginus had seen the opportunity to cut us off. He smelled victory and ordered his men to attack the neck of the bubble. A surge of doubt struck me; did

I miscalculate? Did I get us all killed with my brashness? A spear point struck my shield on the left side, tipping it and opening a gap between Hrolf's shield and mine. A large enemy warrior stepped forward to take advantage of the opening and I struck out wildly. My arm now had room to move and the tip of my seax slashed his throat, splashing me with his lifeblood as he dropped his weapon and tried to stanch the flow with both hands. The blood leaked between his fingers and down his chest as he collapsed to his knees. I kicked him backwards into the man behind him, causing that man to stumble. Hrolf buried his sword in the man's skull, giving us time to lock shields again.

Slowly, I became aware of a lessening of pressure on the pocket we had created and a growing roar coming from the rear of the enemy lines. I looked over my shield to try and see what was happening and ducked back to avoid a spear blade aimed at my face. Ansgar nearly took my head with a wild swing as he killed the spearman ahead of me, and through the space he had cleared I could see that the Vindelici were being attacked in the rear by a new enemy. I tried to make sense of what was happening when I saw a banner that I recognized. It was a black, two-headed battle axe on a yellow background. It was Teutobod's banner. I was confused. The Teutones. Where had they come from? My mind wandered even in the press of the shield wall, then was brought back to the present by a solid blow on my battered shield that pushed my arm back into my chest. Then, like smoke in the wind, the enemy before me vanished. A line of mangled bodies lay piled before us where we had fought so desperately. One moment I could hardly move due to the crush of bodies and the next was as if a dam burst and the Cimbri flowed forward in a rush. All semblance of order on both sides was lost, and the Vindelici turned and fled, pursued by my wild warriors close on their heels.

Over their heads, I could see Teutobod beneath his banner swinging a large two headed battle axe like the one on his banner. Relief swept over me as I realized that after being so close to defeat, we had suddenly won. The Teutones had come from nowhere and joined the fight, surprising the Vindelici with an attack on their rear ranks and saving us from loss.

In the confusion I spotted Reginus standing his ground and encouraging a group of men, probably his retainers, to fight on in the face of the new enemy that decimated his warriors. The Gauls fought desperately until Reginus fell under a tide of Germanic warriors.

The sun had risen well above the horizon and chased away the heavy clouds by the time the thrum of the great war drums of the Cimbri reached the ears of those left in the Vindelici capital. After a time, the sound of fifty thousand voices rose and fell from several miles away as the two sides roared their challenges toward each other. Finally, the loud crash of shields slamming together echoed against the nearby hills, accompanied by the growing roar of combat.

Within the hour, the first runner appeared on the path to the fortress, glancing over his shoulder in utter terror. Fear lent wings to his feet as he sprinted toward the safety of the city walls. Soon, he was followed by more runners, then small groups, and finally a rush of men fleeing the chaos of the battlefield where the army of the Vindelici was dying on the blades of the north men. They had cast down their weapons and shields and ran as fast as their feet would carry them.

Lugius ran at the head of his clan as they pursued the fleeing warriors from the battlefield and he saw the gates standing open, their wide jaws jammed with the crowd of panicked warriors. Men atop the walls shouted a warning to close the gate, but it was too late, hundreds of exhausted warriors relieved to have reached what they thought was the safety of the city were milling about near the gate as the latest group burst into their midst, followed closely by the shouting, snarling, bringers of death.

The unarmed Vindelici, exhausted by fear and the effort to reach the city, were cut down easily. After the massacre at the gate, the victors spread out through the city, going house to house in an orgy of death as their pent-up energy was released on the hapless villagers. They were in a frenzy, killing anyone who was foolish enough to resist and searching for plunder of any kind.

A woman screamed for her children as she was dragged from her home by two warriors. A third tossed a firebrand onto the thatched roof. The flames spread quickly through the dried reeds, leaping from house to house, forcing the people who were hiding in their homes to flee straight into the arms of the invaders.

When I found Teutobod, he reached out with his right hand and when I did the same, expecting a warrior's clasp of welcome, he pulled me into a bear hug, lifting me off the ground and squeezing the wind from me. "Put me down!" I gasped angrily, insulted at the act of familiarity from the older man.

Teutobod was taken aback for a moment, then dismissed my outburst and laughed heartily. "Surprised to see me?"

"Yes," I said, recovering my control. "Your attack may have saved us a terrible loss. Where did you come from?"

"After you departed last year, we had thought to live in peace at Teutobergium, but the Scordisci returned to their raids. We battled many times last summer and endured another long and hungry winter. In the spring, I sent scouts who found your winter camp and followed your trail until they came upon the remains of your great victory over the Romans and discovered that you had crossed the mountains. When they returned, our council decided to follow the Danubius west until we found you, rather than cross the mountains ourselves. We declared war on anyone we encountered and stripped the countryside clean. We burned towns and villages and killed any who resisted us. Like you in Noricum, we took what we needed and left a trail of fire and destruction along the great river from which the weeping will be heard for generations.

"When we passed what was left of Boiodurum, we traveled along your path for a while, but you had left little for us, so when we reached the Isar River we turned south and west, making our own way. I sent my scouts to find you and we tracked your movement along the Danubius. When I learned that the local tribes were gathering to resist you, we moved to your aid. I had planned to meet you for winter camp, but luckily, we arrived when we did."

"Aye, you have my thanks."

"The rest of the world can be damned," he said savagely. "I will no longer allow my people to suffer. From now on, we will be the conquerors. Our wagons are full of grain, our herds are healthy, we will be no burden on you. Together, we shall tread this land without fear. When our tribes are joined, who can resist us?"

Chapter Eleven

After the battle of Manching, we plundered the dead. There were many fine helmets of bronze and iron crested with wolves, boars, eagles, and ravens. There were mail coats, heavy spears, and long swords of better quality than our own. Teutobod's wagons were full of rich plunder he had seized in the wealthy trade city, and ships that had been moored at the docks were now laden with the spoils we had captured. The wide-bellied trade ships would be used to transport the heavy goods farther up the river until we found a way to turn it into silver and gold, though I did not know how far they could go as the river was becoming noticeably smaller the farther west we traveled.

That night, Eldric the high priest, shrieked to the heavens against a background of skin drums echoing through the darkness. His painted face was frightening in the flickering light from a thousand torches. He wore a deer skull on his head, the horns of a young buck stabbing the air with his movements. He shook a pair of dried gourd rattles and danced before the great bonfire, leaping in the air, and thrashing about. With his chant he dedicated half the wealth we had taken to Wodan, and at a pre-arranged signal his priests wielded axes and knives in a bloody sacrifice of two white oxen in the name of Donar, thanking him for the strength he granted us to face our enemies. A pair of acolytes caught the blood in sacred cauldrons, and with sprigs of oak, painted the bows of two of the boats that were filled to the brim with plunder as another score of the aspiring priests threw the carcasses onto the treasures. Piles of straw soaked in oil were placed in the boats and lit afire. Then the boats were pushed out into the calm waters of the harbor to burn until they slowly sunk below the surface as Eldric and his followers chanted their thanks to the gods for our victory.

Though we had won a decisive battle, my mind was unsettled. I should have been flush with the joy of victory, yet I was troubled. I felt lost and indecisive. I had very nearly blundered into a defeat by being too headstrong and only Teutobod's timely and unexpected arrival had turned the battle in our favor and saved us from a terrible loss. My uncertainty was not just about my own abilities, but I was a chieftain now, and I had no vision of our future. I was unable to see what lay ahead. I didn't know what to do. We had been on this quest for eight years and I had been chieftain for more than a year. Every spring we packed up and moved blindly, wandering about until we found a suitable place to make a winter camp, surviving through our abilities, but without a purpose. Inevitably, we made enemies as we invaded the lands of others, and we defeated them soundly, but how much of that was luck?

I ordered a week's halt to treat our wounded and bury the dead, and during that time I sought out Skyld, the high priestess, and my sister Hilgi. My sister, blinded by the plague that had killed our parents, had become a seeress, a prophetess who dreamed glimpses of the future. It was her dream that had set me upon the path that I now walked as chieftain of the Cimbri and had explained both the reason for our troubles and provided the riddle that served to guide us on our quest. It was both a curse and a prophecy, and it left me with more questions than answers. It was my doubts about those answers and about myself that brought me to her that day.

Skyld met me as I walked toward their worn leather tents set up on the edge of our encampment. The ancient priestess seemed as though she were expecting me and showed no surprise at my approach, though I had not seen them for some time and told no one of my wish to talk to Hilgi. Her back was bent, and her dingy gray hair was unkempt. She wore a dirty white shift that looked as old as she did, and her crooked fingers grasped a gnarled stick she used to steady herself. She had frightened me as a boy, and I still felt a shiver whenever I was in her presence.

"Welcome, welcome, Borr," she cackled, amused at my obvious

discomfort. Her lips pursed and unpursed over empty gums and when she talked, they smacked together, creating a distracting accompaniment. "It has been some time, hasn't it?"

"I need guidance," I said impatiently, wasting no time on pleasantries. "Is my sister here?"

"She is there," she replied slyly, turning aside and stretching a thin arm toward a tent behind her.

I brushed past, restraining my revulsion as I passed close to her and drew the flap of the tent aside and entered the gloom. A dim light filtered in through the loose seams and thin spots in the leather, and it took a moment for my eyes to adjust. There were two sleeping pallets piled with dirty furs along either side of the small dwelling. The stink of wood smoke, incense, and unwashed bodies nearly overwhelmed me. Hilgi sat facing me near the back wall, rocking back and forth and humming. This was her world now. She had been an exuberant child with bright blue eyes and shining golden hair, full of mischief and the promise of great beauty, but her suffering at the hands of kidnappers and later the death of our parents and her own sickness had driven her quite mad. Frida and I had tried to care for her, but it proved beyond our abilities, and when Skyld offered her a place of respect within the order of priestesses, it was a relief to me. The priestesses were respected, even feared, for their place in our society and they were provided with food and the things they required to live. However, they lived apart from the rest of the tribe, seldom if ever bathing or caring for themselves. They wore rags, went barefoot except in winter, and never cared for their hair.

The Romans called us unwashed barbarians, but as usual, they had no understanding of us. Grooming was important to our people and most bathed regularly, especially in summer. Keeping hair and beards clean and trimmed was a matter of pride. Men gathered their hair at the top of the head and formed a horse's tail that flowed outward from a leather tie close to the scalp. Other tribes, like the Teutones, gathered their long hair into a braid and then tied it into a knot by their right temple. Most men wore long beards they combed with animal fat to keep it supple. In times of war, they often wove bones, silver bands, or other adornments into their hair and beards to frighten their enemies. The women usually wore their hair long and washed it with a mixture of dried herbs and flowers steeped in warm water, honey, and rendered tallow that left their hair soft and smelling like wildflowers year-round. Clothes were washed and repaired regularly, and in the spring, everyone sported new trousers, shoes, a cloak, or a tunic that the women had worked hard to make over the winter. But the priestesses were different.

Hilgi was eleven years old now, thin and pale from not enough time in the sun. She was filthy and stringy brown hair covered her face. It broke my heart to see her this way. I sat cross-legged in front of her and waited silently for her to acknowledge me, as I knew she would in her own time. After a while, her rocking stopped and her unseeing eyes flickered open, seeming to stare at me. Her pupils were enlarged, making her eyes dark, almost black. It felt as though she were peering into the depths of my soul.

"Hello brother," she said casually, as if I visited her every day. It was a mystery how she knew that it was I who sat before her.

"Hello Hilgi," I replied. "I hope that you are well."

She cocked her head to one side, as if my comment was curious to her. "What troubles you brother?"

I paused for a few moments to gather my thoughts. "I don't know what to do," I sighed. "The curse that you revealed to me provides no answers. We have been wandering for years, fighting, and dying. I don't know where we are going or what our purpose is. I fear I am failing our people."

"You doubt yourself," she said.

"Yes."

"Why? The flood was not your doing. Njoror directed his fury at us because of his hatred of Wodan. We do not have a say in the actions of gods. Nor was the plague your fault. You were not chieftain when the Scordisci attacked us, and yet you led our warriors well. You saw through Carbo's betrayal and led us to victory at Noreia, and again at Manching. Your leadership is not in question."

"But what is our purpose?" I asked. "Are we ever to build our long houses again? Will we ever till our fields and live in peace? Will we ever be able to watch an apple tree bloom in the spring and eat the apples from that same tree in the fall? Or will we always leave in the spring and never be able to taste the sweetness of the fruit that tree has grown during the summer? Njoror's threat of destruction forces us to move every year. To lift the curse, I must convince Rome to invite us into their lands, but how can I do that if Rome is our enemy? They will never welcome us if they view us as a threat."

"Yours is the warrior's path," she said. "You lead our people through your strength and your wisdom, as our father did. The tribe follows you because they trust you. You must learn to trust yourself. You were elected chieftain to lead our people. You were never tasked with lifting the curse. That is a burden you took upon yourself. Perhaps the curse will never be lifted. You were blessed by Donar because he sees his own strength in you. Our people are stronger, more confident than they have ever been. Our herds are healthy, our wagons overflow with gold and silver, our warriors are victorious. We honor and thank the gods with our sacrifices. Every summer we witness new horizons that are waiting to be discovered and every winter we rest. Is that such a bad life? Perhaps the curse will never be lifted. Wodan is named the wanderer because he descends to earth to wander amongst mortals. Is it possible that it is our fate to always wander in the name of Wodan? In his hatred for Wodan, Njoror enlisted Lokke's help to create the curse. Perhaps Wodan has turned it from a curse into a blessing. Perhaps the trickster has been tricked. Perhaps the wanderer is who we have become."

With that, her eyes closed, and she resumed her rocking and humming. She had said her piece and dismissed me. She had given me much to think about, and as I turned away, I gave one last look at my sister. I felt pity for her, yet she did not desire pity. She was content, and what more could I ask?

Skyld was waiting outside and as I emerged, a crooked smile cracked her toothless face. "Did you find the wisdom you desired?" she asked.

I strode past her without replying, and I heard her cackling with amusement as I put distance between myself and the withered priestess.

Hilgi's words had confused me even more, and I needed to think them through.

A shallow ford cut across the Danubius near Manching, and we crossed the river to avoid the wide swamps on the south side.

As we traveled along the wide river valley, I pondered Hilgi's words at length, but they only served to confuse me further. I still had no answers, and I felt as lost and unsure of the future as I did when my father died and left me to lead our clan, alone and unprepared. Finally, I met with Eldric, the high priest. He told me of an ancient ritual called the Utiseta that might help me determine my own path and that of our people.

"The Utiseta is a vision quest that our ancestors observed when they required divine guidance to make important and difficult decisions," he explained. "You must go alone to seek out an ancient place, such as a mound of the old people, and commune with the spirits. If they find you worthy, they will communicate with you, but do not expect the spirit to tell you what to do. They will force you to explore your own soul and to face your fears and your regrets. This can be a terrifying experience, but the answers are within you, and Utiseta can help you find them."

"I need some time alone," I told Hrolf a few days later. "I need time to think. Time to pray for guidance. I'll be back in a few days. Keep the caravan moving and I'll catch up."

"Alone! Are you mad?" Hrolf exclaimed. "The country is crawling with warriors just seeking a chance to avenge the thousands they lost."

"Alone," I repeated.

"At least allow me to have a few men follow you," he pleaded. "They can keep you in sight and come to your aid if necessary."

"No! Do not ask again. And do not think to send anyone to follow me. I'll be back soon enough."

"Why can't you take someone along?" Frida asked later. She was worried. I had been quiet for some time, and she was concerned that I was not thinking clearly.

"Skol will be with me. I need answers, and to get them I need to be alone. Hrolf will be in charge of the caravan, and I'll be back in a few days, a week at most."

She handed me a leather flask of ale and a small bag of dried beef, hard bread, and cheese. I took them gratefully and we embraced. It was rigid and clumsy, and there was little comfort in it. It felt more like what was expected of us as husband and wife, rather than an expression of our love.

I left on foot before it was fully light, clad in my usual buckskin trews and woven cloak. I touched my wolf torque, whispered a quick prayer to my clan totem for protection and with my sword and seax hanging from my belt, I took up my spear and departed into the growing light, with Skol padding softly at my side.

For several days, I simply walked through the forest, enjoying the solitude, eating little, and sleeping on the ground wrapped in my cloak. I was heading into a small mountain range that looked as though it might provide the place I was looking for. I didn't kindle a fire as there was no fresh meat to cook, and I did not wish to attract any attention to myself with the smell and light from a fire. I paused at mid-day to pick some blackberries growing thickly along a rock face at the foot of a large hill and was concentrating on finding the biggest ones when I heard a low rumble. At first, I thought it was thunder in the distance, until I heard the brush rustling in front of me. I knew in an instant that I had made a fatal mistake.

A large brown bear emerged only steps away from me. It was upon me in an instant and I only had time to get an arm in front of my face as its fangs sought to rip out my throat. The bear latched onto my arm instead and I felt its teeth sink into my flesh just before I heard the bones in my arm snap. The beast had bowled me over and was on top of me, savaging my chest with its razor-sharp claws. I was pinned beneath its great weight, and my other arm was entangled in my cloak. I was not able to reach my weapons or even take a breath. I was helpless in its savage assault, and I could hear myself screaming in rage and pain. Regret filled my mind as images of my wife and son appeared. The pain faded, replaced by the fear that I would never see them again. They would never know what happened to me. Darkness crowded the edge of my vision, and I felt my body being violently jerked about. The brute released my arm and clamped its jaws over my face. I gagged from the smell of its fetid breath even as it ripped the scalp from my skull. As my world faded slowly to black, a blur of motion appeared from my right side.

Much later, I awoke to a pitiful whine and Skol licking my cheek. I was disoriented; I didn't know where I was or what had happened, and then everything rushed back at once. The bear! My entire body screamed in pain. I laid still and tried to assess the damage. My head throbbed terribly, and when I tried to lift an arm, I cried out in pain and blacked out again.

More time passed, and I felt the sun on my face, but it was too much effort to open my eyes. I was so tired, so weak. My head pounded like war drums, and after a few moments I surrendered to the fatigue, returning to darkness.

The light was gone when I woke again, and I shivered The pain in my left arm was agonizing. It felt broken. The skin on my fingers felt tight. The movement cracked a scab that formed over my chest wound and warm blood flowed down my side. I could hear the crunch of dry leaves under me, and I reached out weakly to scrape them over me, but they gave little insulation against the cold and soon the fatigue and pain overtook me again.

Time passed and a dim light registered in my throbbing brain. I lay on my back staring up at what looked like rock above me. Cold fingers clutched my heart. *Am I in a tomb? Am I dead? Have I been buried?* I raised my hand before my face, wincing with the effort. *Could I move if I was dead?* I tried to sit up and my body was wracked with pain. *I can't be dead. The dead feel no pain. Where am I?* I lay still, trying to remember, but my memory failed me.

My foggy brain slowly cleared as firelight flickering on rock walls and the smell of burning wood entered my consciousness. I realized that I was no longer covered by leaves but by warm furs and I was lying in a cavern on a thick bed of boughs covered in fresh cut grass.

I tried to lick my cracked lips with a dry tongue and realized my throat was parched as well. The smell of roasting meat reached me and threatened to turn my stomach. I gingerly touched the wound on my chest to find that it was covered by a soft poultice. I tried to move my left arm and discovered that it was splinted and still painful, but the swelling was reduced, and I didn't feel the blood pulsing past it any longer. A shadow passed in front of the dim sunlight illuminating the entrance and my heart jumped in sudden panic.

A voice resonated in the cave. "So, you're awake. It's about time. I was beginning to wonder if you would wake at all. You had a deathly fever and have been asleep for days." His voice was deep and carried no sign of threat. "Calm yourself, I mean you no harm. Your weapons are against the wall behind you. I found you nearly dead and carried you here to bandage your wounds."

The flickering light revealed a serene face peering out from beneath a dark cowl that he pulled back onto his shoulders. Bright blue eyes were set below a high forehead, and a thick mane of gray hair was combed back from his forehead and cut just above his shoulders. The ends of an exceptionally long mustache hung well below his clean-shaven chin. It was thick and covered his mouth, moving as if it were alive when he spoke.

"Who are you?" I croaked through my dry throat, cringing at the pain in my jaw.

"My name is Aldric. I am a bard by trade, a healer when I am needed, a traveler when it suits me, and a hermit when I tire of all that. You sound like you could use a drink."

I looked at him and winced in pain when I tried to nod. He lifted a water skin to my lips, warning me to drink sparingly. Instead, I gulped it greedily, and he snatched it away as a wave of nausea came and was quickly replaced with a piercing jolt of pain in the side of my face. He shook his finger and scolded me, "Until your head injury gets better, small amounts of food and water are best." I scowled at him silently.

"May I examine you?"

I thought about his request and decided to allow it. If he had wanted to cause me harm, he could have done it when I was unconscious, or just left me to die. He peered into my eyes and continued to question me.

"The beast caused quite a lot of damage. How do you feel?"

"That's a stupid question," I mumbled through stiff lips. "Everything hurts."

"Is your vision blurred?"

"I can't see with my left eye."

"It's covered with a bandage. Nauseous?"

I replied through clenched teeth because it hurt too much to move my jaw. "For a moment. It passed. Ow!" I pulled away from his probing fingers and gasped as pain surged with the movement.

"Sorry," he said regretfully. "I set the broken bones in your forearm and treated the bite wounds. You have deep gashes on your chest down to the bone, and several broken ribs. I stitched the cuts closed as best I could and wrapped your chest, but I cannot wrap it as tightly as it should be because of the cuts. You must move as little as possible or risk puncturing a lung. One thigh muscle was detached from the bone, and it remains to be seen how much permanent damage was done. We won't know for a while. All I could do was put it back in its place, clean the wound and wrap it. It should reattach itself, but you will never run again or have full strength in that leg, and you will likely have a permanent limp. You're lucky, though, it missed the artery, or you would have bled out in seconds. You were in shock and not long for death when I found you."

"My face," I gasped. "Tell me."

"It's bad," he admitted. "I did everything I could. On the left side, your scalp was peeled from the top of your head down to your nose, and your left eye came with it. It was still attached, so I popped your eye back into place, laid everything back and stitched up your scalp, but only time will tell if your sight is affected. It's badly swollen now, and the eye is red with blood. When the swelling goes down, we'll have a better idea of the permanent damage. You will have a ragged scar down the center of your scalp and face. Your jaw was dislocated, and you have puncture wounds from the bear's teeth that penetrated your mouth. I set the jaw and treated the wounds; all we can do for now is hope they do not get infected and wait for you to heal."

Returning to his seat across the fire from me, he went on. "So, I've told you who I am. How about you tell me something about yourself?"

I was hesitant to tell him who I really was. We had been ravaging the countryside for months and defeated a large army at Manching, then pillaged the city. If he belonged to a local tribe, his attitude toward me would change, and I was in no shape to defend myself. On the other hand, he could tell by my dress that I was not a local, so I figured I might as well tell the truth, at least part of it.

"My name is Borr," I said, managing to speak through the pain. "My people are from the far north. Years ago, we were forced to leave our homeland and now we search for a new home."

"By attacking others?"

So he knew. "We do what we must to survive, as do they."

An uncomfortable silence descended. I didn't yet know where his sympathies lay, but I was strangely calm in his presence. He moved to the fire and removed a small bronze kettle of broth, then raised my head a bit. He sat beside me and fed me like a babe, letting the broth slowly dribble down my throat because it hurt too much to slurp it or swallow. We sat silently, stealing glances at one another until I rasped, "No more" and he returned to the fire and cut off a piece of meat for himself.

He wagged a rabbit leg and squinted at me. "There was a great battle some distance from here; I assume that was your people. How did you come to be out here all by yourself?"

I suddenly remembered that I hadn't been by myself. I was with Skol, and I hadn't seen him since the attack. "There was a wolf with me. Did you see him?"

He looked at me curiously. "There was a wolf lying beside you when I found you. At first, I thought it had attacked you and you killed it. But after I looked about, I realized that a bear had done the damage to both of you. The wolf bled to death, but it must have chased off the bear before it succumbed to its fatal injury. I did not understand what happened until now. It must have saved your life."

I was unable to speak. I had rescued Skol when he was a pup, and he had saved me more than once. He had been my friend and fellow warrior for the past seven years, always there when I needed him. I thanked him silently for his final sacrifice and wiped away a tear as I prayed for Wodan to accept him to Valhol as the warrior that he was.

"I sometimes use this cave in my travels, and I found you not far from here," Aldric said.

I cleared my throat and winced from the pain of the effort. "How long have I been here?" I asked.

"I found you five days ago."

I walked three days before the bear attacked me. Eight days I had been gone. "My people?" I asked.

"After they defeated the Vindelici, they continued on, ravaging the land. There are columns of smoke on the horizon that mark their progress. It will be a hungry winter for anyone who survived their visit."

"I must go to them," I said, trying to rise.

Aldric didn't move except for an eyebrow cocked up in amusement when I fell back in a wave of dizziness and pain. With a wry grin, he told me what I already knew but refused to accept. I was in no shape to go anywhere and wouldn't be for some time.

"Listen to me, boy. You've lost a lot of blood, and your wounds won't be healed anytime soon. It will take time for the muscles and bones to knit and if you move too much, you'll rip the stitches open. If you move that leg now, you won't just have a limp, you'll never be able to walk again. When it is healed, it will require weeks to gain back the balance and strength you will lose. If you don't die from infection, you might be able to leave here in a few months' time.

"I have nowhere to be, and I would like to learn more about your people. I will stay with you until you are able to travel. When you're fully healed, I will help you get back to your tribe if you like."

"I can't stay here that long! My wife, my son …"

"… already think you're dead. There will be no harm in taking the time to heal properly. You can't miss the trail of destruction they are leaving behind; it won't be hard to find them," Aldric said.

"Can't you catch up to them and tell them what happened? They will send someone back for me."

"It would take me a fortnight to catch them and return with help," Aldric reasoned. "How would you feed yourself, or gather firewood? Besides, even if they came back, you can't be moved without the risks I already told you about. No, we will stay here."

"You don't hate me for the carnage we have caused your people?" I asked.

"My people?" he asked, surprised. "Oh no, I'm not Vindelici. I am of the Tigurini, further to the west. We have no love for the Vindelici. As far as I'm concerned you just tipped the balance in our favor. They won't be a bother to us for years."

I was relieved at that. He was right. I didn't have a choice but to stay put and I was grateful for his offer of help.

"Then I guess it's settled," I said tiredly. My jaw ached from talking and my head was pounding. I closed my eyes against the pain and mercifully drifted into a deep sleep brought on by the valerian root that Aldric had mashed and cooked into my broth.

Chapter Twelve

Over the next few weeks, Aldric and I formed a close bond. At first, I just rested in the cave, regaining my strength. My leg ached terribly, and Aldric brought me the soft inner bark of a willow tree to chew on. It dulled the pain in my head and the broken arm to a tolerable level as well. A poultice of chewed plantain, wild garlic, and honey covered with a piece of clean linen to hold it all in place over the wounds on my chest kept infection at bay. He told me that when he first found me; he'd cleaned the open, bleeding gashes as best he could, and packed them with cobwebs to staunch the flow of blood. This caused a clot to form, and he was able to stitch the sides together while I was unconscious.

We passed the long evenings sitting by the fire talking. I shared my memories of Jutland and the flood that destroyed Borremose, my home by the sea. He had never seen the ocean and was fascinated by the idea of a giant wave that could rise to the height of the tallest tree and cause so much damage. I recalled our decision to leave our homeland and seek out a new life; our journey through the trackless Hercynian Forest, over the mountains of Boiohaemum and the vast plains of Pannonia; and I told him of our alliance with the Scordisci and our battles against the Romans at Siscia and Stobi.

"I know of these Romans," he growled. "Their traders cross the mountains, and our people prosper from their trade, but ten years ago their soldiers marched north and did battle with our neighbors to the west, the Arverni and Allobroges and laid claim to their land. Now they call it … Narbonensis, I think. I have no love for those tribes, but Rome is now on our western border. They have been expanding their power for centuries, first conquering the Italian tribes, then the Celtic tribes on their side of the mountains and the Celt-Iberians far to the west. Now they covet our land, and it is only a matter of time before they come for it as well."

"We have fought them three times and defeated them each time," I said. "Decisively. Yet they are not to be underestimated. I have learned much from a close friend who used to be a Roman soldier, and from our battles with them. They are not the kind of people who accept defeat, they adapt and come back until they eventually win. Their war machines are nothing like I have ever seen and if they are allowed to bring them to bear, they will be devastating to an army of massed warriors such as ours."

I told him of the loss of my parents and so many of our people to the plague that ravaged us in our new home of Haimaz, our war against our former friends the Scordisci, and our decision to journey into Noricum. He asked many questions about the disease, his interest as a healer peaked.

I decided against telling him I was a chieftain. The trust between us was growing, but I wasn't sure how far that trust would stretch if he knew who I really was, so for now, I was just another warrior.

I recounted the betrayal by the Roman consul Carbo, the fierce battle of Noreia, crossing the great mountains and wintering at Boiodurum, then suffering another flood, and our journey into Raetia to fight the Vindelici which brought him to the day he found me.

Through it all, Aldric listened intently, asked many questions, and committed everything to memory.

The weeks passed as my body healed. Slowly I began to feel stronger. I needed something to do besides sleep when Aldric was out hunting or gathering firewood and water. He brought me a branch of linden wood to carve when my broken arm was strong enough, and I carved several small animals to give to my son when we reunited. I was becoming restless from lying still for so long and, against Aldric's advice, I rose to my feet with great difficulty and limped gingerly about the cave, exploring its dark corners. It consisted of a short hallway with a shallow passage on each side of the entrance, and the large chamber in which we lived. Beside the entrance, a luminous white substance appeared to flow down the walls as if the stone leaked milk. Curious, I broke off a piece and crumbled it between my fingers. Confused by the mystery, I continued on.

The floor sloped downward from the entrance to the floor of our chamber, which kept the light from our small fire from being seen by anyone passing nearby. The smoke escaped through a small hole in the roof through which a hazy beam of sunlight would show near midday. On those days, I would crawl under the hole just to feel the warmth of the sun on my face for a few moments.

On one of these searches toward the back of the chamber, I found a depression where a large animal had dug down to create a spot to lie in. It was probably where a bear had spent the winter. The spoil was scattered about, and I found a few odd pieces of bone lying on the surface. At first, I assumed they were the remains of an animal that served as the beast's supper, but when I looked closer, I noticed among the tiny bits of shattered ivory and bone, two pieces that had holes drilled through them. The flat piece had grooves around each hole, and I recognized it as similar to a tool my grandfather had used to make rope. My people had been fishermen and seafarers, and rope was a commodity we could not do without. The other piece was a hollow bone a little longer than the first. It had a vague resemblance to a wooden flute that I used as a child. I knocked the dirt from inside it and wiped off the end, placed it to my lips, and blew. My head jerked back in surprise; it worked! It was very old, and I was full of wonder thinking of the maker who must have lived in this cave long ago and left the items here, buried in the accumulated detritus of centuries.

During the long hours of idleness, there was much time to think, and I spent hours playing random melodies on the flute. I was angry at being disfigured and nearly killed by the bear. The constant pain seared the anger into my soul, and I needed to avenge myself and the death of my loyal friend, Skol. The rope tool provided the inspiration that I had been missing, and that night I told Aldric my plan.

I stayed in the cave for six weeks until we were sure that the leg muscle was reattached and ready to begin strengthening it. My chest and face healed, and the scabs fell off, the pink scars a permanent reminder of how close I came to death. The swelling was gone, and my face had become stiff where the flap of skin was peeled away. The scars stretched every time my face moved and if I coughed or sneezed or even smiled; I felt as though I was going to tear something loose. The vision somewhat returned in my left eye, but was blurred and sensitive to light. It ached continuously, which caused a persistent dull headache that at times became so intense I was unable to think. Aldric fashioned a patch from a piece of deer hide, but when the pain became too much, I laid on my bed, clenching my eyes tightly shut and holding my head, rolling back and forth in pain. Chewing the willow bark kept the light pains at bay, but its effectiveness wore off and the more severe headaches cut through with a terrible intensity.

Aldric had discovered a small patch of mushrooms that he dried and ground into a powder to make a tea. It helped with the headaches and allowed me to sleep better, but the drink made me feel queasy. It was an uncomfortable feeling at first, but I gradually got used to it and the nausea went away. Aldric kept the powder in a pouch around his neck and only allowed me a small dose when he saw I was suffering. He warned me that if used too often, or in too great a quantity, it would become less effective and my body would require more to dull the pain, and he did not want me to become dependent on it for it had an effect on the mind.

The day finally came that I limped gingerly toward the entrance, leaning heavily on the wall. My leg felt weak and tired quickly, but the pain was gone, and the movement felt good.

I emerged into the sunlight and blinked away the brightness that threatened to bring on another headache. The sun felt good on my skin after so many weeks in the dark and smoky cave, and I lowered myself against the rock wall, soaking up the reflecting heat. I tilted my head back against the wall and watched a large thunderhead float across an empty sky. It was an early fall day and the trees had already lost their brightest colors. Leaves fluttered to the ground in a cascade of dull browns and yellows as a warm breeze reversed their direction and picked more up to blow across the ledge in a rustling wave. I took in a long breath of the clear, crisp air and closed my eyes, picturing Frida tending the evening cooking fire with Lingulf playing nearby, and I swallowed a sob of intense emotion.

I was anxious to get started on the journey to rejoin them, but Aldric persuaded me to stay at least three more weeks to strengthen my leg before I set out. I argued with him for days until he convinced me that if I left too soon, I might injure the leg again, possibly worse. My family must think I was dead, and I was desperate to go to them, but I knew he was right, and I didn't like it. My only consolation was that the delay gave me more time to prepare for my vengeance against the beast who had crippled me.

Sitting beside me, Aldric was silent, allowing me to just enjoy being outside. After a time, he broke my reverie to suggest we get started on my conditioning. I gave him a sour glance, and he chuckled and reminded me that the sooner I regained the strength in my leg, the sooner I could be on my way. So, with his help, I reluctantly pushed myself to my feet, testing my weight.

"That's it, just move easily. You've lost some muscle and flexibility. Let's just walk about the ledge today and see how it feels." He held out a crutch he fashioned from a tree branch.

I waved it off. "It feels surprisingly good," I said, shifting my weight from one leg to the other.

"That's a good sign, but don't get cocky."

Just as he said that I stepped on a pebble and my weight shifted, causing me to stumble and a quick stab of pain. Aldric caught my arm and gave me a disapproving look. I returned an embarrassed shrug that turned to sudden anger as I pushed away to stand on my own again. He held out the crutch, and I snatched it from his hand. I hobbled around the ledge, reluctantly using the crutch and silently cursing myself.

We completed the short walk and sat again for a while. "I'm exhausted," I admitted to Aldric. It frustrated me to say so because it reminded me of when I was a weakling youth, unable to keep up with my friends. But at the same time, the thought was strangely encouraging. I realized that I had recovered from my childhood illness and become strong and healthy. That thought gave me hope. I did it before, I could do it again.

I reached down to knead the muscles in my calves. "My legs are aching, probably from not using them for so long," I said in an attempt to lighten my own mood. Aldric, of course, understood all this and remained silent, letting me work through my anger. He allowed me to rest for a while and then positioned himself to stretch and massage the muscles in my legs. When he was finished, they felt much better. The day was waning, and the shade had crept over the ledge at the cave's mouth. The temperature had noticeably dropped, and the smell of rain was in the air.

"I'm hungry," Aldric said, rubbing his belly. "How about some more of that stew?" I nodded and attempted a smile that looked more like a grotesque grimace. The skin on the left side of my face had stiffened, and I had lost the muscle control that allowed me to show emotion. My injured leg was throbbing, and I limped back into the cave and collapsed on my bed, exhausted by the strain.

"You will be able to stand on it more each day, but you must be careful. Take your time, your strength will come back. Tomorrow we will do more and soon, you will be back to your old self," Aldric tried to assure me.

I stared at the fire sullenly and mumbled that I wasn't hungry. The slowly growing pulse in my head foretold of another headache coming on and I rolled toward the cave wall, squeezing my eyes tightly shut.

I woke in total darkness. The scent of wildflowers was in my nostrils and the sound of soft breathing against my chest caused my heart to race. My hand traveled downward over the familiar curves of Frida's waist and hip to rest on her buttocks as she stirred slightly in her sleep. Her hand slid all the way round my waist and one leg slid up my thigh as she pulled herself closer to me. Her head lay comfortably in the crook of my shoulder, and she placed her lips close to my ear. My mind expected words of love, but instead she whispered urgent words of foreboding. I was puzzled at the incongruity of the loving embrace and the dire warning that she conveyed, and I felt a chill creep up my neck, replacing the warmth I felt from her closeness.

"Beware the traitor who lies in wait," came the terrifying words, and then with a gasp that wrenched my soul, the warm breath on my face stopped and her body went limp. My eyes flew open in panic. I woke from the dream in a cold sweat, momentarily confused by the dim light from a dying fire dancing on the cave walls, and realized there was no one lying beside me. What did the words mean? And why did Frida come to me in the night to deliver them? Was she in danger? Who was the traitor? I was filled with questions, and I had no answers.

I continued to have dreams that troubled me. There were more that foretold of danger and things to come, and the repetitive nightmares of the bear attack, but the most agonizing of all was the night I dreamt of returning home. I looked forward to that day with all my heart and in the dream, I walked toward my wife with open arms, only to see her recoil from the sight of me. I wore a patch over my left eye, and the skin of my face and neck was a mixture of black, purple, green, and yellow bruises, the remnants of the severe damage from the bear's jaws. A jagged scar ran upward from the bridge of my nose, parted my hair, and ran down to above my ear where the bear had peeled the skin away. My heart soared at the sight of her, but the smile on my face looked to her like a wicked sneer. A look of horror crossed her face as she saw a thing from Hel. Lingulf hid his face in his mother's bosom and wept in fear. My friends did not recognize me, and I was quickly surrounded by an angry crowd who'd come to defend my family. Frida slipped away between them as they attacked the monster that they saw in front of them. I woke with an ache in my heart and a paralyzing fear that I would never be accepted by my family or my people. I was terrified that I would be alone forever.

Fearing my nightmares might become reality yet consumed with the need to return to my family, I pushed myself hard and my recovery progressed rapidly. We walked to the river and back for a week, then went on a short hunt, and gradually ranged farther and farther out as my strength returned. During the idle nights by the fire, I stretched the injured leg. Aldric rubbed a salve that he had made with herbs and rendered animal fat on my scars to keep them pliable, massaging the tissue as much as I could tolerate. He said that it would keep the skin from shrinking and becoming hard and it seemed to work on my legs and chest, but it was too painful to touch my face.

The three more weeks passed quickly. We exercised daily with our weapons and while my stamina and reflexes had far to go, I had gained back some of my strength, and I at least felt like I could defend myself in a fight if it didn't last too long. Aldric finally proclaimed me fully healed. The bruising on my face and all over my body had faded and was nearly gone, which did much to relieve the worry of my nightmares. The many punctures and lacerations had healed well, but the scars would never fade. He prepared to accompany me back to my people as he had promised, but before we departed, there was something I had to do.

The next morning before dawn, I offered my prayers to Donar for strength, and then I shouldered my buckskin pack. In it was a net I had made by using the rope tool I had found in the cave. Through the weeks, every time Aldric left the cave he brought me back armfuls of nettle, milkweed, reed, and the inner bark of young cedar trees. I painstakingly separated the fibers of these plants and using the skills I had learned when I was a boy, I wove them into strings, then wove those into ropes, and then again into thicker ropes that were as big as my thumb and very strong. Using the skills I had learned as a boy, I tied the ropes into a strong net.

I adjusted my sword and seax, picked up my spear along with two other ash spears I had fashioned, and shrugged my shoulders to settle the pack. It was an overcast day in November that began warm enough, and when we left the cave, we were dressed lightly. After nearly three months, I was finally hunting the bear that had maimed me and killed Skol. We started by returning to the berry bramble as I reasoned the bear's den would not be far. We found it beneath the root ball of a large tree that had fallen years ago, leaving a tangled web of drooping tendrils, grass, and moss that had grown to obscure the entrance to the den that it had dug out beneath the tree. The bear had gone into its winter hibernation, and as we silently approached, I could hear it snoring deep in its lair.

We carefully stretched the net over the opening to the den, listening anxiously to the bear's heavy breathing. When I was tying the top of the net to the root ball, my foot slipped and made a small noise. It was enough to disturb the beast and its snoring paused. My heart stopped and I held my breath. I was exposed at the entrance to the den without my weapons; if the bear woke now, there was little doubt this time the bear would kill me. After a few very tense moments, the snoring began again. We backed away carefully and gathered dry wood, preparing a fire as close to the opening as we dared. When Aldric brought the small flames to life, he added dry leaves, creating a column of smoke that I fanned into the den using my cloak. I was nervous, literally shaking with the anticipation of what was to come, when I heard a snort and then an angry growl.

We backed away and prepared ourselves for what was to come. I was sweating in the cool air, and my heart was pounding so hard in my chest I felt it must burst. My knuckles were white around the shaft of my heavy spear when suddenly, the bear emerged from the cloud of smoke and ran straight into the heavy net, roaring its fear and confusion, and then it saw me and recognized the threat. The beast charged, forcing one of the ropes to the rear of its powerful jaws where its back teeth separated the fibers, allowing its snout through the mesh. The knots around the break held strong as it thrashed its head back and forth and pushed its great weight forward against the restraining webbing, but the anchor points were stretched to their limit and began popping loose one by one. Sensing escape, the enraged bear launched itself forward with a great roar and as the last of the tension was released, it tumbled forward with its forepaws caught in the entangling mesh. I feared that it would roll clear of the net, but the bear's long claws and desperate thrashing tightened the net around its great girth until its struggles lessened and eventually stopped. The beast's tongue hung from one side, and it was panting rapidly, its eyes wide as it realized it was trapped and helpless. I approached warily as it watched me, and as I prepared the fatal thrust, it gave one last attempt to break free. It took all my strength to pierce the thick hide and layers of fat and reach the vital organs, but it was over in a few moments, and as the bear gave a final gasp I whispered to Skol, "You have been avenged, my brother."

I used its brains to tan the hide and fashioned a cloak for myself and new shoes for both of us. Aldric made a necklace of the bear's claws for me, and it hung below my torque. I placed the skull of the beast on a natural shelf in the cave wall in reverence for its spirit. The bear's fat and meat would provide sustenance for us on our trek and as I shrugged into my pack and slung my bedroll over a shoulder, I took a last look about the cavern that had provided us shelter for the past several months.

On the second day, we arrived back at the Danubius and camped near the river. The first day had begun with only a slight limp, but after walking over the rough terrain carrying a pack, my leg ached and I was anxious to stop and rest, though I refused to admit weakness and call for a halt. Aldric noticed me favoring the leg and staggering from time to time, and slowed his pace without saying anything.

It had been nearly three months since the attack and I could still see the trampled vegetation, churned up ground, and deep ruts cut by the heavy carts that told of the caravan's passing. The trail followed the general course of the river, at times coming near it, and at others veering miles away to get around wetlands, riverside cliffs, and other natural barriers. We came across burned out farmsteads and abandoned villages and kept our distance to avoid contact with people who would surely be seeking vengeance. But the land was empty. Only the bare trees held mute witness to the devastation brought on by the Cimbri and our allies. We made good time following the trail and encountered no one for weeks. Though I still had a slight limp, my leg got stronger with time, and before long we were walking at a normal pace.

Several days later, as the sun settled behind the treetops, we approached a ruined fortress sitting atop a steep hill nestled in a gentle curve of the Danubius. The trading boats that had been used to transport the plunder from Manching lie on the bank below the high fortress, as the river had become too shallow for the heavy boats to pass. A wigeon burst unexpectedly from the reeds at the riverbank and with a whir, Aldric brought it down with a stone from his sling. I had seen him use it to hunt small game before and he always kept it at the ready for just such an opportunity. He was a deadly shot, and he had tried to teach me how to use it, but no matter how much I practiced I was never able to master the weapon. We made camp among the abandoned boats, using them as a windbreak for our small fire, and while we ate roasted duck Aldric told me about the ancient city.

"It was called Pyrene," he said. "It has been abandoned for centuries, but the locals say it was once an important trading center and the capital of the local countryside." He told me there were many burial mounds nearby and that it was best to avoid them to prevent offending the ghosts who protected them. The mention of the burial mounds reminded me of the original purpose of my quest, and I decided it was time to tell Aldric who I really was and how I had come to be by myself in the wilderness.

It was the first night of the full moon of the blood month. The time for slaughter, when the meat would keep better in the cold weather and before winter set in. I told him of my father and of my ascension to clan leader upon his death, and my subsequent rise to chieftain of the Cimbri. I explained that I had been in search of a place to hold my Utiseta when I was attacked by the bear, and since then I had been so focused on recovering and getting back to my people that I had forgotten about it.

"I must take the time to complete my Utiseta, or my months of suffering were pointless," I said. "I understand if you do not wish to stay, but will you wait here for me to seek the answers I need?"

Aldric wasn't happy with the idea of disturbing those who rested in the mounds, but agreed to wait for three days. Before dawn I was trudging off in the direction Aldric had pointed. I found a cluster of them northwest of the city and selected the largest one. I reasoned that it must hold the remains of an important man, and I prepared myself as Eldric had advised. I gathered an armload of twigs and climbed to the top of the mound. My heart raced at the memory of the ancient burial mound I had encountered on our journey south after the great flood and the monstrous apparition that had appeared in my dream. My shoulders were tense as I imagined the specter appearing above me at any moment, but nothing strange happened. I was alone.

The setting sun was veiled behind gray clouds in the western sky. I sat cross-legged atop the mound and built a small fire, adding a pinch of incense from a pouch the high priest had given me. Cupping my hands, I pulled the pungent smoke toward me, wafting it up my chest and over my head. Removing a leather wrap from the pouch that held a small bit of dried mushrooms, I popped them into my mouth, then pulled my hood up to cover my eyes. I softly chanted the words that Eldric had taught me over and over as my mind cleared and my breathing slowed. The bright colors of the sunset began to writhe and collide in my head, making me giddy. A wave of nausea came and passed quickly, replaced by a sense of euphoria and finally a great calm as I felt my consciousness leave my body and I found myself floating above the mound.

A familiar stench came to me, and I felt a momentary panic as the horrible visage of the draugar from my youth materialized from the top of the mound and faced me. It floated before me and stared into my eyes with a mixture of recognition and curiosity. The specter wore the same furs and armor as before, only this time I noticed one of the red bits of glass was missing from the front of the odd helmet.

The wraith's lip curled upward in a snarl, and a disembodied voice seemed to come from all around me at the same time. "Who dares to disturb my rest?" the voice demanded.

"I am Borr, chieftain of the Cimbri," I replied, trying to keep my voice from trembling.

"The Red Wolf," the voice replied matter-of-factly.

"I have been called that as well."

"Why have you summoned me?"

"I am in need of counsel," I said.

"And what do you offer me for this knowledge?" hissed the voice.

I had forgotten that Eldric had told me the spirit would want something of value, and with a sudden burst of inspiration, desperately sought the small bit of red glass that I had carried in my pouch since I was a boy. I offered the spirit the object that I had found beside my bed the night I had first encountered the draugar. It accepted the offering with a solemn nod of its translucent head.

"What is it you wish to know?"

"I … seek your wisdom, spirit. I am unsure of my path. I have never felt that I am worthy of the honor to lead my people and I have always been filled with doubt. Because of my weakness, my mother's sister drowned. I failed to protect my family when my wife and child were abducted, and my wife still suffers because of my inaction. I was helpless when my mother and father died from the plague, and I could not care for my sister, who was blinded and driven mad. I failed in my dealings with Carbo, and I allowed myself to be deceived, which placed my people in great danger. My people are cursed to wander the earth forever unless I can convince Rome to grant us land within their borders, but by making an enemy of Rome, I have failed to secure a new homeland for our people, perhaps forever. Wodan honored me as a boy with the dream that led my people south, and Donar approved of my rise to chieftain and gave me the strength to defeat our enemies, but now I am crippled and disfigured. I have lost the favor of the gods."

"Bah!" the voice boomed at me. "The gods do not make mistakes. They chose you because you are worthy. You doubt yourself, yet you are hunno of the wolf clan. You are chieftain of the Cimbri, and leader of the allied army of the northern tribes. Listen well and heed my words. Your people are not lost; they thrive! They follow you because they love you. You have proven yourself time and again. They trust you," it said, emphasizing the last three words. "Stop pitying yourself. You are Borr, named for the father of Wodan! The gods know your name. The prophecy has promised that you will one day be king! Borrix. King Borr. The earth will tremble in fear at the name of the Cimbri and it is Borrix who will lead them.

"You think you have lost the favor of the gods? I shall tell you what you cannot know. Njoror has done his worst to your people. Time and again, they have not just survived, they have become stronger, and he credits you with that. In his frustration, Njoror conspired with Lokke again, and together they conceived a plan to finally destroy you. When you entered the wilderness alone, Lokke came to earth and followed you. Lokke is the trickster, a shapeshifter. He transformed into the great bear that attacked you. But Wodan, the Allfather, watches over you, and he learned of their plan and sent his wolves Geri and Freki to defeat Lokke by giving their power to your wolf-companion who drove the bear away. While you lay near death, Donar lent you his strength and you lived because of it. You are not forsaken; you are chosen as their champion!"

With those words, the apparition shimmered and began to fade. I felt my essence being pulled back toward my body, but before the spirit returned to its eternal rest, it left me with an ominous warning.

"Know that you have powerful enemies. Njoror's efforts to destroy you will be redoubled and he will use everything within his power against you. Rome will seek vengeance for their loss, and they are a formidable adversary. But the greatest danger to you and your people is the traitor who lies in wait."

As those last words echoed in my mind, the draugar descended back into its tomb. I felt my spirit drawn back to my earthly body and opened my eyes. I shivered, not just from the cold, and drew my cloak about my shoulders. The fire had gone out, leaving only several small red embers and a thin trail of smoke. A sudden weariness descended upon me, and as the darkness became total, I fell back onto the cold earth.

A few days later we topped a small ridge and were immediately surrounded by half a dozen warriors armed with spears and shields. "Who are you?" the leader challenged us.

I slowly reached up to pull back my hood and there was a moment of silence while I just stared at him until his eyes widened in recognition. His expression softened and he stepped forward to embrace me tightly. It was my adopted brother, Freki.

"We thought you were dead," he said, overcoming his shock. "I did not recognize you . . . the scars . . ." he said pointing to his own face. "How are you here?"

"It's a long story, first I must see my family."

"And food and ale beside a warm fire," Aldric chimed in. Freki looked at him and back to me questioningly.

"This is Aldric, a good friend," I said. "He found me nearly dead and nursed me back to health. I will tell the tale tonight at the fire. Now take me to my family, brother."

"They are well," Freki answered me, "and they will be filled with joy to see you." Then to Aldric, "We will feast tonight!"

A large bonfire roared in the meadow near the camp and people had come to hear the tale of my return. The news had spread quickly, and hundreds gathered to welcome me home.

A grinning Teutobod strode up to me and clasped my forearm, this time in a greeting of equals. "We thought you were dead," he said, repeating the same words I had already heard a hundred times. Frida was standing by my side and smiling happily. She clutched my arm again when Teutobod backed up and Lingulf clung to my leg. I was relieved that our reunion was nothing like I had feared, and both had accepted my return from the dead without reservation.

I was surrounded by my family and friends. Hrolf, Freki, and Ansgar were there with all my retainers, along with Lugius, Caesorix, and Claodicus and many of their followers. My friend Vallus stood nearby, sporting a grin that exposed his few remaining teeth. Talla and Anik stood beside him. Frida's father Glum had cracked open several barrels of fresh ale and he and Gorm the blacksmith were already drunk and talking with Aldric as they happily re-filled the cups of all those present.

An uneasy silence settled upon the crowd as it parted to allow Skyld, the high priestess, to pass. She shuffled up to me, tapping her staff and sucking her lips in and out over those toothless gums. A look of shock came over her when she came close enough to see my face. She recovered quickly and gave me a sly smile. "The chieftain has returned as I told you he would," she said, turning toward the crowd with a reproving eye. The people shrunk back from her stare, knowing that they had accepted my death despite her assurances that I would return.

She stared at my scars and the patch over my eye. I was growing accustomed to the reaction that my appearance provoked, but this was something different.

"Behold your chieftain!" she cried. "He is loved by the Allfather, who also gave his eye in the quest for knowledge." She turned back toward me again and pointed at the jagged scar in the center of my forehead. "And Donar has marked him with the thunderbolt. He is loved by the gods!" A roar of approval followed her words and ale doused the crowd as tankards were thrust into the air to toast my health.

There was much celebration that night and I leaned drunkenly on Frida as I shuffled to our home. Glum had built a winter cabin for his daughter and grandson, and I fell upon the bed, exhausted and content, and fell immediately asleep. Glum and Lingulf would spend the night elsewhere to allow Frida and I some time alone. It was mid-morning when I awoke to the smell of fresh buttered bread, something I had missed every day while I was living in the cave.

Frida noticed I was awake and brought a generous piece over to me with a warm smile. She undressed and lay down beside me as I chewed on the bread. She ran her fingers across the scars on my chest, making small noises as she examined the new marks on my body. "Do they hurt?" she asked with concern.

"Not much," I assured her. I explained how Aldric had rubbed them with his balm and massaged the flesh to keep the scar tissue pliable. I stretched every day and that helped as well. He had even worked out some exercises for me to move my face and jaw to try to help lessen the pain and keep the scar tissue from becoming too stiff. It was better, and it no longer pulled my lip up, but it was still sensitive, and I flinched when she reached up and touched my face.

"I'm sorry," she said quickly, pulling her hand back.

"No, it's alright." I took her hand and placed it back on my face. Reassured, she traced the length of the scar, curious, and at the same time disturbed by the pain I had suffered.

"Your eye?" she asked softly. I lifted the patch so she could see, and tears welled in her eyes.

"It took a few weeks, but some of the vision has returned. Not all of it though. It's blurry and dark around the edges, and it doesn't close all the way. When it gets dry, a damp compress helps. I can take the patch off in the dark, or when I sleep. At first, I got very bad headaches, but the patch helps, and they seem to have stopped."

She leaned forward and gently kissed the scar on my forehead. "I thought you would reject me," I told her.

"Never," she said. "The scars are reminders of your strength and the sacrifice you went through for our people. They are a sign that the gods love you."

"Skol saved my life," I said sadly. "He chased the bear off but was badly wounded and died protecting me. Aldric found me near death and dressed my wounds. I owe him everything. He is a good friend. He even buried Skol for me," I said as a tear ran down my cheek.

Frida held me as I grieved for my friend and after a few moments, I turned to her. I pulled the furs over us, and we made love as if it was our first time.

The sun was high when I emerged from our cabin and surveyed the encampment. Hrolf was loitering nearby, waiting for me.

"How are you feeling?" he asked.

I smiled. "I am well, my friend. I have a clear mind and a new outlook."

"So, what did you learn on your quest?" he asked. "Was it worth it?"

"Oh yes," I replied. "It was worth it."

A new confidence filled me with hope. Njoror's curse doomed us to wander the earth, but it did not say we had to do it aimlessly. In the spring, we would continue our journey, always seeking a path forward. Aldric's people lived in the west. For now, we would go west until the future revealed itself. We would add the Tigurini to our list of allies, then we would see what the future might bring.

If destiny brought us back into contact with Rome, I would ask for land again, in the continued hope of finding my people a new homeland. But if they refused us again, I was not sure my response would be to peacefully move on. I would not be insulted, and I would not be betrayed again.

Someday, I will be king, and the earth will tremble at the name of the Cimbri.

Chapter Thirteen

December 112 BC

Aldric, Hrolf, Teutobod, and Vallus were at my fire to discuss what would happen when we contacted the Helvetii. Aldric had told me he was of the Tigurini, a tribe that along with the Verbigeni and Tougeni, formed the coalition of the Helvetii.

"We're not far from my people," Aldric told me. The wind howled outside, and a draft blew through the cabin. He rubbed his hands vigorously and held them toward the flames. "A week's journey south will bring you to the Swabian Sea," he said, his face lighting up at the mention of the vast inland sea. "From the west end of the sea, the Rhenus River flows west and then makes a great bend northward. It is the northern boundary of my people. Travelers say it continues many leagues north to the Oceanus Germanicus, though I have never journeyed there."

"How will they respond when we cross the Rhenus?"

"Whispers of your journey have crossed the mountains with traders. Boats carry the news up and down the rivers swiftly. There are few who have not heard of you. My people are aware of your quest. The legend of Borr and the Cimbri have traveled throughout the land. Word of your battle at Noreia has encouraged the tribes that are resisting Rome, and some will see you as an ally in that struggle. Others, as the Taurisci did, will reach out to Rome for help. With your permission, as soon as the weather allows, I will return to prepare them for your arrival. I have some influence with my tribe. I will suggest that they ally themselves with you."

Vallus cleared his throat to get my attention, and I nodded at him. "Before you make decisions on the future, might we review what has happened up to now and what we know about what is before us?" I nodded again and he rolled out the vellum map that he clutched under one arm. I had not seen it for years and I was surprised at what I saw. It showed wear at the edges and was thin in spots where he had made changes, and there were several blotches where the ink had gotten wet, but the line could be clearly seen where he had traced from our home in Jutland along the Albis River to the Danubius and into the lands of the Scordisci, as far east as Pannonia and south to Macedonia. He had marked the sites of our battles at Siscia and Stobi with an X. It was a record of our journey, and Aldric stepped forward to gaze at it with keen interest.

A line diverged from the Danubius at Teutobergium and followed the Dravus River west into Noricum. An X represented our battle with the Romans at Noreia and the line crossed the Alpes to Boiodurum, then followed the Danubius again until another X indicated our recent battle at Manching.

"Here is where we are," he said, using the point of his small eating knife to indicate the spot on the map where our camp stood. The area north of the Danubius was marked only with a group of trees and labeled as the vast Hercynian Forest. The western edge of that dark forest was the Rhenus River and to the west of that the map was blank except for the word Gallia. The Rhenus rose in the Lacus Venetus, what Aldric called the Swabian Sea. Farther west, the map showed a second large lake at the northern foot of the Alpes, Lacus Lemmanus, which birthed the Rhodanus River. It snaked its way south all the way to the coast of the Mare Nostrum through the Roman province marked Gallia Transalpina.

"The blank area to the west is Gallia. I have never been there, but with Aldric's help, I have already begun to fill in some detail. When we cross the Rhenus where it rises at the head of the Lacus Venetus, or Swabian Sea," he said, nodding in deference to Aldric, "we will enter the land of the Helvetii, more specifically, the Tigurini.

There is a second lake further southwest, even larger than the first, and he tells me this is where the Rhodanus River rises. The Rhodanus then flows southward to the coast of the Mare Suebicum and the Greek trading port of Massalia. Many years ago, I told you how the Romans defeated the Allobroges and Arverni."

"I remember," I said.

"Their lands are now part of the Roman province of Gallia Transalpina. They border on those of the Helvetii, who are feeling the pressure of Rome's incursion as Rome fortifies those borders. The Romans covet their lands because they have heard rumors of gold to be found in the rivers and streams."

"Is this true?" I asked Aldric.

He shrugged his shoulders. "There are some who find gold in the waters or on the riverbanks, but not much. Most give up on it, as it takes a lot of time and effort to find even a small amount of gold. The Tigurini are not rich by any means."

"Nevertheless," Vallus continued, "the rumors abound through the army and all the way back to Rome."

"The Helvetii confederation are wary of a Roman expansion into our lands, and our borderlands are closely watched," Aldric said.

"What about Gallia?" I asked, pointing to the word on the map. "Are those tribes enemies or allies of Rome?"

Aldric and Vallus both started to speak and stopped. Vallus gestured for Aldric to go first. "It varies," he replied. "There are many tribes in Gallia, and the politics are different with each one. Alliances are made and remade regularly. Many want the fabrics, wine, fruit, and other trade goods that come up the rivers from Grecia, Italia, Africa, even as far as India. Others resent the presence of foreigners who come to conquer and demand tribute. There is unrest in many of the tribes, even in the areas under Roman control, yet they fight each other as often as they fight Rome."

Teutobod had been following the conversation but said nothing. "What do you think, my friend?" I asked.

He opened his mouth to speak, then paused. Finally, he said, "We will always be grateful to you for your help when we arrived in Pannonia."

"As we are for your help after the great flood, and again at the battle with the Vindelici," I said.

"Still, it is through the generosity of your people that we have avoided great suffering. We joined you willingly, and we intend to share in your struggles as well as your successes. The Teutones fear no one, but we cannot be at war with everyone. If we can form an alliance with a local tribe like the Tigurini, and possibly others, it would only benefit us. We would increase our numbers and our strength, especially if we are to face Rome again in the future."

I glanced at Hrolf, "And you brother?"

"I agree with Teutobod. We cannot fight everyone, and we cannot afford constant war. But Rome has made it clear that we are not going to be welcomed and we will likely have to fight them again. I think we should reach out to the Tigurini."

"Your thoughts echo my own," I said to them all, chewing on my cheek for a moment in contemplation. "Then it is settled. Aldric, as soon as it is safe to travel, I want you to go to your people and inform them that we come in peace and wish to talk. We only request space enough to camp next year, and we will move on again in the following spring as we always do. Hrolf, you will lead a delegation to accompany Aldric and speak on my behalf. We can discuss further details with them after we arrive."

"Teutobod," I said. "A moment?"

"What is it?" he asked when everyone had left.

"I'm not sure how to approach this subject," I said tentatively. "I've known you for years. Since my people began this long journey. You were a great friend to my father and have been to me. Our tribes have been allies and helped each other through some very tough times."

"What are you getting at?" he asked.

"If our tribes are to face the future together, it will be difficult to have two leaders."

Teutobod's expression turned hard.

I held out a placating hand. "Hear me out," I said. "Please."

He calmed and let out a heavy breath. "Go on."

"Decisions will need to be made. Negotiations will need to take place. If we are to ally our tribes, there must be one voice to represent us. You know as well as I do that more than one chieftain will cause friction. If we are to be traveling together, facing the same challenges, we must come to an understanding who represents us, with one voice."

"And what do you suggest?" Teutobod asked drily.

"The allied tribes and various factions that have joined the Cimbri have sworn to follow me as their chieftain. Some have gone so far as to ask to be adopted into the tribe."

Teutobod bristled visibly and made a growling noise in his throat.

"Let me be clear. I am not suggesting that you submit to me. We are equal allies. What I am asking is that if you continue with us on this expedition, that you agree that I will be the war chief of all." He appeared that he wanted to say something, and I raised my hand again, asking for patience. "The Teutones will remain independent, and you will retain the respect you deserve as their chieftain. The smaller contingents will remain under my leadership as the chieftain of the Cimbri. It would be a combined effort in all ventures, and we would share equally in all hardships and divide all gains evenly between the two. But I am asking you to agree that when the talk is done, when the debates are finished, when the plans are agreed, that I will be the voice that represents us all. That I will be the war chief of the allied tribes. And if we gain future allies, I ask for your support to recognize me as the war leader for them as well. I give you my word. You will be consulted with every major decision that concerns us all."

Teutobod stared at me for a long moment. I could not read his expression as he thought over what I had said. Eventually, he spoke. "I cannot make that decision alone. I must hold a council."

"I understand. Yule begins in a week. It is the time for the assembly."

"I will come to you with an answer after the assembly," Teutobod agreed.

Chapter Fourteen

Rome

Spring 111 BC

When Jugurtha received the news that war had been declared he was totally shocked. He had been utterly convinced that all things were purchasable in Rome, and this had been unexpected. Better than anyone he knew what war with Rome meant. He had spent years commanding the Numidian auxiliary cavalry under Scipio in the Numantine war. He had seen the power of their siege engines, their fortifications, and their manpower. He knew the abilities of their generals. War with Rome would be costly in every way. In a last attempt to avoid hostilities Jugurtha sent his son to Rome to negotiate on his behalf. Still convinced that Rome's favor was for sale to the highest bidder, he sent chests of gold and silver, pearls and gems, with instructions to bribe whomever it took to prevent an invasion.

This time, however, Jugurtha's overtures were ignored. When the delegation arrived, the senate decreed, "Unless they came to surrender Jugurtha's kingdom and himself, they must quit Italy within ten days."

Thereafter, the new consul Lucius Calpurnius Bestia, who had been assigned to prosecute the Jugurthine war, readied his army. While Bestia had many admirable qualities, both mental and personal, he was a greedy man. His desire for wealth and influence was well known, and had it not been for the law that pre-determined the commander before he was elected as consul, Bestia likely would not have been chosen, given Jugurtha's history of bribing officials.

But Bestia was shrewd, and he selected as a legate the very same Marcus Aemilius Scaurus that had been sent to meet Jugurtha the year before. He knew that Scaurus' reputation would blunt the objections any might have with Bestia's assignment.

Lucius had been in Rome now for over a year. He had been assigned to a garrison within the city that provided special services to members of the senate and other officials. Occasionally, the unit was called on to provide crowd control for large events, or security for members of the senate, especially during times of unrest when the mobs of angry citizens created a threat to their safety.

For months after the murder of the Romans at Cirta, the soldiers had been a regular sight at the Curia Hostilia when the senate was meeting. Lucius had been standing at the door to the senate house one day when Gaius Marius climbed the steps to yet another session. As he passed Marius' gaze locked onto Lucius' face. Marius possessed a prodigious memory, and he was well-known for remembering everyone he met. He was able to instantly recall where and when he knew them from, a skill that was very useful to any military officer or politician.

"Lucius Aurelius, isn't it?" he asked. "I believe I gave you those gold armilla that you are wearing."

"Yyyyes sir," Lucius stuttered, his eyes staring straight ahead.

"What is a hero of the Battle of Noreia doing here guarding these 'great' men?" he asked.

"I was assigned to the Rome garrison after I recovered from my wounds, sir."

"Really? Hmmm," Marius mused for a moment before continuing into the senate house.

Lucius glanced sideways at his companion standing on the opposite side of the great doors and let out a breath of relief.

That evening Lucius was summoned to his commander's quarters. "How the hell does a man like Gaius Marius even know you exist?" the centurion asked incredulously. Lucius recognized it as a rhetorical question and remained silent. His commander shook a papyrus scroll in Lucius' face. "These are orders signed by his hand assigning you to his personal staff. You are to report tomorrow morning to the general's own home. I don't know how you pulled this off Aurelius, but you had better make the best of this. After that business in Noreia you were lucky to escape with your life. You have the night off to pack your belongings and say your goodbyes. And Lucius."

"Yes, sir."

"I'm sorry to see you go. You're a good soldier. Make the best of this opportunity. Marius can be your path to success."

Chapter Fifteen

June 111 BC

Divico called himself king of the Tigurini, a Celtic sub-tribe of the Helvetii confederation. The Tigurini lived across the Rhenus River from what the Romans called Germania. It was a land of unsurpassed beauty. Snow-capped mountains towered above emerald-green meadows filled with brightly colored wildflowers. Silver streams of cold glacial melt spilled from the canyons to feed the small rivers, which in turn flowed into the pristine waters of the Swabian See, and then issued forth into the river Rhenus. We crossed the river above the great falls of the Rhenus, whose roar could be heard for a mile or more. We followed the guides that Divico provided us to the area he had selected for our winter encampment. It was only a few weeks' travel from our last camp, but I reckoned that it was sufficient to meet the demands of Njoror's curse.

Hrolf waited for me while I crossed the ford at the head of the caravan. "Divico has invited you to join him at the midsummer feast," he told me as I curbed my stallion next to his.

"That's in a few days," I answered.

"He has tentatively proposed an alliance and wants to make it formal."

"We shall see," I said.

Divico was a large man. As tall as me, but with a heavier build. He was young, about my age, but carried himself with the confidence of a man born to leadership. His scars told of his experience in battle, and he took the time after we met to boast about each of them. I learned very quickly he was full of pride for himself and his people, and not without reason. He was an accomplished warrior and a popular leader. Aldric sat at the high table on his right, Teutobod and I to his left.

The hall was large and high roofed. Smoke from the open hearths lingered about the ceiling as it fought a drizzling rain to escape through the hole in the roof. Divico had served a grand feast to welcome us, and food abounded on the surrounding tables. Two haunches of venison, a goose, and a whole pig turned on a single spit over the largest fire while several large fish baked on flat rocks near the coals. Chickens, ducks, and pheasants were suspended on hooks, dripping their fat into the glowing embers, each drip causing a small flame to burst forth and creating a mouthwatering aroma as the birds roasted. Several cast iron cauldrons bubbled with savory stews and loaves of bread were constantly replaced on the tables as the men sopped the stew and fat and shoved it into their mouths, greasing their heavy mustaches in the process.

Men sat at benches on the pounded dirt floor, and banged on the tables with their open palms, calling for the serving girls to bring more ale, and bring it they did, as the cups were drained quickly. The hall was filled with the raucous voices of the warriors of the Tigurini and the Cimbri and Teutones. More men lingered outside the door and under a thatch-roofed pavilion, as all could not fit into the hall.

Aldric had told me he had influence with the Tigurini. What he had neglected to tell me was that Divico was his younger brother.

"We have different fathers," Divico explained. "His was the shaman of our tribe who died of a disease not long after Aldric was born. My father was the son of a chieftain who took notice of the beauty of our mother. He married her and adopted Aldric. Two more sons died at birth and a daughter was born before I was. In time, my father became chieftain, and when he died, I took his place. Aldric should have been the heir. But he was content to be his own man and abdicated to me."

"And your sister?" I asked.

"There," he pointed toward the back of the hall, where a tall woman laughed loudly at a crude jest. Her blond hair was cropped short in the style of the men around her and she wore a gold torque around her neck, indicating her high status in the tribe as both a warrior and a member of the ruling family. "Her name is Errani, which means peaceful woman, but she is nothing of the sort. She is loud and boastful and has a reputation in battle as fierce as any man. She has never married and is without children and she is content with the ways of the warrior."

It was obvious she was comfortable in the presence of so many men and that they considered her an equal.

Divico was a gregarious man, with an honest face absent of guile. "My brother has told me much about you, and it is an impressive tale. Especially when he found you half-dead and nursed you back to health. You surely would have died were it not for his help."

"Aye," I acknowledged. "I'm very grateful to Aldric." Aldric looked uncomfortable, which in turn made me suspicious.

"We are well met, you and I," he went on. "It is fortunate that we meet as friends, rather than as enemies. Those that meet you as enemies do not seem to live long enough to regret it." He gave a half grin and left that statement hanging as he took a long pull from his cup.

"It is lucky for both of our tribes that we have the space to accommodate your many followers," he tipped his cup toward Teutobod, who scowled. He already felt left out of the conversation between Divico and myself, and the implication that he was my follower didn't sit well.

"Is something wrong with your friend?" Divico asked.

"He is not my follower, he is the chieftain of the Teutones, and he is my equal. You would do well to treat him so."

"Of course. My apologies to you both."

Teutobod growled his acceptance.

"In any case, I am happy to provide the space that you need to regain your strength through the winter, and I have guaranteed safe passage through our lands when you move on in the spring."

"You have been more than generous," I replied.

"And we are happy to do all this for our new friends. As I said, Aldric has told me of your … adventures … in Pannonia, Noricum, and Raetia. He has also told me of the curse that prevents you from rebuilding your homes. I wonder … what are your plans for the coming summer?"

"We have not discussed any details yet," I said. "We will move on in the spring, that much I know. But where? That I have not decided yet."

Divico was reclining in his high-backed chair, a finger tapping his chin as he considered my words.

"There is uncertainty in southern Gaul," Divico began. "Since the Romans defeated the Arverni and Allobroges ten years ago, they have been pressing their influence in our direction. They have claimed a border of their northern province of Gallia Narbonensis that comes against our own lands. Some of their bolder citizens have already crossed that border and hold great estates in the lands of the Arverni. That is how the Romans work. They encourage their merchants and settlers to enter new lands, promising them the protection of the Republic, and punishing any locals who dare to fight against it. Eventually, they claim the need to protect their citizens and send their armies to kill and to conquer, then claim the new land as their own."

"What does this have to do with us?" I asked, slicing off a large piece of cheese.

"Much of southern Gaul is divided by the Roman influence in their lands. Many can see the ambition that Rome holds for more land and tribute, others see opportunity for trade and power. The Raurici and Arverni want to push west into what is left of the Aedui, who are allied with Rome and are seen as traitors. I want to attack the Romans and push their border back south to the Isara River, away from our lands. The other tribes of the Helvetii confederation are preaching caution and don't want to provoke the Romans, and I do not have the strength needed to attack on my own."

"And you want us to join you," I concluded.

"Yes! Think of it. Your people and the Teutones, more than forty thousand warriors, added to that of the Tigurini, the Raurici, and the Arverni. When others hear of this coalition, more will join. After we punish the Aedui, we continue south and push the Romans back. It is time the Romans were taught that they are not welcome here. Your wagons are full of plunder from your travels. I want that for my people, and so will the others. The Roman estates in Gaul are ripe for the taking, and the Gauls living in Narbonensis are rich as well. Silver is plentiful. Horses and slaves will make us all wealthy."

Teutobod was listening intently now, interested in the possibility of gaining plunder.

I did not tell them I had been considering approaching the Roman governor of Narbonensis with another offer of service in return for land. It was just an idea forming at the back of my mind, and I did not wish to box myself in with options just yet.

I wasn't surprised by Divico's proposal. I had half expected him to ask us to help fight the Romans, but I could not help but think about how that arrangement had turned out with the Scordisci. My thoughts swirled. I needed time to think, and Divico came to my rescue. Smiling broadly, he said, "Obviously you will need time to consider my proposal. Take as long as you need. You have the rest of the summer and all winter to think about it and discuss it with your people and your allies. Whatever you choose, you are free to stay in your camp through the winter and you will have safe passage through our lands."

Chapter Sixteen

Rome

Marius petitioned Bestia to accompany him to Numidia as his legate. Again, as when Carbo turned him down and marched to his defeat, Marius was passed over in favor of Scaurus, another member of an ancient family. It was always thus. The aristocrats always looked out for each other and looked down on those who rose to prominence through their own abilities.

"Well," he thought to himself, "like it or not, if I'm ever to be consul, I'm going to have to play their game. If this were a battle, I would find a way over or around these obstacles."

Marius' military mind went to work. As much as he detested the political intrigues, the family connections, and the dirty money that were a daily part of advancing within the Roman political system, he began forming a plan. He had advanced as far as he was going to get, based only on his intelligence and ability. In their world, that wasn't enough.

He began by assessing the people he knew, separating them into categories. Who did he know he could trust, who did he think he might be able to trust, and who did he know he could not trust? Who were those that might be in a position to help him, and of those who would be willing or unwilling to do so? Marius had a great deal of money to implement his plans, but how to do so without revealing his intent? His actions must be anonymous. Marius began cultivating contacts from all walks of life and slowly he built a vast political machine. He refined his political platform.

He knew that he had much more in common with the plebeians, the common people who were represented in the senate by the populares, than with the nobilitas, the born aristocrats with long family lineage, most of whom sat in the senate themselves or were represented by the optimates.

Marius had already established himself as a populares. His personal background, the laws he had passed, and his support of other populares had solidified that. Now, he put more thought into how he could use that to his advantage. The plebians were the largest voting bloc in Rome, and provided the elections were truly fair, if he could win their total support, he would have an easy path to the consulship.

There were many people in Rome dissatisfied with the status quo. The senate had dulled the edge of many of the Gracchi reforms that benefited the common citizens. In the past twenty years, many of those who had stood up for the people and against the aristocrats had suffered horrible fates, some being torn apart by vicious mobs or being thrown from the top of the Tarpeian Rock. Those memories were still fresh, and the people were ripe for a new leader who they identified with. Marius decided to broaden his appeal by cultivating his image as a man who came from humble roots and rose to the pinnacle of success through his own efforts, owing nothing to any man.

He began by quietly and anonymously funding Gaius Memmius, a fiery tribune of the people who was making dangerous enemies by calling out corruption in the senate. It was he who spearheaded the call for war against Jugurtha in the face of those who had vigorously defended the prince for so long.

Memmius had accused Lucius Opimius and Marcus Aemilius Scaurus, two former consuls of receiving bribes from Jugurtha along with many other senators and influential people. He called for an investigation into these bribes, but thus far had been blocked by those very same powerful people.

Then Marius hired rabble makers to whip up the public through a middleman, thus leaving no trail back to him. Men who stood in the market squares and supported Memmius, men who thought they were doing the work of the people, while they were secretly working in Marius' favor.

He already had a reputation as someone who would stand up for what was right. Back when he was a young tribune, he proposed a law to reform the election process that would weaken the power of the senate. The consul Cotta made a motion to dismiss this law and to bring Marius before the senate to answer for his actions. When he did, Marius, as tribune, threatened to have Cotta arrested. When Cotta turned to Metellus, the other consul for support, Marius called for the officer outside the doors to come and arrest Metellus. When no support was shown toward them, the two consuls were forced to concede, and Marius won an important victory that established his reputation as a man of the people who had the fortitude to stand up to men of much greater power.

Marius then began to reach out to the military. He had spent more than twenty years in the army and had many friends. He was known as a soldier who knew and cared for his men. He was an intelligent leader and a keen strategist, and his talents lay not only in the tactics of war, but in the logistics and intelligence required to win.

He carefully floated the ideas of certain changes to the military, feeling out how his ideas might be received. He found that there was some dissatisfaction in the ranks. Many of the frontline troops had been fighting the Germanic and Celtic tribes for years, and they wondered about making changes to the tactics that had been used for centuries. Tactics that served Rome well against enemies that fought much the way they did, in ordered phalanxes on neat battlefields, but did not work so well against the wild barbarians who charged in mass formations, relying on surprise, strength, and violence of action. Marius began forming his own ideas of changing the organization of the army, how best to limit their vulnerabilities, capitalize on their strengths, and account for the different tactics of these new enemies who they were obviously going to be facing for some time in the future.

But one thing was still missing. Though Marius was an equite, the first rank of commoners and quite eligible to serve as a military officer, he would never be a noble. The aristocrats always looked down their noses at anyone who did not have a line of ancestors represented by marble busts in wall niches lining the entryway to their fine houses. Consuls, generals, senators, lineage running back for hundreds of years. If Marius could make it to the office of consul, he would be the first in his line to do so. A new man, as it was called. Then he would be considered as one of them. But until then, his lack of pedigree worked against him.

This was something he must address, and the only way to do that was to marry into a noble family.

During all this, Marius built his own personal staff. Men who were very loyal to him. Men like Lucius Aurelius. Lucius was a young soldier, a veteran of the Battle of Noreia, and he was grateful to Marius for the opportunity that he had given him. And Marius saw potential in young Lucius. He had the perspective of the foot soldier, the man in the ranks that Marius valued. He talked with Lucius often. Marius recognized that this was an intelligent young man and knew that he could use him in the future for important tasks.

One day, the general called for Lucius to attend him during a visit to his doctor. Marius had been afflicted for years with varicose veins in both legs, and being somewhat vain, had decided to do something about them. The general was famed for his courage and endurance for pain, and he proved that one day when Lucius stood by while Marius discussed military subjects seemingly without concern as he thrust his leg out and allowed the surgeon to go to work. Marius endured the scalpel without making any outward expression of pain. When the surgeon completed the first leg and suggested he was ready to repeat the operation on the second leg, Marius simply stated, "I can see that the result does not justify the pain. That will be enough." Marius stood and walked out, followed by an amazed Lucius.

Chapter Seventeen

August 111 BC

Wherever I found myself, the rhythmic sound of the blacksmith's hammer comforted me. The pulsing ring of metal on metal always returned me to my boyhood home of Borremose, before it was destroyed by the great flood. In those days, Gorm was a simple village blacksmith who worked in his smithy from dawn till dusk, hammering out the iron and bronze weapons, cooking pots, hinges, brackets, and tools that were crucial to our survival.

It was a sound that echoed in every village and settlement across the many leagues we had traveled no matter what tribe or nation, even in the Roman camps, the hammer and anvil always sounded the same. Now, as I walked with Hrolf toward the forge works, the sound was multiplied many-fold as Gorm's apprentices learned the new techniques of iron-working that Divico's smiths were teaching. The forge works were some distance from the settlement to keep the noise and acrid black smoke away from the living areas, and further still, a thin white smoke drifted from inside the forest's edge, where the charcoal pits smoldered.

The sound of chopping axes was accompanied by that of wood splintering as trees toppled with a resounding crash. Wood filled ox-carts plodded toward several new mounds in various stages of completion. Men prepared a large area by scraping down to the dirt, onto which hardwood would be stacked vertically, as tall as the tallest man. Then more carts brought loads of leafy green vegetation that was laid on top of the wood and yet another train brought clay from near the river, which was then packed around the mound about as thick as a man's hand. Vent holes were created around the bottom of the mound about a pace apart, and a hole was left at the top of the mound, where a fire was lit. The embers from that small fire would burn downward into the mound and ignite the stacked wood. Once the fire had taken hold, the vents and fire hole would be closed up, dousing the flames and trapping the heat under the ground.

Young boys then watched the mound. Smoke always found its way through, and occasionally a vent formed, and flames emerged, indicating too much air had gotten into the mound and the fire had flared up. A few handfuls of dirt plugged the vent and smothered the emerging flames, so that the wood continued to burn slowly under the mound, creating a great heat that turned it into charcoal.

It was difficult and dirty work. Especially for those who opened the pits and took out the charcoal. A gray dust arose as they raked it out and bagged it in burlap sacks to be taken to the forges. The men were covered in the dust and for days after coughed and sneezed it out of their lungs.

Some distance away from the charcoal heaps, a churning black smoke revealed where a group of clay chimneys had been built under the close supervision of Divico's smiths. The Tigurini used similar clay chimney furnaces to smelt the impurities from their iron, but they were larger, drafted better, and burned hotter due to the increase of forced air through a larger leather bellows. This allowed more iron to be smelted during one process, an important difference, as each bloomery was destroyed when the iron had been smelted.

A pile of the iron ore that we had captured in Noricum lay nearby, and men swung large hammers to break the nuggets of raw ore into smaller pieces that would be dropped down the chimney directly into the extremely hot fire. When it was deemed complete, the chimney would be broken apart and the bloom withdrawn. It would then be hammered to remove the slag and shaped into ingots and bars to be used later in the forges.

As we walked along, Gorm appeared. "Come to check on me?" he jested.

I smiled. "Just walking the camp. How is the apprenticeship coming?"

"Very well!" He was obviously pleased. "We are learning much from the Gauls and turning out a respectable amount of work. I don't think we will ever be as talented as they are for creating beautiful things, but weapons, tools, and armor don't need to be beautiful."

"You've quite a talent for organization, Gorm," Hrolf said, waving his hand toward the expansive forge works. "This is impressive."

There were many blacksmiths throughout the alliance, but I had charged Gorm as the master smith. In the years since we had left Borremose, Gorm had taken on a very different role than just the village blacksmith. He was charged with overseeing large projects, such as constructing the vessels we required to cross the large rivers that we could not ford, and he organized the teams that repaired our wagons while on the march. Now he supervised the forges, and he relished the challenges and responsibilities. He was a natural leader and an excellent manager.

"Have you been to the wagon works yet?" he asked.

"I have not."

"Come, there is much to see."

So, we walked together beyond the forges to the wagon works. There were stacks of raw planks for the sidewalls, men making wheels, and a group of teenaged boys were peeling the oak poles for the cart tongues. Axles were piled to one side and on a makeshift tabletop lay the iron brackets, chains, hooks, hinges, straps, and bolts used to repair and construct them. Several men were repairing and making new yokes and harness for the oxen. It was another impressive operation that Gorm had created.

"We've learned much from examining the Roman wagons that we captured. I've started using iron straps to strengthen the axles, so we should have less breakage."

Hrolf turned to me. "What of the silver and gold that we took, and the armor and weapons?"

Gorm looked at me expectantly. "I've traded the gold and silver ore to Divico," I replied. "His people will smelt it and give it back to us in coins, for a fair price. It will be easier for us to transport, and more easily used as well. I've also given him much of the spoils, such as the mail that is too small for our warriors to wear and the swords and helmets they won't use. The Gauls are talented at making mail and they will be able to make it larger for their use. That is how I got him to agree to teach us their metal-working techniques, and seeing all this, I believe it was worth it."

Gorm spoke up. "I've also been visiting their mint to learn the process they used to make the coins. I've got my hands full with everything else right now, but someday the knowledge will come in useful."

Chapter Eighteen

October 111 BC

I had taken to walking alone in the evenings to think. I left my bearskin cloak on its peg in the wall and wore a simple hooded woolen cloak as I wandered about the encampment, so that I would not be recognized. As I walked, I came upon a gathering of people around a large bonfire. The smooth tones of Aldric's voice came to me as I neared the fire.

"Listen closely and I will tell you the story of the Cimbri, and of a sickly child who grew to become a famous warrior and unlikely leader, and one day the chieftain of a great alliance of the northern tribes."

He was reciting a story, my story, our story. I hardly recognized the tale as he embellished it a great deal, but at the core, it was all true. It was the words that I had spoken to him during my time of healing in the cave we shared for so long, and now I understood his interest in my tale. With great solemnity, he told of the flood that drove us from our homeland and began our years' long journey southward. He recalled that I was chosen by Wodan to deliver the message of encouragement and prophecy that gave my people hope. He spoke of the time I nearly drowned trying to save my sister Hilgi and Nilda, my mother's sister, and how the river water had miraculously cured my lifelong sickness; how we spent weeks crossing the dark Hercynian Forest and our battles with the Boii. He recited the story of how I found Skol and we had become lifelong friends and warrior brothers. He described the battle of Siscia in detail, and the fight at the battle of Stobi when I won the wolf headed torque that encircles my neck. And he told them of the death of my father and how I came to be a leader during the great plague on the plains of Pannonia and through a war with the Celtic Scordisci. His tale followed our journey into the mountains of Noricum, and how we won a great battle against the Romans, then crossed the Alpes and camped near Boiodurum where we suffered another flood. He recounted the journey through the swamps along the Danubius and he became animated as he pantomimed the battle of Manching.

He paused, and his deep voice took on an even more dramatic tone. "But the great warrior, Borr, was troubled by self-doubt. He was humble and did not feel as though he deserved the mantle of leadership that had been thrust upon him, and he did not feel up to the challenges that lay ahead. He was confused by the curse of the sea god Njoror that prevented him from finding a homeland for his people, and he wanted answers. In his quest for knowledge, he walked into the wilderness, searching for the answers he so desperately desired, where he was attacked by the trickster god Lokke in the form of a great black bear."

The crowd collectively gasped at the ferocity of the attack and the description of my wounds. They fidgeted uncomfortably at how I lingered for weeks near death and communed with the gods. He reassured them that Skol had saved me with the power of Wodan's wolves. The crowd murmured with awe when they were told Donar had lent me his strength to recover and to eventually kill the bear and return to my people.

"He wears the claws of that bear on a necklace about his neck, and the skin of that same bear is now his cloak. He bears the mark of Donar's thunderbolt, and he sacrificed an eye to gain wisdom, as the Allfather himself had done. He vanquished the Scordisci, the Romans, and the Raetians, and he has cheated Hel herself for his soul. Have faith in him, my friends, for he needs your belief that he can lead you. Pray for him, for he needs the continued blessing of the gods."

I realized that I was fingering the necklace of bear claws as I listened. I had forgotten that Aldric was a bard, and now I saw for the first time what an extraordinary storyteller he was. His audience was captivated, and as his tale came to an end ,I quietly stepped backward, away from the light cast by the fire. The listeners applauded enthusiastically and came forward to shake his hand or clap his shoulder to express their thanks for the story.

As Yuletide approached, people did not seem to have the same enthusiasm as most years. Many people were expressing doubts about our journey. It had been ten years since the great flood drove us from our homes and we had suffered much. Some of the clan leaders were outspokenly critical, and Lugius led a faction of malcontents who were beginning to cause trouble. It was no secret that there was unrest, and Eldric attempted to put it to rest before it was time to make oaths.

"Rumors have reached my ears that some of you are disheartened. That you wish to return to your homes or to claim a piece of land and settle. Some have even expressed that they no longer believe in our chieftain, despite everything he has done, everything he has suffered in our cause. To you I bid listen, listen closely, and you will be reassured that our path is the righteous one. You will be convinced that our chieftain is the only one who has the power and the wisdom to lead us."

Eldric drew himself up and deepened his tone. "In the beginning, there was only Ginnungagap, the great abyss. No light, no sound, only the chaotic void that stretched across the endless primordial universe. At opposite ends of this nothingness, the ice and frost of Niflheim hurtled toward the fires of Muspelheim. Immeasurable eons passed until the two collided in a great cloud of steam that rose and froze again, over and over, until from the countless layers of ice, rose Ymir, the first of the frost giants.

"Ymir searched the cosmos for sustenance until he found Audhumla, the giant cow that had been formed from the ice as well.

Ymir drank of her milk, even as she nourished herself from the salt that she licked from a great block of ice. In time, a man was revealed from the ice. His name was Buri, and he was very different from Ymir, whose countenance was fearsome and cold, while Buri was handsome and strong. Buri was the first god. Ymir hated him at once and the two immediately became enemies for all time, launching the eternal war between the giants and the gods, which would last until the days of Ragnarök.

"Buri begat Borr, who married Bestla, a giantess, and they in turn had three sons, Wodan, Vili, and Ve, the first of the Aesir. In the cosmic war between giants and gods, Borr's sons overcame Ymir, whom they killed and tore asunder. The Aesir gods used the remains of Ymir to create the land of Midgard, and Wodan created man in order to fill Midgard with life.

"The gods created Asgard for themselves, the city of light from which they watched over Midgard from their grand halls and shining towers. Wodan, ever in search of greater wisdom, one day came to the well of Mimir. When asked what he would sacrifice for the prize of divine wisdom, he plucked out his own eye and offered it to Mimir, who granted him a single drink from the well. Wodan often descended to Midgard, where he disguised himself to walk among men. It is on one of these many visits that he met an earthly woman, and together they begat a son, who fathered another, and the line continued, until Borr was born.

"Now, you already know that we were cast out of Jutland by the vengeful god Njoror. The god of the sea and of sailors who once was a friend to us, the people of the coast. But when Wodan took Njoror's ex-wife Skadi for himself, Njoror became angry, and sought to injure Wodan in some way. Because the Allfather was too strong, Njoror struck out against the Cimbri, the sky-god's favored people, and sent the great flood against us. Then he conspired with the trickster god Lokke to lay upon us a curse that prevents us from finding our own homeland. Since then, he has struck out at us several more times in an effort to finally destroy us, but Borr has led us through those difficult times, and today we thrive.

"We are not lost. We cannot be. For Borr is named for Wodan's father and descended from the Allfather himself. And like Wodan, he has sacrificed an eye in the quest for wisdom. With this wisdom comes great power. The power to lead our people to many victories, to convince our people of what we must do to survive. This will be difficult, as they will not always understand, but Borr's strength, given to him by Donar who has marked him with the thunderbolt, and the wisdom granted him by Wodan for the sacrifice of his eye, will convince our people as well as our enemies that we are favored among the gods."

His speech had an immediate effect on the malcontents and I received a steady stream of oath makers throughout that evening. The stability of the tribe seemed to be restored.

January 110 BC

For months, I searched for an answer to Divico's proposal. I wanted an end to the violence and was not keen on entering into direct conflict with Rome if I could avoid it. I wanted to lift the curse by getting them to invite us into Italy so that we could finally build our lives in one place and let our children grow without the constant threat of warfare. I prayed often to Wodan for guidance and yet I was unable to decide on a course forward. We had lost hundreds more people in the flash flood at Boiodurum, and half our cattle herd had been washed away. The loss was beginning to show as the herd that was left dwindled and the numbers of our people grew.

When a solution finally presented itself, it came from an unexpected source. One evening, deep in the heart of winter, a loud knock came on our door. A man wrapped in furs stood in the doorway. His name was Skapti. "Lord, please, I must speak with you." I invited him in from the cold, ignoring that he had called me lord. I was becoming used to it. He stamped his feet to get the blood flowing again and shook the snow from his shoulders as he removed his fur cloak. He nervously told me that he represented a group of people that included members from the many different tribes that had joined us over the years. He was not Cimbri, but some in his group were. They had become disillusioned with our quest and asked my blessing to return home in the spring.

"Have you considered the curse?" I asked him.

"We have, lord. Those Cimbri among us feel that if they part from the main body that they may no longer be held under the curse and they are willing to take the chance. The others felt that as they were not part of the Cimbri at the time of the curse that they might be spared. No one is sure, lord, but we all wish to try. We are tired, lord. We want to build our homes and till our fields, raise our children and grow old in the shade of the same trees."

"I will consider your request. Come back with the new moon to hear my decision."

The next day I met Hrolf for a walk through the camp as we often did. He was silent, waiting for me to begin the conversation with whatever was on my mind.

"Divico's proposal is intriguing. In one way, I feel we owe him for the respite he has allowed us by granting us this land and the help he has provided. He has made it clear we are not obligated to join him on this summer campaign, but if we don't, he won't be able to move against the Aedui or the Romans this year, and that is what he hopes to do. I do not see a gain for our people. Just more warfare, and not really a solution to the curse."

Hrolf paused to lean against a snow-covered cart. "What do you intend to do about the faction that wants to return home?"

Skapti had mentioned something that I had not thought of. Could it be possible to fool the gods by simply changing the name of our tribe to avoid the gaze of the gods? It would not be the first time such a thing was done. Before our people moved north to Jutland, we were not called Cimbri. It happens all the time, and now that we were such a collection of mixed tribes, might it be a solution? I believed that it might be worth exploring the idea.

"In the spring, we will go north. We will follow the Rhenus to the northern sea and we will see if returning home is possible. Divico will have to deal with his own problems."

My decision had been made and when I told Divico, he was disappointed but gracious. He understood our desire to return home. When the people were told they were overjoyed, and the rest of winter was filled with the anticipation of returning home.

Flickering orange light from several bonfires reflected brightly off the snow as Frida and I walked with Lingulf to the shore of the small lake near our encampment. Our breath gusted in great clouds in the crisp mountain air, and we gratefully accepted a cup of warm spiced mead from a serving girl as we approached the fires. The high peaks loomed above us like gray ghosts against the moonless black sky through which the twinkling stars peered down from the heavens.

It was a night of great beauty, and the air was filled with the sounds of revelry as songs were sung and tales of adventure and bravery told around the large fires. I saw Aldric recalling our journey to a crowd of smiling faces, enthralled to hear their own adventures repeated in such a tale. Out upon the lake teams of oxen had dragged the snow clear of a large area in which a number of children and a few adults were gliding across the ice, bumping into one another in a contest of speed and balance as they raced from one side to the other.

During the idle hours of early winter, the Tigurini had shown our young men how to fashion a bone blade that was attached to the foot, which allowed them to glide across the ice. They drilled holes in the shinbone of a cow through which they threaded a rawhide strip that was tied around their foot. The bone was polished smooth, and then waxed with bees wax, or beef tallow, until it gained a golden sheen that would glide across the ice.

The boys formed two teams and played a game of last-one-standing. The players used a wood pole tipped with an iron spike to push themselves around the ice by placing the tip between their feet and pushing themselves forward, often at great speed.

The teams started at opposite ends of the cleared area and raced toward each other, their objective to knock the opposing team members off their feet until one team had no one left standing. One player hit a patch of rough ice that caught his bone blades, causing him to fall before he reached his opponents. Another pushed too hard with his pole and his feet went out from under him. He got up slowly, rubbing his bruised backside and groaning. The ones that managed to stay upright collided with each other, trying to knock the other down and often resulting in both of them falling. It could be a rough game and there were minor injuries, but there was much laughter, and all had great fun.

When Lingulf saw the other boys out on the ice, he immediately wanted to join them and pulled urgently on my arm. "I want to do that, Papa!" he cried. "Look, there's my friends," he said, pointing to two young boys with their fathers on the edge of the arena.

"You can't play with the older boys yet, but I'll go out with you so you can see your friends," I told him.

We strapped a pair of bones onto his feet. They were too big for him, but I got them tight enough so that I could pull him around a bit. He was thoroughly enjoying himself when we heard a shout. "Stop!" a man shouted at his son as he glided past the torches that lined the arena. "Stop!" came the shout again, now laced with fear. The boy suddenly dropped from sight as he broke through a patch of thin ice and a woman's scream came from the shoreline. Without hesitation, his father jumped in behind the boy. Ansgar had been nearby with his own son, and we rushed to their aid, yelling at our boys to stay where they were. Ansgar lay flat on the thin ice, crawling carefully out to the edge of the open water, while I held his legs and two others held mine. More men rushed to help and were motioned to stay back. Suddenly, the boy erupted from the icy water and into the waiting hands of Ansgar, who used his great strength to haul the boy out and onto the ice as the others pulled us all back to safety. His father never surfaced. He gave his life in the last effort to save his son. The boy's mother fell helplessly upon her knees as Frida took charge, ordering the other women to strip off his clothes and wrap him in a wool blanket, rubbing his arms and legs and chest to get the blood flowing. A spasm shook his small body as he coughed up water and began crying and calling for his mother. The incident was a tragic end to the evening, and the revelers made their way home, silent and somber in the knowledge that life was so very fragile and at any moment, happiness could be snatched away without warning.

JEFF HEIN

Chapter Nineteen

Villa of Gaius Julius Caesar

January 110 BC

Gaius Julius Caesar, son of Gaius Julius Caesar and father to another Gaius Julius Caesar, was the severely indebted patriarch of the Julii, an ancient family that had recently declined in fortune and influence. He was entitled to a senator's seat due to his exalted forbears, and he himself had reached the office of praetor, but the effort to fund his last election had severely depleted their remaining fortunes and driven him deeply into debt. The Julii had a long history of holding the highest offices in the Republic, but no one had achieved that most prized position of consul in nearly fifty years. The family had declined in fortune and influence. Today Caesar struggled just to pay the debts he owed.

"I suppose you are wondering about the reason I invited you to my home this evening," said Caesar.

"It did come as a bit of a surprise," Marius admitted, waiting for the senator to explain as they casually strolled through the atrium of Caesar's home. He knew Caesar only as a fellow senator and had never had a personal conversation with him.

Caesar was hesitating, unsure how to proceed. He could not shake the embarrassment of what he, a patrician of a most ancient and noble line, was about to ask a man with no notable family history. He took a few more moments to gather his thoughts, then consoled himself that at least Marius was an equestrian, and a well-known and successful one at that.

"I wish to make a proposal that may be of benefit to us both." Puffing up his cheeks and blowing out a breath of air, he finally got directly to the point. "I have a daughter in need of a husband, and you are in need of a wife."

Marius raised an eyebrow and the corner of his mouth twitched just slightly.

"I have watched you and witnessed your ambition and I must say that you are an impressive man Marius. You have great reputation as a soldier, and your support of plebeian causes has made you popular with the people, but you must know the real power lay with the noble classes. You have made few friends among them, and I mean no offense, but due to your lack of family history, you will likely never be accepted into their circles on your own. A marriage to my Julia will provide you with the respectability you need to pursue your goals."

Marius, normally unflappable, was momentarily speechless. This was the last thing he expected to hear, but he had to admit he was interested to hear more. As was his way, he remained silent and allowed Caesar to continue.

The older man glanced sideways at Marius, still uncomfortable with the conversation. "You should know she is widowed and has two young boys. I would expect you to take them in and care for them and provide for their education. It would, of course, be your choice to adopt them or not. I just wish to ensure my daughter has a husband and my grandchildren have a father."

Marius was forty-seven years old, Julia only twenty, but in arranged marriages that mattered little. Roman marriages were often more for political advantage and alliances than romance. Caesar's proposal was nothing unusual.

"I will need some time to think about this," Marius said.

"Of course," Caesar replied.

Some days later, Marius walked alone along the shaded lane that led to his family's estate in Arpinum. The tall cypress trees along the dirt road created alternating bars of shade and light as the setting sun cast long shadows across his path. The rhythmic crunch of gravel beneath his sandaled feet accompanied his thoughts as he pondered his life's direction.

He had reached the heights of success within the military starting at the tender age of seventeen and had learned his craft well from Rome's last great general, Scipio Aemilianus.

He had a spotty record on the cursus honorum the pathway to political success with service as a military tribune, two stints as plebian tribune, but then lost his bids for questor and aedile. He later won election to praetor and spent an uneventful year in Rome, but then, as pro-praetor, was appointed governor of Hispania Ulterior where, through his military successes and acquisition of mining rights and other interests, he became a very wealthy man.

Marius' humble birth was looked down upon by the patricians and he was considered by many to be a turnip-eating country bumpkin who rose to prominence through luck and association with more competent people.

In a nutshell this was the problem he faced. He had a reputation; he had wealth; he had checked all the boxes to progress to the next level, but he still was not accepted in their world. If he ever wanted to get elected as consul, now was the time to address that. He was getting long in the tooth.

None of the overtures Marius had made over the past year had panned out. He had not been able to find any unmarried women of noble birth whose fathers were interested in marrying them to him. But now one had come to him.

Gaius Julius Caesar was the head of an ancient household that had fallen on hard times. The family's wealth and influence had dwindled, and an eligible daughter presented the opportunity to correct this.

For Caesar, marrying his daughter to Marius was an opportunity for an influx of sorely needed cash from one of the wealthiest men in Rome and for Marius the marriage was a chance at gaining the respectability he needed to be accepted to the inner circles of patrician society.

The girl was twenty and already a widow. She came with two sons, Quintus and Gnaeus, explaining why Caesar was willing to approach a man of lower rank with a marriage proposal. Marius had turned it over in his head many times throughout the day and could not find any downside.

Villa of Gaius Julius Caesar

March 110 BC

Julia was surrounded by a gaggle of her friends, all talking and giggling over each over with anticipation of the celebration. Two were styling her hair in the tradition of a Roman bride, while two more held a hand, brushing and polishing her nails. A cosmetae, a female slave that specialized in the application of makeup, sat on a stool between Julia's knees applying the dusting powder composed of white chalk, crocodile dung and white lead. This foul-smelling concoction gave her skin the desired tone of white preferred by aristocratic ladies.

The early morning sun shined through the open window and il-luminated her plain features, her expression in stark contrast to the festive mood. She was a demure woman by nature, not comfort-able with public appearance or undue attention. Since the death of her husband, she had led a quiet and lonely life at her family's estate, mourning him for the respectable amount of time and then more. Theirs had been an unusual marriage as they truly loved each other, and his death was a great blow to her and her children. He had been a wealthy man, a merchant. She had not had the obligations of a great house and was able to care for her household and raise her children in relative quiet.

The arranged marriage to Marius, a man more than twice her age, brought a mixture of emotion. The few times they had met, he seemed so severe, so distracted. He seldom smiled and he had few friends. She was grateful for the security that it would provide her and her sons, and she knew that the arrangement solved her father's financial woes. She had wondered how her father would pay her dowry until she overheard them discussing it one evening and learned that it would be paid back to Marius out of the substantial gift of money that he presented her father in exchange for her hand.

When her father told her of the arrangement, he explained that it was her name that Marius was marrying. The prestige that came with the Julii name was important for his political plan and Marius had assured him she and the boys would be well cared for. But he had told her she would be expected to run the household and hold the dinners and other entertainment required by the wife of a senator.

A rapid clapping of hands startled everyone in the room as her mother entered, calling for attention. "Everyone out," Marcia said, smiling broadly. "It's time for the dress!"

A flurry of girls erupted from the room leaving mother and daughter alone except for the slave girl that carried her wedding dress. Marcia laid a hand on her daughter's shoulder and with the other, reached to tip her chin up and looked into her eyes. "You will be happy again," she said, understanding what was bothering Julia. "I'm sure of it. This is a day to rejoice. I know you still mourn your husband, but we must accept that he is gone. Life must go on and this is a solution that is good for you and your children."

"I know, mama," she answered dutifully. When she heard the sadness in her daughter's voice, Marcia had to fight back the tears that threatened to ruin her own cosmetics.

"Here," she said, blinking away the wetness. She reached out to the slave girl and took the dress. "Let's get you dressed. You're going to make a beautiful bride."

In a short time, Julia was ready. Her dark hair was coiffed into the tutulus style, held in place by a tiny iron spear that was meant to drive away evil spirits. A wreath of flowers circled her brow, and a lacy veil covered her face. Around her waist, over the showy white dress, she wore a thin belt that Marcia tied into the knot of Hercules, the symbolic knot that her new husband would untie to consummate the marriage. With a sigh, her mother smiled at her and embraced her again. Julia reached up and dropped her veil over her face. Together, they turned and walked out the door.

All eyes turned toward Julia as she entered the room. *She really does present a beautiful picture*, Marius thought, standing by the priest in front of the altar. The room was filled with nobilitas grudgingly paying their respects to the ancient family of the Julii and by extension Marius. A gaggle of smiling military officers hovered in the back of the room, the better to be the first to the banquet tables and wine pitchers when the formalities were complete.

"Wherever you are Gaius, there am I Gaia," Julia completed their vows as Marius slipped the gold ring upon the fourth finger of her left hand, the one in which it was believed the vena amoris ran straight to the heart. Marius turned back to the altar and offered a small prayer to Jupiter, asking to bless the marriage.

After dinner, the bride's parents stood at the entrance to say their goodbyes. Marius and his friends pretended to pull Julia from her mother's arms and the whole procession followed them to his house, as they were showered by various nuts. When they arrived, Marius picked her up and carried her across the threshold where they would begin their lives together.

Chapter Twenty

Germania

April 110 BC

Alarge fire at the center of a clearing deep in the Wodan-wald cast long shadows deep into the dark night, reflecting from the new leaves of an ancient oak that had stood sentinel over the sacred site for centuries. Thousands of warriors had gathered at this place to hear the prophet who had been traveling through the wilderness for months, calling for war.

A murmur of surprise rose from the crowd as a man seemed to appear from nowhere, standing beside the fire. The man spread his arms and turned for all to see him. He was tall and thin, and naked from the waist up. His ribs showed through thin skin, and he had painted the runes of Lokke and Fenrir onto his chest. He was pale and bald, and he had blackened his teeth and lips with charcoal and darkened his eye sockets and his nose so that he looked like a walking skeleton. Those closest to him could see that within those black circles, white scabs covered the center of his eyes such as afflict the very old, but most astonishing of all were the scars on his back. As he turned about, a gasp followed through the crowd as a bright red image of the world tree, Yggdrasil, was revealed. Its roots began at his beltline, its bole alongside his spine, and its branches spread across his shoulders.

His gait swayed as he circled the crackling fire as if one leg was shorter than the other, and he dragged one foot slightly. His skull-like face stared malevolently into the crowd of surrounding warriors, and his head twitched toward his shoulder now and again with an involuntary tick. Those brave warriors, men who had faced death many times and thought themselves afraid of nothing, looked away in sudden fear, avoiding the prophet's piercing gaze.

"Three times!" the prophet shouted suddenly, drawing everyone's eyes back toward him. "Three times Donar has tried to strike me down! Three times I have survived! The first left the mark of Yggdrasil, the great ash tree, around which all life exists. The tree whose death Donar fears, for when that tree dies, all the worlds will die with it. The second bolt nearly blinded me, yet I still see through a veil of white. The third was meant to kill me, and it succeeded! But when my soul met the goddess Hel at the gate to her realm, she knew that I was favored by her brother Fenrir, the wolf-god, and she sent me back to the world of the living."

Murmurs of disbelief rippled through the crowd and the prophet allowed a moment for it to quiet, nodding his head knowingly.

"You question my story," he said matter-of-factly. "I understand. It is difficult to believe." He looked down, still nodding. "Even I did not understand at first. I was no one special, just a common warrior. Like you, I hoped that one day I would die in battle and the Valkyries would carry me to Wodan's hall to greet the friends and enemies of my life and eat, drink, fight, and die to wake the next day and do it all again until the end of time. But Donar knew who I was and tried to destroy me before even I knew my fate.

"One special night my life was forever changed. Fenrir, the great wolf, came to me in a dream. He told me that long ago the gods had learned that the scions of Lokke would one day bring about the end of the world of gods and men. How in fear of that fate, Wodan cast Fenrir's brother Jormungand into the great sea to become the serpent that encircled the world, and then forced Fenrir's sister Hel into the underworld, where she became queen of the dead. Wodan feared Fenrir most of all, and he and the other gods bound him with unbreakable chains, then tethered him to an immovable boulder, where he was cursed to lay until Ragnarök drew near.

"Ragnarök, the end of days for gods and men. The earth will quake, mountains spit fire, the oceans will boil, and the skies darken. But before it begins, there will be signs of its coming. Chaos will rule in the days before Ragnarök. The winters shall be cruel, wars will be endless, thousands will die from disease and starvation, even the Aesir shall suffer as those who worship them lose faith. Fenrir will thrive in this chaos. He will grow larger and become stronger from the fear and sorrow and pain, and when the chains thought to be unbreakable are finally broken, Fenrir will search out Wodan to avenge himself for his imprisonment. Lokke will lead the frost giants of Jotunheim against Asgard's warriors, Hel will lead the legions of the dead and Jormungand, the sea serpent, shall slither upon the earth, leading the monsters of the world to the final battle.

"Like you, I have heard this story many times, but never from a god who was destined to bring it about. It was then that Fenrir told me he desired my help. But what could I possibly do? How could I help a god?

"Fenrir told me that the end was nearing, but that it was not coming quickly enough. He commanded me to abandon my own ambitions. He was impatient for his revenge against those who bound him, and he named me as his prophet. He told me that the growing chaos in the world of men brought him strength, but that he needed more. He growled his instructions and tasked me to sow the chaos that would give him the strength to finally break his bonds. Fenrir promised in return for this service, that when our world collapses into the cosmos and is forever destroyed, when the gods of Asgard are dead, that he will build a new Valhol, on the ruins of that shining city, and that I would lead those that joined me to live there, forever. To feast, to fight, to drink and to love, and to hear our feats and our names repeated in song.

"And so, I set upon my task to spread the words of Fenrir, to bring him the strength he desired. But such a thing cannot be hidden from the other gods. This is why Donar has tried so hard to stop me. And he would have, if not for the protection of Fenrir and Lokke," he said, pointing to the runes on his chest.

"Like all men, you and I will die in the final battle. But the loyal warriors of Fenrir will rise to live again!"

A great roar erupted from the gathered warriors, who raised their voices to the dark sky. A thunder of spears, axes, and swords beating on shields accompanied them, and then, without warning, the sky flashed brightly, as a single bolt of lightning reached down from the heavens, leaving its image upon every watcher's eye when the sky returned to an inky black.

Chapter Twenty-One

Spring 110 BC

We prepared to move as we had nearly every year for ten years. Flowing down from the heights of the Alpes the Rhenus bent to the north, and we entered a large river plain between two low mountain ranges. This was the land of the Raurici, allies to the Tigurini, who had also promised us safe passage.

We were able to leave earlier than usual because Gaul enjoyed shorter winters and firmer ground than we had previously traveled. The land was more open, with large tracts of coppiced oak, linden, and willow forests interspersed with cleared fields and natural meadows. The numbers that moved north along the Rhenus were immense. The caravan now included the entire population of the Cimbri and Teutones and the smaller tribes, clans, and family groups that had joined us along the way.

The further north we walked, the wider the valley got, and the horde spread across the entire plain. Not long after we crossed the boundary of the Raurici we began seeing the remains of burned-out villages and homesteads. Much of the land we passed was deserted. Soon we entered the tribal area of the Triboci, then the Nemetes, and finally the Vagiones where we halted in the shadow of the Donarsberg, a flat-topped mountain named for Donar, the thunder god. The berg dwarfed the surrounding hills and rose high above the river valley, and an ancient oppidum of the Vagiones sat atop the mountain. Our encampment covered the land below the mountain from horizon to horizon.

The next day, I took Teutobod, Hrolf, Ansgar, Aldric and five other men up the trail to the city and stopped a hundred paces from the gates. None of my men had shields and I spread my arms wide, empty handed, to show that I only wished to talk. We had been watched as we approached and it did not take long for the gate to open, and a man who I assumed was their chieftain rode out to meet us. He was dressed in a fine coat of mail and a long sword hung at his side in a bronze scabbard so highly polished it shone like the sun. A thick gold torque circled his neck, and he wore a fine bronze helmet topped with a snarling boar that looked as though it could come to life and leap right off his head. He was followed by nine warriors, also only armed with swords.

He curbed his horse a few paces before mine. "Who are you?" he demanded.

"I am Borr, chieftain of the Cimbri and war-chief of the allied tribes," I replied. "And you?"

"Wiglaf. King of the Vagiones."

His eyes widened when he noticed the scar on my forehead and the claw marks on my chest. I was simply dressed, wearing only my buckskin trews and leather boots, with a sword in a leather scabbard hanging at my hip on a wide belt. The air was cool, but I seldom wore a shirt these days as the scars on my chest were sensitive and the rough clothing rubbed on them uncomfortably. I did not want to threaten him. I had come only to talk, but the presence of so many unknown warriors on his land had put him understandably on edge.

"Why do your warriors fill my valley?" he asked indignantly.

"My people are returning home, and have stopped only to rest," I said. "We are simply passing through your lands and will be gone in a matter of days."

"You are not with the Suebi," he said matter-of-factly.

"No. Though there may be a few among us. We have gathered people from many different tribes on our journey. Is that who has been ravaging your lands?"

"Yes," he paused thoughtfully. "Come, let us talk over some food and drink," he invited as he turned his horse back toward the gate.

"The wolf-warriors have been terrorizing my people. They come in the dead of night and kill everyone, including the livestock, ripping them apart in horrible ways and causing as much suffering as possible, then they burn everything and return across the river. They are savages. Some say they are half-man and half-wolf. There is a priest that leads them, who claims he is a prophet of Fenrir, the wolf-god. He wishes to hasten the coming of Ragnarök by sowing as much chaos as he can. He believes that he places himself in Fenrir's debt by doing so and he and his followers will survive the destruction of our world and be resurrected to a new Valhol."

Wiglaf advised us to move on quickly, as being behind strong walls was the only defense from these wolf-warriors, and that our people camping on the open river plain would be vulnerable to them. Most of his people had already moved west to avoid them, and the rest lived within the walls of the oppidum. The land around was bare and offered little, and I was inclined to agree that we should move on as soon as we were rested.

Two days later a rain sodden Treveri delegation appeared at my tent. They looked cold, tired, and bedraggled from the weather, but their leader was determined to complete the task their king had assigned him. He stood tall, his blonde hair cut to the shoulders in the way of the Gauls. His blue eyes shone with intelligence and pride, and his manner was easy and full of confidence. His name was Oslaf, and I liked him immediately. "My king wishes to know what your intentions are. If you plan to attack us, you should know our people are prepared for war and we will resist any invader to the last man."

Aldric had told me that the Treveri were a large tribe that lived further north along the Rhenus. They were of Germanic origin themselves and had pushed westward across the Rhenus decades ago. Now, they were resisting the push from the tribes who had replaced them in the east, the same Suebi confederation from which the prophet gained his wolf-warriors.

"You can assure your king that we are not seeking a war," I began. "We are returning to our home in Jutland. We have been on a quest for many years and my people are tired. We only wish to go home."

Oslaf repeated the story that Wiglaf had told me of the wolf-warriors and how their settlements closest to the river had been raided. He offered the same advice as had Wiglaf. Move on as soon as you can. He told me that Treveri scouts had conducted patrols across the river for weeks and had reported movement throughout the forest up and down the river. Tribal groups were assembling near the defeated or abandoned fortresses whose former occupants had been displaced. The Suebi, Marcomanni, and others were pushing westward because of the Boii who were pushing them from farther east. Warriors gathered in large groups as their priests conducted sacrifices and inflamed the tens of thousands of warriors for the coming war.

"There is great unrest in Gallia. The frontier along the Rhenus River is in flames. There are rumors of a cult of warriors led by a mysterious prophet who turns these men into beasts, half man and half wolf, that hunt only at night, bringing terror."

"I have heard of this prophet," I said.

"He claims to be a prophet of Fenrir, the giant wolf-god of the Germanic tribes who is destined to bring about the end of the world, and he is urging the forest tribes to war to hasten the chaos."

"I know of Fenrir," I replied drily. "How is it that you know him? Your gods are different than ours."

"Many of the tribes that live along the northern Rhenus came from the forests to the east. Years ago, the Treveri crossed the river and pushed out those who lived here. We brought the old gods with us, and we still worship them. There are many places named for Donar and Wodan."

Oslaf sat back while a servant filled his cup, then leaned forward and continued. "Many Germanic tribes settled into northern Gallia north of the Seine and west of the Rhenus and once the land was conquered, we made peace with our gallic neighbors. Now we are in turn being attacked by the forest tribes that filled the space behind us. Our people are moving westward, away from these raids, which is creating conflict as they push against other tribes. It is leaving a wide strip of open land that the woodland tribes are sure to see as an opportunity to settle permanently."

"What does this have to do with me?" I asked guardedly.

"Your arrival is fortunate timing. If your warriors were added to ours and the other Rhenus tribes, we may be able to stop this invasion. Together, we can push the Suebi and their allies back to where they came from. I am asking that you help us." He sat back in his chair, took a healthy drink from his cup of ale, and waited for my reaction.

I told Oslaf I would give him an answer the next day, but that was just courtesy. I already knew my answer was no. I had no wish to enter into a war that I had no stake in, and I planned to stay only one more day. Mindful of his and Wiglaf's warnings, I had doubled the guard and ordered mounted patrols along the river, but that night the ominous warnings proved true. Somehow, they had appeared in the center of our camp, and I woke to screams in the early morning darkness. Bright light flickered against the walls of my tent and as I flung open the flap, I saw that several tents nearby burned furiously. A man ran from the nearest tent, his hair and clothing on fire, his screams shredding the air, and as I watched a great hulk of a man chopped down into the burning man's shoulder with an enormous axe, ending his screams forever. Hundreds of dark figures moved through the camp, slaughtering anything in their path. They had come from the river to hit the center of our encampment. Chaos surrounded us as women and children fled in every direction and my warriors, roused from their beds, looked for an enemy.

The enormous warrior turned toward me; his face shadowed by the bright fire behind him. He took a step toward me and my breath caught for a moment as a flaring light revealed the snarling visage of a wolf where the man's face should be. Could this be one of the half-man half-wolf warriors I had heard of? My mind froze with fear and my heart pounded in my chest. My family was behind me, protected only by the thin leather walls of our tent, and this beast was stalking toward us. My only choice was to defend them. I swallowed my fear and stepped toward him, circling in the open space between the burning tents, trying to draw him away from my wife and son.

With an animal-like howl he rushed me, and I realized that in my haste I had left my shield in the tent. I parried his powerful swing, and sparks flew as sword met axe, clanging loudly. The heavy axe was knocked only slightly aside from its target, my unprotected head, and just missed my leg as the strength of his swing carried the axe down and into the ground. I allowed the recoil of my sword to carry me around in a tight circle and spinning on my left foot, I came around with both hands on the hilt to chop into the man's neck with all my strength, nearly severing it in one stroke. He fell to his knees, then flopped onto his side, and as he hit the ground the wolf's head cape that he wore was knocked askew. Relief washed through me. He was a man, not some monster, and he was killed as any man could be.

Hrolf appeared at my side, covered in blood. "Are you alright?" he asked me. I was gasping for air and nodded when I realized that the noise had changed. The screams of fright and shouts of rage had turned to moans of anguish and weeping. The raiders had disappeared as quickly as they had attacked, leaving only destruction in their wake. As the gray light of dawn revealed the carnage, we found that they had killed dozens and wounded many more. Most of the dead were innocents who did not have a chance to defend themselves. A separate group had attacked our cattle and driven off hundreds into the river, where many had drowned.

When one of Oslaf's companions approached me around midday, I was talking with Teutobod. I asked him where Oslaf was. "Dead," he said. "Killed in the raid."

"Tell your king the Cimbri and Teutones will join him in punishing these savages."

―――――――

Several weeks later, on the first night of the hay moon, under a blanket of near total darkness provided by a thick layer of clouds that concealed even the thin light of the stars, we crossed the river. Over one hundred thousand fighting men crossed the Rhenus that night. We met no resistance as we melted into the dark forest on the far side, but the dawn's diluted light revealed the Suebi and their allies waiting for us a mile from the river behind shield walls that bristled with spears. They had created a line of fortifications by felling trees to disrupt our charge and it was a difficult battle, but our numbers overwhelmed them. After days of savage fighting and heavy losses on both sides, they withdrew from the river's edge into the forest, and we let them go in order to treat our wounded and care for our dead. Great battles raged up and down the river as the Cimbri and our allies pushed the enemy back.

By the waning moon we had advanced to a line twenty miles from the river and occupied villages and oppidums up and down the new frontier. The Teutones crossed near the mouth of the Neckar River and fought their way up the slopes of a thickly wooded area that the locals called the Wodanwald. After a three-day battle, they took a particularly strong outpost high on a hill above a sharp bend in the Main River. The Teutones suffered many casualties and took their revenge upon the captives with a bloody sacrifice to Donar. Teutobod's warriors crossed back to the west but later returned to the ruined fortress to erect a tall sandstone marker that commemorated the battle where they had lost so many.

Some of the other allied tribes occupied forts and villages that created a connected buffer zone on the east side of the river, and I pulled the Cimbri back to the west. Teutobod decided to set up winter camp near the Donarsberg and a week after the final battle, the Cimbri continued north.

The Treveri, grateful for our help in the Suebi war, granted us safe passage through their lands. On the trek north, we passed a large slate hill across the Rhenus from us. Our Treveri guides were on edge for several days and later that night as I walked the camp, I heard them telling the story of the Loreley.

"For ages past rivermen tell of the Loreley, a beautiful maiden who sits atop the great rock above the river Rhenus, brushing her golden hair in the moonlight and singing a melancholy song to her lost lover. Her warrior was killed in battle and when she learned of this, she came to the rock. In her great sadness, she threw herself from the heights into the river below. On certain nights, a strange glow comes from the top of the mountain. Men say it is she who sits there in the moonlight, brushing her shining hair and keening her grief to the passing sailors who become so enraptured with her beauty and song that they lose their wits and are drawn to their deaths on the rocks below. As they sink below the waves, the last thing they see is a glimpse of the siren as she welcomes them to her watery grave."

I shivered at the thought and made a small sacrifice to Rhenus Pater, the god of the Rhenus River, thanking him for watching over my people as we had traveled along its length this summer. I was much relieved that we traveled by land and not by water.

We crossed the northern boundary of the Treveri at the Maas River and entered the domain of the Ebrones, a Belgae tribe who were on friendly terms with the Treveri and had granted us a tract of open land for our winter camp. Along the way, I had used some of our gold to buy grain and wine for the winter, and barrels of a strange food called olives. They were new to us and had a pleasantly salty taste that made my mouth pucker up and crave more, and they went especially well with a tankard of ale. I liked the ones that were picked green and soaked in lye water to remove the bitter taste, then stored in brine.

Lingulf, now six years old, sat on my lap one night talking and laughing as he told me about his day. Frida stood at her loom, weaving and looking on with a contented smile. He giggled uncontrollably as I popped one of the small green fruits into my mouth, chewed the meat off of it, and spit the pit into the fire with an exaggerated sound. It sizzled in the embers for a few moments until it burst into a sudden yellow flame and burned intensely, lighting up the room briefly.

"I want to try, Papa," he said, snatching one from my hand and popping it in his mouth. He was still giggling and when he took a quick breath, he sucked the olive into the back of his throat, blocking his airway. His eyes went wide in panic when his breath caught and tears flowed. He tried to scream but only managed a horrible gagging sound. I froze for a moment, unsure what to do, then held him at arm's length and shook him, to no avail. His lips were turning blue and red splotches had darkened around his eyes when Frida flew to my side and snatched him from my hands, flipped him upside down and pounded his back until the thing dislodged and fell to the ground. A loud wail erupted from the boy, who clung tightly to his mother, sobbing from the pain and fear of what had just happened.

I met Frida's eyes with a pang of guilt, but she reassured me with a nod that all was well as she comforted our son, whose eyes were now heavy as he fell asleep, safe in his mother's arms. I stood awkwardly in the center of our cabin and watched as she laid him down in his bed and returned to embrace me, now comforting me as she had our son. I held her tightly as relief flowed through the both of us and we thanked Freya, goddess of the hearth, for the life of our son that could have been taken from us so quickly.

We were a few days' ride from the Oceanus Germanicus, and I sent a party to the coast to buy smoked fish and salt. It had been an abundant year ,and they returned in a few days with their carts full. We had arrived in time for the fall eel run and at the first sighting of the slithering fish roiling the water as they returned to the sea, our people were elated at the thought of enjoying a tradition we had not been able to do since the first days of our journey.

Frida was happily preparing a basket with food and drink, some knives, and a few woolen blankets when I padded silently up behind her and slipped my arms around her waist. She jumped and turned, giving my shoulder a light smack in admonition. Then, with a smile and a quick kiss, she returned to her task.

"Do you remember the night we met?" I asked, leaning against the wall beside her as she worked. I snatched a piece of cheese out of the basket when she wasn't looking.

"Of course, I remember," she said. "You were blind to me no matter how much I tried to get your attention. You just kept talking with your friends and getting drunk."

I chuckled. "That was the first time I ever got drunk, and I suffered for it the next morning. But I saw you. I couldn't take my eyes off you," I said wistfully, reaching out to touch her hair. She wore it the same as I remembered that night. She had been through so much since then, walking thousands of miles, enduring extreme cold and heat, deadly enemies, the birth of our child, then being kidnapped and assaulted, and yet she was the same beautiful young girl that I met so long ago. I had changed in so many ways, and she remained the same. The rock our family relied upon. I was so grateful for her, and I felt the guilt of not showing it enough. It was always the same. The feelings welled in my heart but could not find their way to my lips. But she knew. Her dark eyes looked back, tenderly searching the depths of mine as we silently communicated our love. We had finally won back our closeness. After years of merely existing beside each other, we were finally in love again. She rested her head on my chest and reached for my hands as we stood quietly, our hearts beating together in our tender embrace, just enjoying the shared moment.

"There will be a party leaving soon to go back to Cimberland," I said.

"I have heard that," she said. "There is much talk of it."

"What do you think?" I asked her.

"Will the curse follow them?

"I don't know." I feared that it would, but how could I know?

"I have decided to keep the rest of the tribe here while a small group checks it out, but I want to go with them with enough warriors to guarantee their safe passage. I will return before winter sets in."

When we got to the river, Lingulf ran off with his friends as Frida set to work making a drying rack and her father, Glum, gathered wood and kindled a fire. Aldric and I shoved a few birch torches into the sandy gravel along the water's edge and as darkness fell, the flickering light revealed the surface of the water churning as the eels began their nocturnal migration. Born in the high mountains far to the south, he was familiar with the migration of the eels, but near the source of the Rhenus they were not so numerous. The transparent young eels swim the length of the Rhenus from the Oceanus Germanicus hundreds of miles upriver each year, all the way to the great falls near the Swabian Sea where the Tigurini live. They wriggle their way over the rocks and wet grass next to the turbulent falls on their instinctive journey upstream to new freshwater homes where they stay for several years, gradually changing color to a beautiful yellow gold as they mature, then silver, before they make their final journey back to the sea as a fully grown adult.

Aldric was astonished at the countless snake-like fish as they slithered and tumbled over each other in their headlong race for the sea. Like me, he was using a leister, a three-pronged fishing spear with backward facing barbs that we had fashioned earlier. He shouted with childlike delight when he speared his first eel, a large one about the length and girth of his arm. Two others that were entangled with it dropped back into the water when he lifted it over his head and onto the shore as the fish struggled mightily to escape. The look of pure joy on his face made me laugh like I had not laughed in a very long time, and for a while, I felt like a boy again.

Lingulf pounced on the eels we threw onto the riverbank and deposited them into a nearby barrel where Glum salted them to remove the slime and kill them, and then Frida deftly cleaned them and lay their long bodies over the drying rack. Within an hour, the racks were full, and we paused the harvest to eat and sit by the fire.

We all basked in the joy and comfort of being close to family over a pot of Glum's sweet honey mead and reminisced for a while of the night we had all met so long ago. Lingulf sat on the ground, his arms wrapped around his legs and chin resting on his knees, fascinated by the stories he had heard before and always welcomed again. It was a time to pass on the history of our family to my son, and I began the tale of my father, Haistulf, and how he had met my mother, Ishild. He was the son of the hunno of the wolf clan and she was the pretty daughter of one of his father's retainers.

I told him of Freki and his twin brother Skalla who had become my brothers when their parents were killed in the great flood and about my mother's sister Nilda, who had drowned on our journey, and my father's brother Grimur, who had left us so long ago and never was seen again, and his other brother Lothar who had died at the battle of Noreia. I told my son of the plague that had taken my parents, and Skalla, and Grimur's wife and son, and so many more of our people when he was just an infant. And I told him of my sister Hilgi, who was now a priestess, a seer, a prophet.

It was not the heroic tale that Aldric wove of our survival and victories over our enemies, but a more intimate story of the people who came before him.

"What about Uncle Hrolf?" he asked me.

"Well," I began, "we met your uncle Hrolf on a night much like this. Weeks after the great flood, we had traveled into the land of the Teutones, and they, along with our friends the Ambrones, saved us from a terrible winter by giving us food and clothes. We went fishing for eels and Hrolf laughed at me because I could not hold on to the eels that struggled out of my hands. He was the one that showed me to use a piece of cloth like I showed you, and we've been friends ever since. That was also the night that I met your mother," I said.

"I know," Lingulf said. "You didn't notice how pretty she was because you were drunk," he said with a giggle.

I shot Frida an embarrassed look, and she blushed and gave me a self-conscious grin.

"I heard you talking before," the boy said.

"Big ears," she said.

Glum, his belly shaking with mirth, laughed loudly and nearly fell off the log he was sitting on.

"Your grandfather is the one who is drunk," I said, and we all laughed again. "And now it's time for little boys to be in bed." I snatched him up from the ground and he squealed with delight.

One thousand people headed east, accompanied by another thousand warriors. We took no cattle and traveled in mostly open land near the coast with scattered plots of scrub forest. We were watched from a distance but allowed to pass unmolested. After several weeks, we crossed the western boundary of Ambrones territory and were met by a group of scouts who escorted us to their capital. Amalric was still their chieftain. It had been ten years since I last saw him, and he was as I remembered; tall and powerful, in total command of his people, and a gracious host.

He was eager to hear our story, and I regaled him with our adventures since we last saw him.

"I am sorry to hear of your father's death," he said sincerely. "He was a great man, and now you are the chieftain in his place. It is good that the son succeeds the father. But I'm afraid you have returned in vain."

"What do you mean?" I asked.

"Several new tribes have moved onto the peninsula. They killed many of those who remained when your people left. The Saxones have taken over the lands of the Teutones, and the Angles pushed farther north. They used to live to the south and east beyond the Odra River but are being pushed by other migrating tribes. The world is changing swiftly."

"I know. Just this summer we fought a war with the Suebi, who were being pushed out of their lands by the Boii," I told him. He nodded and continued.

"Another unnamed tribe of warriors arrived from across the sea," he started. "Maybe they crossed from Scandia or farther east, I don't know, but they are calling themselves Jutes because Jutland has become theirs. They are the ones that now live in your villages and homesteads. They are all savage tribes, and they harass our borders constantly. The Albis is a natural boundary, but they raid our cattle and farms and disappear back across the river. These tribes far outnumber my people, and I believe they are planning an invasion of my lands in the spring. Your arrival was unforeseen, but fortuitous."

"Are there any of our people left?"

"A few made it to our borders seeking refuge, and I granted them land. They have a village to the west of here. I sent a messenger to tell them you have arrived."

Amalric told me that because of the pressure from the eastern tribes, he had been considering moving his own people. News of our journey had reached him from time to time and he knew of our victory over the Romans at Noreia. I told him of our encampment just weeks from here. He brightened at the prospect of joining forces, and we made plans for the Ambrones to join us in the spring.

With Amalric's news of our homeland, the group who wished to go home came back with us, as did those who were pushed out by the Jutes, and we all returned before the first snow.

"What is it?" Frida asked when I twitched sharply and threw the covers back, concern plain in the tone of her voice.

"I didn't mean to wake you," I hissed at her, swinging my legs over and sitting on the edge of our sleeping pallet. I hadn't meant to sound angry, but I did. A stabbing pain behind my left eye had jolted me from sleep.

She placed a hand on my back, and I tensed; the pain in my head was so intense that every nerve in my body was on fire.

"I'm sorry," I said more gently. "It's another headache."

I hurried out the door into the cold winter air, naked. The headaches had returned weeks ago, now accompanied by attacks of severe pain throughout my body. I had discovered that cold helped and as I gulped the night air, exhaling clouds of mist, I broke the thin layer of ice on a bucket outside the door and scooped the frigid water onto my head and face, gasping as the water trickled down my chest and back, the pain slowly fading in its intensity.

Frida stepped outside and reached up to drape my bearskin cloak about my shoulders. The warmth was comforting, and the pain ebbed to a dull echo of what had awakened me. "The pain is so severe," I said. "I thought they were gone for good." She stood with me for a while until my breathing had returned to normal. With her arm around my waist and mine across her shoulders, she lent me her strength as she guided me back inside.

Chapter Twenty-Two

Rome

December 110 BC

"Congratulations Gaius!" Publius Rutilius Rufus toasted the birth of Gaius Marius the Younger. "I hear he is a healthy and happy boy. I pray to Jupiter that he has a long and prosperous life."

Marius smiled so seldom he was nearly unrecognizable, sporting a huge grin as the room acknowledged the toast. He was uncharacteristically jovial, smiling and laughing with those who attended another reunion of the veterans of the Numantine war. When those present returned their attention to their own conversations, Rufus and Marius talked alone.

"He is a blessing," said Marius, "but I have found that I cannot tolerate babies. The incessant crying, feeding, and shitting is driving me insane. I must get away from the city. I wish Albinus would get on with these elections so I can petition the new consul for a position on his staff. Perhaps this time it will be different."

"Indeed, you have been busy behind the scenes," Rufus replied knowingly. "Many are surprised that you did not run for consul. Why is that?"

"I'm not ready yet. When I run, there will be no doubt I will win. I've made progress toward my goals, but it is not yet time."

"Marrying Julia was a brilliant strategy. I trust it has not been too painful?"

"It has not. She has been a most loyal and willing wife. In fact, we are becoming rather close. That was unexpected. I had simply planned on a marriage of convenience, but I have found she is an intelligent woman and beautiful as well. She is proving to be a fine companion."

"I'm happy for you Gaius. Truly. You deserve something in your life besides a cold bed and hardtack."

Patting his belly Marius chuckled, "I could use some hardtack. This city life is making me paunchy. It's high time I went back to a cuirass and pterugis and put away this toga."

"So, what do you think of the war in Numidia?"

"Bah! Such incompetence." His mood shifted sharply. "It's proof that sending these aristocrats achieves nothing. If the senate were serious about punishing Jugurtha, they would put me in charge."

"Quintus Metellus is running for consul. He'll probably get Numidia as his province."

"Hmmph. Another aristocrat," Marius complained. "Although, I must admit he has the reputation of being honest enough not to be susceptible to Jugurtha's bribes. It doesn't hurt that he comes from centuries of family money."

"He's also a competent general," Rufus suggested. They had served together with Metellus in Numantia, and the three held a grudging respect for each other's military skills.

"I suppose he's capable enough," Marius said.

"I'm glad you agree," Rufus said. "On your left." Rufus tipped his chin over Marius' shoulder to indicate someone was approaching.

"Marius, Rufus," Quintus Caecilius Metellus greeted them. "I would like it if you joined me at my home for supper tomorrow. We have some matters to discuss, and I prefer not to do it here."

The two simply nodded and Metellus walked on.

"What do you make of that?" asked Rufus.

Marius frowned after Metellus. "I don't know yet."

Spurius Postumius Albinus had been sent to carry on the war against Jugurtha after Bestia returned without having brought the war to an end. Rumors circulated that Bestia, like so many others before him, had succumbed to the flattery and bribery of the Numidian prince and had made little effort to bring him to task. Albinus had followed suit. Despite making a big show of his preparations for war when he reached Africa, he sat in Utica with his legions and made proclamations, had meetings, and allowed himself to be deceived by Jugurtha, who constantly promised to surrender and then delayed. Once again, Jugurtha seemed to have bought himself out of a war. When the summer had passed and it was near the time for the consul to preside over the elections in Rome, Spurius Albinus departed, having accomplished nothing of significance, and left his brother Aulus in command of the army in Africa.

Aulus saw his brother's absence as an opportunity. He was an ambitious man, and he was not satisfied with the lack of progress in the war. When Spurius was delayed in Rome, Aulus rolled the dice. He led his troops out of their winter barracks and marched on the town of Suthul, Jugurtha's treasury and residence. Aulus prepared a siege and while his attention was drawn to containing Jugurtha's forces, the prince, now declared king as his rivals had all been killed, escaped the surrounding legions, and lured the Romans away. Jugurtha promptly defeated them and surrounded the survivors. Jugurtha offered Aulus terms which allowed him to save the rest of his army, and though this was a distasteful end to Aulus' efforts, he agreed to quit Numidia and pass under the yoke. This humiliation proved too much for the senate, and the war with Jugurtha was renewed.

When the elections were finally complete, Quintus Metellus had secured Numidia as his consular province while the second consul, Marcus Junius Silanus, would remain in Italy. Metellus immediately began preparing to depart for Africa. Marius and Rufus had accepted his offer to accompany him as his legates, each to lead one of his consular legions. The three had often served side by side watching each other with interest as they climbed the cursus honorum, the pathway to reach the highest office. Born only three years apart, Metellus was the oldest and the first to be elected consul. Now they used those talents and connections to build an army that would finally bring Jugurtha to justice.

Chapter Twenty-Three

March 109 BC

The headaches had stopped again, and I was feeling much better. I held a gathering of the leaders of all the clans and allied tribes, and it was then an important decision was made. Skapti, the leader of the faction who wished to return home, approached me with another proposal. They now wished to stay where we were and establish a colony.

"We are made up of members of many different tribes. We have Cimbri, Teutones, Boii, Langobardi, Semnones, and a dozen others. Before we knew of the curse, we all came to consider ourselves Cimbri under your father's leadership, and now yours. But we are tired. The old ones want to die on land they call their own and our young ones want to raise their children in one place. We ask your blessing to establish a new tribe that will encompass all of us under one name. We believe this may allow us to avoid the gaze of Njoror and allow us to finally live in peace."

"And what do you propose to call yourselves?" I asked.

"We intend to build a new fortress. The name will be Aduatuca, and we will call ourselves the Aduatuci," he said, drawing himself up with pride in the name. "It is the Gallic word for fortress, and we will be the fortress people. We have already found a nearby hilltop with a source of water to build it upon."

"We are a free people," I said. "You may stay or go as you please. I give you my blessing to do what you like. How many are you?"

"There are as many as three thousand who have let it be known that they would stay, lord," he replied nervously.

I considered that number for a moment. An idea was forming. Three thousand men, women, and children weren't enough to protect themselves from outside pressure, and with the migration of other tribes that was happening, I was worried that they might be overrun. I had long been thinking on the challenge of our growing caravan. The old, the sick, the wounded and crippled, all slowed our movement and required the help of many of the able-bodied to complete each day's march. We had lost much of our herd since Boiodurum, and endless marching was making them lean and stringy. Reducing our numbers and building a permanent base could be the solution to many of our problems. Most wanted to keep their identity as Cimbri, but creating a new tribe of the ones who wished to stay just might prevent Njoror's curse from punishing them.

I instructed the other leaders to look for volunteers to start a new colony. I pledged to come to their aid if ever needed, but they had to be willing to renounce their old tribal names and adopt the new. Nearly ten thousand decided to stay.

As soon as the weather allowed, fifteen thousand men under Gorm's direction began the construction of the fortress. By the time we were ready to move south, stone walls framed by timber in the fashion of the Celtic oppidums were complete. A ten-foot-high rock faced wall, backed by a thirty-foot-wide rampart, surrounded the hilltop enclosing an area of more than two hundred hectares. The Aduatuci would complete the timber gates, watchtowers, and palisade, and construct the interior buildings after we had gone.

I ordered a large stone vault constructed within the walls that held the treasure that we had accumulated. The fortress was a stronghold that I could return to as needed and though they considered themselves a new tribe, they understood that I was their patron and one of their duties was to guard my treasury. Most of the cattle remained, and the Aduatuci were tasked with growing the cattle herd, training oxen, and providing a tribute of grain and beef each year.

There was an air of excitement and apprehension as we prepared to depart the camp. Friends and families wept as they parted. But in the end, it was a good thing. The main body of the caravan was reduced, and those that were too old, crippled by war or injury, or just tired of our journey, were able to set down roots. Of course, it remained to be seen if they would survive the summer, as they were now waiting to see if they had avoided the curse as they hoped.

During Yule an assembly of the headmen of all the allied tribes had decided that now that their lands were secure from the threat of the Suebi and their wolf-warriors in the east, it was time to move against the Gallic tribes to the south who had aligned themselves with the Romans and eventually to push the Romans themselves back to the coast. It would be war on a scale not seen before. As the snows began to melt, I sent an ultimatum to the Roman governor of Gaul. Grant us lands within your borders or we will ravage Gaul, forcing more refugees into Gallia Transalpina, upsetting trade, and causing terror throughout the land.

The weather continued to warm, and when the Ambrones crested the eastern horizon, we turned our faces south and marched along the Maas River. I rode near the front of the caravan, with Hrolf, Ansgar, Freki, and the newest addition to my advisors, Aldric, at my side. A dozen of my other retainers rode close behind us. Anik and Tala walked with Vallus and Frida farther back in the column. The numbers we left behind at Aduatuca were more than replaced by groups of warriors and adventurers who joined us from the Treveri, Vagiones, Nemetes, and Triboci, who we had allied with last summer in the war against the Suebi, and who all had ancient ties to the Germanic tribes to the east. The Teutones met us in the low mountains separating the headwaters of the Maas which ran north to the Oceanus Germanicus, and the Saone whose waters flowed south into the Rhodanus and down to the Mare Nostrum near the Greek trading port of Massalia.

Leaving the Maas behind we entered the lands of the Lingones, ancient enemies of our allies. Their capital city sat atop a high limestone bluff above the river valley to our west. We met their army on the river plain below the city and slaughtered them. The Treveri, avenging some ancient atrocity offered no mercy, killing those too old or too sick to have value, and enslaving the women and children. They dumped dozens of corpses down the wells to poison the water and piled their carts high with silver and iron ingots, metal pots, tools, weapons, mail, and helmets. It was reminiscent of what the Suebi had been doing to the Treveri just last year.

We marched on the next day, coming to the Saone and turning south until we arrived at the mouth of the Doubs River, where we met the Tigurini and others of the Helvetii confederation, along with the Raurici. They had walked from their homes in the foothills of the Alpes through Sequani territory, where they defeated a substantial army.

Our allies kept their autonomy, and their tribal leaders retained their authority, but they looked to me as their war leader. My reputation had traveled far and now I had become the war chief of dozens of allied tribes.

The Cimbri led the way as we burned our way south. Much of eastern Gaul lay in ruin. Wherever our warriors tread, columns of smoke rose to the sky, marking our advance. Large trains of wagons and carts filled with plunder lumbered back toward our home cities, flanked by long lines of slaves and warriors sent to guard them. Yet our thirst only grew. The great alliance numbered more than two hundred thousand now, half of which were warriors ready for war and eager to enrich themselves and gain reputation.

Some tribes pledged homage and offered tribute to stave off destruction. Others resisted us and were overwhelmed. Waves of refugees fled southward before the approaching horde.

The Cimbri clan leaders moved with their warriors and Teutobod rode with his own people, as did Divico of the Tigurini and other leaders of the lesser tribes. Most of the Cimbri leaders and their retainers rode the more robust, thick bodied horses common to the people of the north. The Gauls rode the taller, sleeker horses that they were famous for breeding, but the majority of our warriors walked.

The many tribes were distinguished by different hairstyles, manner of dress, and their distinctive shields. The Cimbri wore their hair gathered at the crown of their head, the bulk of it flowing backward like a horse's tail, many had long braids falling from their temples. The Teutones favored their long hair tied in a knot above the right ear. The Gauls and Celts wore large mustaches that drooped at the ends down past their shaved chin while the northern warriors grew thick beards that fell upon their chests. I was an exception in that I was unable to grow respectable facial hair and chose to remain clean shaven, rather than endure the embarrassment of my thin, patchy, calico colored beard.

The northern tribes still wore mixtures of animal skins and furs, and dark colored rough woven clothes made of wool or linen. By far the weapons favored were the ash hafted battle spear with a leaf shaped point, a short sword or seax, and characteristic oblong or six-sided wooden shields brightly painted in the traditional colors and designs of their clans and tribes. The boys and younger warriors carried the lighter throwing javelins, and many of the young ones favored the captured Roman swords.

The Gauls wore mail and bronze helmets and carried long swords. They favored axes over short swords as a second weapon, though many carried both. Their smiths had the skills to make mail that fit them better than the small Roman Lorica Hamata we had taken from the defeated legions at Noreia. Our warriors disdained the heavy coats, preferring to go into battle shirtless, or even naked. The Celtic tribes of the lower Danube who had joined us wore colorful cloaks knotted about their neck or fastened with a metal cloak pin. Their finer woven clothes were often striped or checked in more colorful patterns than their northern cousins, and the design of their spears and seax were slightly different, but no less deadly.

We were a mixture of different peoples, clothing, and customs, and had an understanding of each other's languages through years of living together.

Common to all were the neck torques and arm rings of twisted bronze, iron, silver, and even gold. The size and thickness varied with the wealth and prestige of the warrior. The more precious the metal, the greater the deed that earned it, and the wealthier the leader that gave it. It was a visible way to recognize the value of our warriors and was a symbol of rank and bravery. Young men were awarded a less valuable version when they reached manhood, but the more elaborate designs and more precious metals were coveted by all.

The bronze torque that I wore was taken years ago from a dead Roman officer in Macedonia and given to me by Hrolf, my Teuton friend and now general of my army. I cherished it as a symbol of my first real battle and the opposing wolf's heads reminded me of my wolf clan heritage and our conflict with Rome, the people of Lupa, the she-wolf.

The horde swarmed over the land, trampling the green of early summer. The alliance now numbered more than two hundred thousand souls from a score of tribes, more than half of which were warriors ready for war and eager to enrich themselves and gain reputation. Even though we left many behind with the Aduatuci, tens of thousands of carts and herds of cattle and other livestock followed us to provide for the campaign.

The Arverni had joined us and together we pushed out their neighbors, the Aedui, who retreated south into Roman territory. They were a large tribe disliked by the other Gauls because they had sided with the hated Romans when the Arverni and Allobroges had been conquered.

The caravan moved behind the warriors and the older men and teenaged boys were tasked with protecting our families and belongings. Our women could defend themselves as well and were hardened by their life on the move in the open air among the threats of hostile tribes and the whims of nature. We had crossed raging rivers, dense forests and swamps, vast plains, and soaring mountains. The cultivated lands, hard packed trails and roads, and hardwood forests of Gaul were a luxury compared to where we had traveled over the past decade.

Only ten years, I thought. It seemed like a lifetime ago that we had left our homes in Jutland, devastated and forlorn. We had traveled so far, lost so many. Cursed by a jealous god to forever wander in search of a new homeland. *Will we ever find a home?* I wondered. It was a question that dogged me every day, and it was the answer that I so desperately sought for my people. We had been repelled by the Scordisci, refused by the Romans, and battled many hostile tribes. The curse of Njoror demands that Rome welcome us, for if we enter their land without that invitation, we will be destroyed. The jealous god has shown his willingness and ability to do that when he sent the tidal wave that destroyed our homes in Jutland, the illness that killed a third of our people, and the flash flood at the foot of the mountains near Boiodurum. I had no doubt that the curse was real, and I knew that I must continue to seek the invitation of Rome to settle within their borders. But the curse only required they welcome us into their lands. It did not specify their motivation for doing so.

The headaches had returned. They were coming with more frequency and more intensity. I had many sleepless nights and often the pain lasted for days without relief. Only the mushrooms that Aldric offered gave me relief, yet he held them back, always repeating that it was not wise to become dependent on them. The pain made me angry. The lack of sleep left me short-tempered. More and more I thought only of causing others pain, such as what I suffered, and so I ordered my warriors on a path of destruction. I pushed away those that cared for me. Frida kept Lingulf from me when I was at my worst. Even my old friends kept their distance. Only Hrolf stood steadily by my side, regardless of my occasional fits of rage.

I knew that our rampage in Gaul would be heard in Rome like thunder rippling through the great mountains, and I depended on that to bring them back to us. This time, the idea of welcoming us into their service must surely be more desirable than meeting such a great army on the battlefield.

We continued south, spreading from horizon to horizon until we came to the Rhodanus River. This was the northern boundary of the Roman province of Gallia Transalpina. We crossed the river and advanced as far south as Vienne, the stronghold of the Allobroges who had been conquered by the Romans a decade earlier. A small garrison of Romans fled at the sight of the vast host of warriors, and this is where we paused. On midsummer's eve, I held a council of the important men of the alliance to decide what came next.

Chapter Twenty-Four

Narbo, Gallia Transalpina

Late March 109 BC

Freki walked beside the centurion that led the Cimbri delegation through the iron gates of the governor's estate, across
the paved courtyard and up the wide stairway toward the
recently completed building built of honey-colored stone beneath
a pink-tiled roof. It had taken six years to complete the palace, and
it was truly a wonder to these men who lived most of their lives in
the open or in small cabins.

Narbo had been founded as the capital of the new province of
Gallia Transalpina at about the same time the Cimbri had begun
their journey from Jutland. Much of the surrounding city was still
under construction, growing constantly as retired legionaries, Celtic, Greek, and Roman merchants, and people of every color and
stripe and every profession flocked there in the hopes of becoming rich in the prosperous new trading port.

The tall, fair-haired warriors climbed the steps to the wide portico,
where a guard saluted the centurion, then stepped aside to let them
pass. The officer's hobnailed caligae echoed on the marble tiles as
they passed down the wide hallway and turned to enter a high-
ceilinged room where two more guards flanked the doorway. In
the center of the floor was an image made from tiny colored tiles
of a man in a water chariot pulled by a pair of porpoises. He was
holding a trident and chasing a heavy-breasted maid who had the
tail of a fish. Freki and his companions struggled to control themselves but remained stone faced even as they took in the wonders

that surrounded them.

The large room was empty save for a table piled high with parchments and scrolls. Two men were bent over the table and straightened as the delegation entered the room. One was a tall man, thin and balding and with a stoop in his slender shoulders that made him look older than he was. He introduced himself as pro-praetor Lucius Cassius Longinus, former governor of Gallia Transalpina. He had an open face that invited trust and a manner that encouraged conversation. He introduced the second man as Quintus Servilius Caepio, the current praetor and governor of Gaul. Shorter, stockily built and with a full shock of dark hair, they were opposites in appearance and demeanor. Caepio wore a scowl that seemed to be his permanent expression and he bore no diplomatic mannerisms, as did his companion.

Longinus had been sent to Africa two years earlier as a praetor with the task of bringing Jugurtha to Rome to testify in the corruption trials of prominent Romans. The following year, he had been assigned as governor in Gaul and had only recently been replaced by Caepio.

"I have come to deliver a message from my chieftain," he said formally.

Freki looked at one of the men who accompanied him to translate.

"Yes, so we have heard," replied Longinus, smiling. "What is it?"

Freki handed him the parchment, which Longinus unrolled on the table for Caepio to read. The color drained from Longinus' face while Caepio's turned a dark red. Longinus straightened and glanced toward Freki and before he turned back to the delegation. Caepio took a moment to compose himself and coughed to cover the anger in his voice. "I will see that your message gets to the proper people," he said in a clipped tone. "Is there anything else?"

"I am to wait for a reply," Freki said. "I require food and accommodation for my men and myself."

Caepio nodded at the centurion. "It will be taken care of," he replied, dismissing them.

"Sir?" the centurion asked uncertainly.

"Yes?"

"They arrived with one hundred warriors who are camped outside the city."

"See to it. centurion," the governor impatiently snapped.

Rome, April 109 BC

"This letter arrived from the governor of Gallia Transalpina just three days ago," announced Marcus Aemilius Scaurus. The princeps senatus held the parchment scroll above his head. "It is written in Latin in a crude but legible hand and is signed by the leader of the allied tribes that have invaded Gallia Narbonensis." A murmur rippled through the Curia Hostilia.

More than two hundred senators had come to the emergency meeting in the senate house and the only sound in the large room for several heartbeats was the crackle of the charcoal burning in the braziers. Suddenly, the room erupted into a flurry of voices. Senators stood, shouting at each other and flapping their arms about. Scaurus had anticipated this reaction and waited patiently until his voice could be heard over the din.

"Silence!" he shouted several times. "Sit down!" Slowly the assembly controlled their outburst and one by one regained their seats.

Most of the senators present had been in this very room four years ago during the trial of Gnaeus Papirius Carbo, who had lost two legions and their auxiliaries to the Cimbri, nearly fifteen thousand dead and wounded and the rest routed. All of Rome had panicked at the threat posed by the barbarian horde that was poised in the mountain passes above Aquileia and every one of them expected to see the wild north men storming the gates at any moment. The senate had called up every able-bodied man in and near the city to guard the walls. It was a month before they were confident that the threat had disappeared like the smoke rising from the brazier before them.

"Quiet!" Scaurus shouted over the remaining voices. "If you will allow me, I will read the letter," he said with a note of derision.

Greetings to the senate and the citizens of Rome

Four summers ago, your general Carbo confronted us in the mountains of Noricum and demanded that we leave the lands of the Taurisci and return to our homes. I told him of the flood that had destroyed our homeland and that we had been wandering since and had no homes to return to. I explained that we were not seeking war with Rome and offered friendship and a military alliance in return for fertile land for my people.

Even though he denied my offer of alliance, we agreed to leave as he requested. When we departed, he betrayed his promises and attempted to destroy us. We discovered his deceit and defeated him in a decisive battle that left his legions destroyed. Those legion's standards stand outside my tent as I write this letter.

Since that battle, the tribes north of the Alpes and on both sides of the Rhenus have witnessed our power. Many tribes have fallen. Many tribes have sworn themselves to my banner, and I am conducting a campaign throughout Gaul that will demonstrate our resolve. I am prepared to continue this campaign into Gallia Narbonensis if necessary. I will camp at the confluence of the Rhone and the Saone near the Gallic city of Lugudunon to await your reply. I expect to hear your decision by mid-summer.

Once again, I extend to you our friendship. As a sign of our good faith, my representative has returned the standards of your defeated legions to your governor. In return, I ask only that the people of Mars grant us land within your borders to settle and rebuild our homes and villages. I offer our warriors to serve as allies and auxiliaries to your army. It is still my intention to live in peace with Rome. But be warned. I will not be betrayed again.

*I am Borr, chieftain of the Cimbri and war chief of the allied northern tribes.
I await your reply.*

Again, the room erupted into chaos. This time, it was the consul
who demanded silence. Marcus Junius Silanus had been elected as
the junior consul and had been in Rome since he took the curule
chair back in January. Afraid that he was destined to serve out his
position as simply an administrator rather than gain fame as a successful general in the field, he saw his opportunity. The senior consul Quintus Caecilius Metellus had already been given command
of the army assigned to Africa to force Jugurtha into compliance.
He was even now in the south of Italy preparing his army to cross
the Mare Nostrum, and the wars in Illyricum and Macedonia were
being waged by pro-consuls who had been in command there for
years.

Metellus came from a long line of consuls and generals and had his
own personal reputation as a competent military man and a man
of honor and integrity. Silanus was a Novus Homo, a new man, the
first of his family line to be elected to the highest political office
in the Republic. The future and reputation of his family were at
stake. Silanus did not have the family name that helped guarantee
political success. Moreover, he did not have the military experience
that others did. But this new threat provided his chance. A victory
over this northern threat would cement his own legacy and assure
the grand future he planned for his sons and their sons.

When the room had quieted again, the consul acknowledged Gnaeus Mallius Maximus to speak. "These are the same barbarians that
ravaged Noricum and defeated Carbo four years ago. Fears of an
invasion flew for a year after Carbo's failure. The panic eventually
died down, but rumors were heard now and then of their passing north of the Alpes. Last summer there was a large border war
along the Rhenus and if the rumors are true, the same tribe that
defeated Carbo and now threatens Gaul is the very same that led
an alliance against the forest tribes that were pushing west across
the river.

213

"Again, they have suddenly appeared from the north and threaten a province of Rome. They have been moving south along the Rhone and are now encamped around Vienne in northern Narbonensis. They have conquered local Gallic tribes, many of whom joined them and have been pillaging all of southern Gaul for months. Refugees have been flooding the borders, overwhelming the local garrisons and townships. Trade has been disrupted, Roman citizens living in Gaul have been murdered, and now, now they threaten an invasion of Narbonenis if we don't give them land. Their army is encamped less than two weeks' march from Massalia. Something has to be done."

Someone in the back shouted out of turn. "Our armies already employ warriors of many different nations as auxiliaries. Why not accept their offer of alliance?"

"Yes," shouted another. "It would prevent us from opening another war in the same year. Our treasury is running low, manpower is low. We have ongoing wars against the Celts in the east, conflict and rebellion among the Iberian tribes in Hispania to the west. Metellus is preparing for war in Numidia to our south. Why would we want another war in the north with these barbarians?"

"You would forget Carbo's disgrace? His defeat has never been avenged," Silanus answered to murmurs of agreement. "You would ignore the chaos they have already sown in Gaul and Narbonensis? Now they threaten us with war if we do not grant them land. When did Rome bend the knee to the will of barbarians? What would that say to our other enemies? I say no! Give me imperium to take my consular legions north. I will at the very least block their advance, and if necessary, repulse the Germanic tribes that are pushing south into Gallia Narbonensis."

Like Carbo, Silanus was given imperium to prevent an incursion only. He was not authorized to start a war. He was not to initiate hostilities unless he was attacked. But he was given full authority for a show of force. He was to deliver a firm message that the Senate did not accept their offer of alliance and wished only that they return to their homes in peace.

Silanus felt disappointed and yet relieved at the same time. He had the opportunity to handle a significant crisis and to command an army in the field, but he was under no illusion that he was a military man. He knew that his experience was limited and that he was no tactician. But knowing his own weaknesses served him well, as he chose a competent man to be his legate. The same Gnaeus Mallius Maximus who spoke first in the senate meeting. Maximus came of humble blood as did Silanus, and if he were ever elected consul, he too would be a New-Man. The two worked well together and shared a mutual respect that they did not enjoy when involved with the members of ancient families who boasted magistrates centuries back.

"Prepare the legions," Silanus ordered his legate. "We march in one week along the Via Aurelia."

Southern Italy, April 109 BC

Quintus Metellus addressed his senior officers the evening before they departed for Africa. "The Senate has tasked me with ending the war in Numidia. You are all aware of the failures of Bestia and Albinus and the accusations of bribery and treachery that surround everyone involved with this debacle so far. I selected each of you because of your personal and military reputations. You are some of the best military minds in Rome. We all served under Scipio and benefited from his leadership example. Scipio was known as an honest man as well as a brilliant strategist and tactician, and it is my intent to repeat his success and bring this war to an end.

"Make no mistake, Jugurtha is a brilliant general. He has wealth and influence even in Rome. He learned his military prowess under Scipio as we did. He is a formidable enemy, and this will not be an easy task. Numidia is an important province that supplies Rome with a large portion of our grain supply. This is not a war against the Numidian people, but to remove Jugurtha. My strategic goal is to deny Jugurtha the support of his own people by turning them against him. At the same time, helping them to understand that continuing on his path is a guarantee of destruction similar to their neighbor, Carthage.

Marius and Rufus were both surprised to see Gauda at the meeting. He was a half-brother to Jugurtha, born to a different mother. Both were sons of Mastanabal, brother to the last king, thus Gauda was Jugurtha's last rival to the throne of Numidia.

Gauda had petitioned Metellus to join the Roman forces that were to fight Jugurtha. Gauda had tried to claim the kingship of Numidia without the approval of the senate, and Metellus refused to recognize that claim; but he did allow him to command a group of Numidian cavalry to support his legions.

The next morning, Metellus and his legions sailed for Africa.

Chapter Twenty-Five

Gallia Narbonensis

Freki had spent two months at Narbo before the sound of trumpets announced the arrival of the consul. Silanus rode his horse at the head of his legions, followed by his signifers and senior officers. The sound of their hobnailed sandals striking the stone-paved streets echoed between the new buildings. Row after row of soldiers marched along in scarlet cloaks, their helmets and mail glittering in the afternoon sun. Silanus was dressed in his parade finery, bronze helmet and cuirass polished to a high shine. He rode straight-backed and tall, aware of the eyes that watched him pass.

More than the soldiers, Freki was impressed by the number of supply wagons and artillery pieces that creaked by, their iron-rimmed wheels rattling over the stones, followed by the auxiliary cavalry, slingers, and archers that brought up the rear. He had not been witness to the size of the legions they had defeated at the battle of Noreia because that was a battle of individuals and the Romans were overwhelmed by the Cimbri's greater numbers. The artillery had not played a part because Borr had sent a dedicated force to ambush them, taking that threat out early in the fight. The Roman commander had limited his own archers, slingers, and spearmen by placing them in the forest instead of the open, where their weapons would have been more effective. Seeing the order and discipline of the legions in front of him, Freki gained a new respect for what they would be facing the next time they fought.

As the column passed the governor's palace, Silanus and an entourage of staff officers, slaves and other servants broke off and entered the courtyard. The rest of the legions continued to march through the town and established a camp a mile west of the city.

"Welcome Consul," Caepio greeted Silanus in the courtyard where he had assembled his own guard. "Your quarters are prepared and servants are waiting. I have prepared a feast for this evening, or it can wait if you would prefer to rest after your journey."

"I prefer to get straight to work. Where is my headquarters?"

The palace was large enough to provide comfortable quarters and workspace for both senior magistrates and their staffs and Caepio provided counterparts to brief the consular staff. Turning to his staff officers, Silanus ordered them to immediately begin preparing the legions for a month in the field. "Gather supplies and make repairs. You have two weeks. I want to be marching north by the first day of Iunius."

They saluted and with a "Yes, sir!" moved out smartly.

To Caepio he said, "I understand the delegate from the barbarians is still here awaiting my answer?"

"He is."

"I want him brought to me. Immediately."

"Yes, sir!" Caepio responded enthusiastically. He was long ready to see the barbarian put in his place.

When Freki arrived, Silanus spoke without malice but left no room for argument.

"You may inform your chieftain that I will meet him at Vienne on the first day of the next full moon. Fourteen days. There, I will deliver the Senate's answer to his request. He may bring no more than fifty men."

Chapter Twenty-Six

Numidia

June 109 BC

Upon their arrival in Africa Albinus immediately turned over command to Metellus who went straight to work. The months lost waiting on the delayed elections, then recruiting and training his legions in Italy and getting them to Africa had set Metellus back half the campaign season. In addition, when they arrived, they found the legions that had been left in Africa were in terrible condition. When Bestia returned to Rome two years ago, he had left his legions behind on the pretense that they would keep a peace that he had never achieved. Now they, along with Albinus' legions, were occupying winter camps outside Utica. Their defeat and humiliation at being forced to walk under the yoke had broken them.

Metellus put Marius directly in charge of restoring the Africa legions to readiness. After a day spent interviewing the officers and walking through the camps, Marius joined Rufus for dinner. "They're in bad shape," he complained. "The camps are in disarray. The stench is terrible, the walls have not been fortified, and the watches are not being kept. The soldiers walk into town or elsewhere whenever they please and the civilians mingle with the soldiers inside the camp. Mules and pigs wander about. The prostitutes are even working inside the walls."

"Sounds like you've got your work cut out."

"Yes, and that's not all. They haven't been paid for some time and they are compensating themselves by looting the countryside. The locals are lining up to complain about it and demand reimbursement. This is a mess."

"Well, Metellus gave you free rein to get them ready. What are you going to do?"

Marius began by removing every officer and placing them in the lowest ranks. He hand-picked men from his own legion to take their place and formed a corps of officers loyal to him, then issued orders to remove all camp followers and other civilians from the camps. No soldiers were to have servants or beasts of burden. All freelancing was forbidden. The camps were torn down and the men marched to a new site where they constructed new castra. He instituted an exercise program that included daily marches and made them carry all their weapons and tools. During the marches Marius himself appeared first in the front, then in the middle, then in the rear, to ensure that all his men saw him taking part and encouraging them. He carried the same load as they and he marched the same miles. He dug in the trenches and placed the stakes beside his men. He trained with shield and gladius and threw the pilum, and he required all his officers to do the same. He marched them daily, dug fortifications, moved castra, and trained them in battlefield movement. Marius restored the iron discipline that marked the Roman soldier, and he did not otherwise punish them. With the restored discipline came pride as well as loyalty to the general that worked beside them.

When Marius had first joined the legions in Numantia, they were in much the same condition, and he used what he had learned when Scipio had taken over. Metellus, who had also participated in Scipio's restoration of the Numantia legions, watched and approved.

Marius used the opportunity to teach his young officers the way Scipio had taught him, and he kept Lucius Aurelius by his side, using him as messenger and liaison, even confidant at times. He had special plans for this young man.

Over time, the legions remembered their pride and their readiness was rebuilt.

Having learned of the consul's preparations through his network of spies and knowing of his reputation for integrity, Jugurtha began to worry. He too had begun his military career under Scipio as the commander of an auxiliary unit of Numidian cavalry, and the Romans leading this army were all associates. They knew him and he knew them. The king sent deputies to meet Metellus to propose his submission, asking only for the lives of himself and his family and offering to surrender everything else he owned to the Romans.

But Metellus would not be fooled. He knew Jugurtha for the faithless negotiator he was and instead attempted to turn Jugurtha's ambassadors against him. Offering them large rewards for delivering Jugurtha to him, dead or alive. Metellus would only settle for Jugurtha himself and, in the meantime, continued to prepare for the war that he knew was unavoidable.

Chapter Twenty-Seven

July 109 BC

I sat by an open fire, silent in the company of my closest friends, pondering the possibility of Rome agreeing to our request. Freki had brought the message from Silanus and that night the war council agreed to send a party to meet with him. I knew the Cimbri were eager to settle down and the Teutones as well. But the rest were just as eager to continue their rampage in Gaul, killing their enemies and anyone who they perceived had wronged them in the past. The plunder and slaves flowed back to their villages, and they were becoming rich. I also knew that many wished to push into Narbonensis and extend the war to the Romans.

Hrolf finally broke the silence. "Do you really expect them to swallow their pride after their loss at Noreia and welcome us into their lands?"

"I don't know what to expect," I answered. "I hope that they will accept us. They wish to talk only because they fear us. It would suit them better to make an alliance rather than fight."

"Their pride has been injured," Vallus put in. "They will want compensation in some way. They see you as a threat, not an ally. They are not concerned with your reasons for leaving your homelands and coming here. It's unlikely they would welcome such a large military force into their lands."

"Compensation! Hah! They betrayed us," said Lugius. "They betrayed us, and we crushed them for it. I'm sure they are pissed-off about it, but we hardly need to pay them for their betrayal."

My head was pounding again. I rubbed my temples and took a deep breath, exhaling loudly as I stood. "I have made the request. If they deny us, we will be forced to turn away again, or face the curse. We cannot enter Italy. I won't put our people in the way of another flood or plague. I also don't wish open war with Rome when our only solution to the curse lays in their hands. But mark my words, if we are betrayed again, they will be the ones to pay."

Frida was sullen as she stuffed half a loaf of bread and a chunk of cheese into a small sack. "Why must you go? Why didn't he just send his answer with Freki? I don't trust them."

She came to me and wrapped her arms around my waist, laying her head against my chest. "I have a bad feeling."

"Don't worry," I said, stroking her hair. "Hrolf will be beside me and we are taking a guard. I don't trust them either. They have nothing to gain from betrayal, and everything to fear. They know we bested them the last time they betrayed us, and we are even stronger now. Why would they take that chance?" I hoped I sounded more confident than I was.

"Anyway, if they refuse us again, we must turn away. The curse prevents us from forcing our way onto their land."

Silanus formed his legions near the city of Vienne. A contingent of one hundred warriors accompanied the allied leaders to the meeting and now stood at a respectable distance from the Romans.

Silanus openly stared at the Cimbri chieftain striding toward the praetorium. The barbarian's heavily muscled body was covered in scars, and he walked with a slight limp. A jagged scar ran from inside his hairline to the bridge of his nose and a leather eyepatch covered his left eye. His chest was bare, revealing four wide furrows where the flesh had been gouged below his right breast. A bronze torque tipped with opposing wolf heads encircled his neck and below that hung a leather thong strung with the claws of the beast that Silanus supposed had maimed him.

Silanus was no coward, but the single steely gray eye that fixed him in a piercing stare was unnerving. The consul sat in a comfortable chair behind a low table laden with food where a second chair sat. When Borr was seated, a servant brought him a cup of wine.

"Consul, my people tire of their wandering. It has been more than ten years since we were forced from our homes, and we have traveled far. On behalf of my people, I ask that the Senate grant us land to live upon. Land to raise our children, farm our fields and raise our livestock in peace. In return we will serve Rome. Our hands and our weapons shall be yours for any purpose you wish. It is my understanding that you are engaged in several different wars even now. You could put us to use immediately if you chose to do so. We are fierce fighters, and we are much better friends than enemies."

Behind Silanus stood Maximus, his legate and Longinus, the former governor of Narbonensis, and now the second legate to Silanus. All three bristled at the veiled threat and Maximus moved his hand toward the hilt of his gladius.

Silanus sat motionless, save for a hand raised to calm Maximus. His face betrayed no emotion as he listened. For a fleeting moment, the idea of recruiting these savage warriors to fight for Rome appealed to him. Then finally he said, "Rome has no lands to give and desires no services. The Senate has denied your request for land and your offer of service. You are ordered to return to your homeland and to cease pillaging Gaul."

Borr sat, his expression unreadable. He had expected this answer yet held out hope that his request would be honored. His head was throbbing and at the consul's words, distant hope turned to sudden anger. He leaped to his feet, towering over the consul. "Rome does not give me orders," he said savagely, pointing his finger at Silanus.

The hiss of steel sliding from scabbards sounded as the Roman guards drew their weapons.

Hrolf, Teutobod, and Divico stood behind Borr and answered the threat as their own steel leaped into their hands.

"Stop!" Silanus shouted. "There will be no bloodshed today." He ordered his men to lower their swords. "Go," he said to Borr. "Turn your army around and go. In two days, I will do the same. There is no need for further bloodshed, but if you seek it, you shall find it."

Chapter Twenty-Eight

I seethed as we rode away. What I had heard, I had expected to hear, but I was the chieftain of a powerful alliance, and the insults were unbearable. If I was ever to convince Rome to accept us, there was nothing left to do but turn around and try again later.

We left the Roman camp late in the day and were forced to make a camp before we had traveled far. I was deep into my thoughts, staring into the fire, and at first, I did not see the warriors that rose from the ground just a hundred feet away until Hrolf reached out and touched my arm in warning. Suddenly, the entire company was attacked by hundreds of heavily armed warriors. The attack was well planned, and Teutobod, Divico, Hrolf and I had been cut off from the rest of the guard. My warriors fought like demons, but they were outnumbered ten to one, and the fight could not last long. Looking back, I saw their defeat was imminent and realizing there was nothing I could do, I vaulted onto my horse. "Split up!" I shouted and kicked my heels back. My stallion leaped forward, knocking an opponent to the ground as my sword cut down into the neck of another wild-eyed warrior who was reaching out to grasp my leg. Teutobod and Divico followed suit and spurred off in different directions. Hrolf tried to follow me, but before he could get away, a sling-stone slammed into his helmet just above his ear. He swayed deeply to one side and nearly fell, but he clung desperately to his mount and managed to get away. He and the others disappeared into the night.

I let my mount pick his way, trusting to his instinct as we entered a copse of trees. I was not hurt, but the night was dark, and I was fleeing for my life. The thought struck me that the warriors that had attacked me had not carried weapons. They were all trying to pull me off my horse, trying to capture me. With that realization, it suddenly registered that I was riding too fast, but before my body could react to the thought, a limb struck me straight across my chest. I fell hard on my back, the wind knocked out of me. I gasped for air for a few moments and listened as the hoofbeats faded into the distance.

The stars and moon were covered by a blanket of clouds and in my haste to get away, I did not know which direction I had fled or where I was now at. I must get back to the camp, but I had to wait for daylight, or I could stumble back into whoever ambushed us. I crawled to the base of a large tree to rest. My mind was reeling. The Romans had betrayed me again! How could I be such a fool? But was it the Romans? Could it have been Gauls out for revenge for the destruction we had brought upon them? My men were likely all dead, and I had seen Hrolf wounded. I had no idea about Teutobod or Divico. The headache had worsened and was pounding. It was difficult to think. I sat with my head in my hands and squeezed my eyes tight shut, trying to will it away. But to no avail. The pain made me angrier, the frustration of being refused again made me despair for my people and the thought of betrayal turned my heart cold.

This is what becomes of trying to make peace. Well, there will be no more peace. I am the chieftain of the largest alliance this land has ever seen. Fierce warriors of dozens of tribes, all anxious to make a name for themselves. After this there would be no hesitation. No negotiation. I will never again ask Rome or anyone else for permission. I have been chosen by Wodan and marked by Donar. I am a favorite of the gods. It will be war.

The night's clouds brought a light spatter of rain while I sat beneath my cloak at the base of that great tree, and it threatened to become a storm when the wind picked up just before morning. The blackness faded into light and dark shadows as the gray light of dawn slowly revealed the forest I found myself in. The pounding in my head had subsided a bit, but was still a dull throb. As soon as I could see, I started off in the direction my horse had run. My hair plastered to my forehead and water ran down my back. I pushed on through the underbrush until I began to see space between the trees in front of me. I was coming to the edge of the forest and before me lay a small meadow. Standing halfway out munching unconcerned on the grass stood my horse. The reins hung down to the ground and trailed as he wandered about in a small circle.

I looked about and seeing nothing that concerned me, I stepped into the open. The horse looked up and recognizing me, went back to cropping his breakfast. I was a few paces from him when I noticed his leg was tied to a stake. Too late, I realized I had been trapped. Twenty men surrounded me, all with clubs. I didn't have time to draw my sword before I was struck low in the back, then again under the chin as I dropped to my knees. I was still conscious as the rain of blows continued, again and again, until darkness claimed me.

When my eyes opened, I found myself lying on the wet grass staring at a pair of Roman sandals. My head was hurting terribly, both from the headache I still suffered and from the blows it had received. I squinted into the light in an effort to quiet the throbbing. A laugh penetrated the haze.

"So, the barbarian lives. A pity. But perhaps he will be of use. Put him in the cage and let us be out of here." Then darkness pulled me back.

My body jumped off the floor of the wagon I was in and jolted me awake when I crashed back down to the wooden planks. The axle had dropped into a small stream bed and thrown me into the air. Iron bars surrounded me, sunk deep into the thick planks of the floor and the ceiling. There were iron cuffs around my wrists and ankles with chains connecting all. My weapons were gone, as well as my cloak and the bear claw necklace. For the first time in many years my bronze torque was not about my neck.

A Roman soldier drove the wagon behind a pair of army mules and looking about, I saw other legionaries marching alongside. A group of warriors formed a guard around the wagon, but strangely, they did not look like Gauls. Their hairstyles, clothes, and weapons appeared to be from the eastern forests. A Roman officer and a frightening looking priest rode up behind the cart when they saw that I was awake.

The priest was vaguely familiar. He wore a mocking smile and had a fearsome appearance. "At last," the priest said, "I will have my revenge."

I was puzzled by his statement. His voice had a familiar sound to it, but I could not place his face as someone I had known. Although his skeletal appearance and his milky eyes would have made it difficult for his own mother to recognize him. Suddenly, I was aware of who he must be.

"Fenrir's prophet," I said flatly. It was his plans that I had spoiled when we pushed the Suebi back across the Rhenus River. I was beginning to form a picture of what happened. "In league with another Roman liar who said we could go in peace and then ambushes me like a coward."

"Promises to barbarians mean nothing," the officer said dismissively.

The Romans were uneasy whenever they looked at the priest. Vallus had told me the Romans had their own religion. In fact, there were many within the Republic that were tolerated, but the wild men of the north intimidated them, and the fierce gods they worshiped even more.

"After what you did to Carbo, we are not about to trust your word that your army will withdraw. You are our insurance that it will."

The back of my neck tingled, and I glanced at the priest, who was staring at me and smiling while he fingered my bronze torque at his throat.

Keeping my eyes on the priest, I spoke to the Roman, "You fear me so much that you had to enlist the help of the Suebi?"

The priest chuckled but otherwise was silent, and the Roman scowled.

"We need no help to capture or kill the likes of you. It is simply the fact that barbarians think differently when they think at all. They are all bluster, muscle, and emotion. He advised us on how you would react, and he proved correct," the officer said, reluctantly acknowledging the priest's role.

I said nothing. The throbbing in my head was excruciating, but I was determined not to show it. Shortly they became bored and rode away, and I was free to slump my head again and try to endure the pain.

Chapter Twenty-Nine

That evening, Hrolf arrived back in the camp an hour or so after Teutobod and Divico. The blow had stunned him, but he suffered no worse than a tender bruise on his temple. Teutobod had already assembled the war council, and they were loudly discussing what to do.

"Borr is dead or captured!" Teutobod said. "We must avenge him and the attack on our delegation that traveled under a truce. The Romans cannot go unpunished."

Divico was worried about attacking the Romans. Several factions had already expressed that without Borr's leadership, they were returning home. "We don't know what happened to Borr," the king of the Tigurini said. "We can't let the alliance break up. We need to elect a new leader that will keep the tribes together. Only temporary, of course, until Borr returns."

Hrolf stepped into the circle of elders and signaled that he wished to speak. The rest quieted down. "I was injured in the fight and lost my way." He turned his head to display the bruise. "This morning I awoke to the sound of marching and the squeal of axles. Hidden by some brush, I saw a small caravan of Romans and what appeared to be Suebi warriors marching south. A wagon with a cage carried a single man. A prisoner with fiery red hair and an eye patch. Borr lives, and the Romans have him."

Teutobod jumped to his feet. "We must break camp immediately and pursue them!"

"I agree," Hrolf said. "But as has already been said, we need a single leader in Borr's place for now."

Divico stood. "I say that Hrolf should be our war chief until Borr returns. He has done it before, and the people know him."

"I have no argument for that," replied Teutobod.

"Nor I," called out another.

"Is anyone opposed?" asked Divico. None were.

"Then this is what we will do. It's already too dark to set out tonight. Gather as many mounted warriors as we can to ride at dawn. We must catch up to them before they reach the safety of Silanus' camp. The rest of the army will follow as quickly as possible, followed by the carts and livestock. We must protect the families, so leave at least a thousand men with them."

Few slept that night as the fires burned high and the camp was filled with the sound of stones scraping the edges of swords and spears. Shields were checked to ensure they were sound, and food was prepared for the march.

Just as the dawn revealed enough light to distinguish shadows, the mounted warriors thundered out of camp behind Hrolf, followed by tens of thousands of fierce Germanic and Celtic foot warriors.

Chapter Thirty

An urgent horn sounded the alarm from the back of the caravan. Pro-praetor Quintus Servilius Caepio, governor of Gallia Narbonensis, turned just as two thousand horsemen topped the ridge behind them and thundered down into the valley they were travelling. "Go!" he shouted to the wagon driver. "Go, go, go! Get him to the camp!" Pushing the centurion's shoulder, he ordered, "Get the wagon to the camp!" Caepio's plans were suddenly falling apart.

The Suebi warriors ran for the nearby trees. The prophet's horse turned in place, its feet churning up the dirt as the beast felt his rider's uncertainty. The man's head turned in several directions, trying to decide what to do. Fearing he might lose his chance at revenge he urged his mount forward and drew his sword. He thrust at Borr through the bars, but the movement of his horse and the jostling of the wagon spoiled his aim. The sword caught between the bars and dropped to the floor of the wagon.

Freki split off with half the riders and swept down upon the fleeing Suebi. Spears pierced the panicked men and swords and axes slashed down, cutting through iron shield rims and splitting willow boards. Some who threw down their weapons in order to run faster reached the safety of the trees, but most left their bones to lie in the open meadow.

It was a race to the top of the next ridge where the Roman camp lay another mile beyond. The sentries atop the camp's walls sounded the alarm, and the legions were forming, but they would be too late. Hrolf descended upon the hapless caravan with a thousand horsemen, clods of earth flying into the sky as they charged and falling back to the ground as so much rocky hail.

Realizing they would not make it to the camp, Caepio shouted, "Testudo!" ordering the defensive formation used by the legions to repel an attack. The disciplined soldiers stopped and turned, facing their shields up and out. Taking in the chaos and seeing little hope for a victory, the prophet galloped away, desperately hoping that a lone horseman would not attract the attention of the savage attackers.

A wedge of horsemen drove between Borr's wagon and the rest of the Romans. Hrolf leaped from his horse and using a lead-weighted war axe, beat the lock from the bars. Borr stepped to the ground and raised the sword above his head and a roar of victory was heard all the way to the Roman camp.

He took his friend into a tight embrace and slapped him on the back. Then turned toward the formation of Romans surrounded by his warriors whose numbers grew by the moment as Freki's men returned from the chase. The line of shields rippled and quivered as the certain knowledge spread amongst those men that they would likely not survive. In the center stood Caepio, who could see his own death in the eyes of the warriors that faced him.

"Steady," he said softly to his men. "Hold. Have courage."

Borr raised his sword and pointed it at the young tribune.

"Tell Silanus that he failed. Tell him that you failed. Tell him . . . that the only thing he has succeeded in is making Borrix an enemy. An enemy that he will not escape. An enemy that will destroy him. And an enemy that will strike fear into every Roman heart before I am done!" It was the first time I had used the title. But it felt right. Borrix, King Borr, king of the Cimbri, war chieftain of the allied northern tribes.

"Mount!" he said. "Let them go. For now."

Chapter Thirty-One

Silanus turned to his legates. "Thanks to Caepio's failure to capture their leader, this Borrix, the tribes will surely attack. I don't know what possessed him to act on his own, but he has cost us the advantage. We march with the dawn. Prepare to strike the camp." Caepio stood in the back, staring at the floor furious with himself.

"March where, Consul?" questioned Maximus. "And why? We haven't even engaged them yet."

"Send messengers to the garrisons in Massalia and Narbo," Silanus said. "Tell them we need every soldier in Gaul to meet us at the confluence of the Isara and the Rhodanus."

Maximus continued to protest. "We have two full strength legions and two auxiliary legions. We have the strength to fight them right here. We have a camp, we have the artillery, and we have enough food and water. Why expose ourselves on a march? We will be more vulnerable." Maximus glanced toward Longinus, silently asking for support.

Taking the cue, Longinus said, "Maximus is right Consul. We should stay where we are and let him come to us."

"No!" Silanus shouted. "We march in the morning. You don't know how many there are. My spies have just returned and they reported the size of their encampment. There are near two hundred thousand men, women, and children. Half of that warriors, and they are already headed this way."

The color drained from Longinus' face. Maximus was speechless for a moment. "One hundred thousand warriors," he said flatly.

Silanus slammed his fist into the map table. "Now, prepare your legions to move."

Chapter Thirty-Two

The leaden sky was lightening while we watched the castrum from the ridgeline to the east. My warriors had marched thru the night to reach us. The unmistakable sounds of Roman legions breaking camp had begun two hours earlier when the mournful sound of the brass horns echoed off the nearby hills and woke the camp. The shouts of officers rang in the damp morning air as they prodded their men to eat, strike the tents, gather their gear, and pack the carts. The men wolfed down a cold breakfast of crumbled cheese wrapped in a flat bread and a few gulps of posca.

The legions had years of experience in the field, and it would take more than the threat of a barbarian attack to rattle them. They moved out with practiced speed and confidence.

When the baggage trains had been loaded with the bakery, smithy, troop tents, and other equipment, they began to break down the camp's defensive perimeter. The sharpened stakes planted in the protective ditch were removed and bundled to be used again the next night. Caltrops were recovered from the ground surrounding the camp. Hundreds of shovels reduced the berm back into the ditch that it came from so that the fortification could not be used by Rome's enemies.

The cavalry scouts pounded out the gate past the artillerymen who were preparing their ballistae for transport, on their way to reconnoiter the route and take positions to the front and flanks. The sun was clear of the treetops when another blast from the trumpets signaled it was time for the main body to move out. The legion that would lead the march for the day stepped forward, led in song by each maniple's junior centurion who belted out a bawdy cadence to which his soldiers replied in voices that echoed into the new day as their hobnailed caligae stamped in unison on the packed earth of the Gallic road. The chants overlapped one another and from a distance became an unrecognizable rise and fall of voices that flowed along the long line of men. The sound was joined by the squeal of the axles of heavily laden carts and wagons and the bellowing of oxen and braying of mules. The first legion was fol-lowed by Silanus and his entourage of staff officers, signifers, and musicians.

Next came the second consular legion, followed by the baggage carts, siege train, and other rolling stock. Behind them marched the two auxiliary legions providing the rear guard for the consular army.

Freki and his horsemen lay in wait for the scouts and when they'd departed the safety of the fort and ridden into the hills, he took them by surprise. The five pairs of riders had not yet separated, and they were surrounded by overwhelming numbers and killed swiftly, leaving Silanus blind.

The Cimbri came out of the east, the rising sun brilliant behind us as we topped the ridgeline and careened down the hillside in a mad rush, crashing into the second legion. The red soldiers were blinded as they looked up the slope toward the sound of twenty thousand warriors screaming their battle cries. It was not slow; it was not subtle. There were no drums to warn them, nor trumpets. It was a headlong charge, brash and unorganized, and terrifying.

I did my best to stay in the lead, but my injured leg caused me to lose ground as the youngest and strongest outpaced me. Still, I reached the Roman lines seconds after the shields crashed to-gether. The impact they felt when we hammered into them rippled through the entire formation. The legions had little time to respond before we were in the fight. Some had turned to make a shield wall, but it was unorganized and left gaps that we exploited. They had been marching in column. The maniples of Hastati, Principes, and Triarii were out of order when they turned to meet us, creating confusion in their ranks.

Their horns blared a warning and the entire line moved to support the legion we had assaulted, but as they formed their ranks to march against us Teutobod's twenty thousand raced down the opposite slope and smashed into the lead legion with irresistible force. They were forced to defend themselves even as Amalric's fifteen thousand Ambrones warriors hit the auxiliary legions in the rear. The Tigurini and other allies were tasked with preventing the ballistae and other large weapons from being deployed as well as capturing the trains.

At least one of the Roman officers had anticipated such an attack and dispersed the lighter scorpions on wagons throughout the formation. The scorpions fired iron tipped bolts the height of a man and as big around as my arm with fearsome power. The weapons had been fastened to the wagon beds and weighted down with sandbags to absorb the recoil when the weapon fired; and when the column stopped to defend themselves the crews chocked the wagon's wheels to prevent it from rolling.

The huge bolts cut deep channels in our tightly packed assault, so powerful that they pierced several men at one time, scattering the men nearby and causing chaos in the charging ranks. I had seen the Romans practicing with the scorpions when I was a young man and had gained a respect for their power, but we had never faced them in battle. I had thought to avoid them this time by attacking the siege trains while they were in the march, but this was new. They were numerous and effective, and the Romans guarded them well.

We hit them hard, and we hurt them badly, but I stuck to my plan and signaled my men to pull back. At the sound of the carnyx, they disengaged and vanished back across the ridges as quickly as they had appeared. They were becoming accustomed to the new tactics and responded to the signal.

The Romans recovered quickly, loading their wounded onto wagons, and resuming their march, but they left many dead upon the trail. At the sight of so many enemy warriors, doubt had begun to set in, and they felt a new sense of urgency to get to safety. This time, the column moved out at a faster pace.

"We hurt them," said Hrolf. "They are already wondering if they will make it home."

"Aye, but I still don't understand why we stopped. We should hit them and kill them in one big strike," said Teutobod.

I had planned the night before for the leaders to meet after we pulled back from the fight, and we stood on the ridge watching the column move through the valley.

"Look at them," I pointed. "They are in a panic. They fear us. This is what we want. Not just to kill them, but to make them afraid. To make them fear our power. We will continue to follow them and attack in lighting strikes. Attack, kill, withdraw, and attack again. Each time giving them time to think about it, time for the fear to grow. Time to anticipate the next attack. It is three day's march to the battleground where the Allobroges and Arverni were defeated twelve years ago. That is where we shall finally destroy them and avenge that defeat." Those with us from those two tribes cheered.

I ensured there were always men within sight of the Roman column, and I sent my cavalry to sting them while they built their camp. I placed units to guard the water sources so they could not replenish their water skins. I wanted them to see us, to fear us. I wanted them tired and thirsty. I kept Teutobod and his warriors in front of the caravan, calling and jeering at them as they fell back then surging forward to threaten them. When the Romans reacted defensively, he pulled his men back. The Ambrones picked away at the rear of the column. Stragglers were killed or captured. We were tiring them out, slowing them down, and turning their hearts cold with fear.

The first night I ordered campfires to be lit within full view of their camp to keep them thinking how many we were. The pinpoints of firelight seemed as numerous as the stars in the sky and surrounded the entire column.

The next day they left their camp standing as it was, not bothering to knock it down. No scouts were sent out. There was no need. They could see us in the distance. We made another attack while they crossed a river in the next valley. We hit them like before, but this time we feinted toward their infantry and attacked the scorpions. I wanted them taken out of the fight. We lost men, but most of the fearsome weapons were destroyed. They had left their larger siege weapons and much of the baggage train at the camp to allow the column more speed. Now we only faced their infantrymen and what was left of their cavalry. Amalric and Divico's warriors had thoroughly depleted the auxiliary legions. Our constant attacks and withdrawals never allowed the Romans to mount an effective defense or counterattack.

The legion's tools had been left behind with the baggage train, and there was no castrum the second night. Many of the legionaries simply sat down where they stopped and rolled up in their cloaks, exhausted, thirsty, and cold. Near midnight, the screams of a hundred prisoners pierced the darkness as priests lit the tinder of a wicker man they had built on a hilltop a half-mile ahead of the caravan. From their position in the valley, the orange flames seemed to be floating in the night sky and the screams of the dying reached them on a warm summer breeze that brought a chill to their spines.

By morning, the breeze was cooler and rain clouds hung low in the sky when the few hundred remaining Romans passed the smoking remains of their comrades. They had awoken to discover that their general had deserted them in the night. Silanus had taken his senior officers and what cavalry remained and stolen away into the darkness while his men burned. Rain spattered, then quickened, then began to fall in sheets. The refreshing water seemed to revive them, and they picked up their pace. A shout from the front announced that the Isara River was in sight, and they began to run. The white stone tower built by Ahenobarbus to commemorate his victory over the Gauls appeared in the shadowed valley, surrounded by a pile of rusted and broken weapons and shields; and the men dared to see it as their salvation, knowing that this was where the legion of Gaul was supposed to meet them.

I had deliberately held my men out of sight until that final moment. Just as the Romans dared to hope for their survival, the carnyx blew their mournful wail across the valley. More and more horns joined in, and the sound gradually rose above the noise of the rain. Most of the Romans had cast aside their shields in their headlong flight, even swords and pila. Few still wore their mail or helmets. They were naked to our blades, and like the riders of Wodan's wild hunt, we descended upon them from the hills, determined to kill them to the last man.

Epilogue

The messengers that Silanus dispatched never arrived. No legions came to meet him.

The morning after the final battle dawned clear and bright. In the east, two limestone peaks, each crowned with a circlet of thin white clouds, towered over the long massif that dominated the land. In the shadow of these ancient sentinels, the Cimbri and their allies turned away from their victory, their lust for battle sated. Denied the homeland they sought and forced by the curse that ruled their lives, they turned away from the mountain passes that would have taken them into the fertile valleys of northern Italy and vanished back into the mysterious north.

HISTORICAL NOTES

The village of the salt people is today's Hallstatt, Austria. The region was known for its salt mines for thousands of years before the local mines fell into disuse around 400 BC, probably due to an earthquake that collapsed or sealed off the mines. The mining moved to other locations in the Salzkammergut area, but Hallstatt has maintained a population throughout the ages. Located between the Hallstatter See and the Dachstein Massif, Hallstatt gave its name to the early Celtic Iron Age culture in Europe from 800 – 450 BC. Today it is one of the most highly visited sites in Europe.

The Heuneburg is believed to be the ancient Celtic city of Pyrene, named by Greek author Herodotus. It is located in southern Germany on a large hill above the upper Danube River. Borr passes by the city which fell into ruins centuries before his arrival, and the mound graves of the ancient Celts on his way westward to rejoin his people. There is an open-air museum and reconstruction of the hillfort open to visitors today.

In his work "The Gallic War", speaking of the Aduatuci living at the oppidum of Aduatuca, Julius Caesar wrote, "The tribe was descended from the Cimbri and Teutoni, who, upon their march into our Province and Italy, set down such of their stock and stuff as they could not drive or carry with them on the near side of the Rhine, and left six thousand men of their company therewith as guard and garrison."

Hohle Fels cave is one of the many limestone caves in the Swabian Alps of southern Germany. The cave was formed during the White Jurassic Age over 150 million years ago. Artifacts have been found in the cave that were created by human hands as far back as 40,000 years and the bone flute and rope tool that Borr finds and uses during his recovery are just two of them.

In "Rise of the Red Wolf" Borr sustained several injuries during a bear attack. He is found by a healer who sets his broken bones and treats his wounds. His new friend packs the wound with spider webs to stop the bleeding and then cleans it and stitches it up, placing a poultice of honey and garlic mixed with chewed plantain over it to stave off infection and promote healing. The chemicals in saliva and the crushing of the leaves by chewing activate the plantain's natural properties that also promote healing by drawing out infection and assisting with preventing infection. These are several ancient treatments that were used then and are recognized even today as having actual medical benefits. Honey and garlic are well known for their anti-biotic qualities. Willow bark has salicin in it, a chemical similar to aspirin and was chewed by the patient or boiled to make a tea for pain relief and anti-inflammatory treatment. It could also be applied as a topical treatment to a wound for pain relief by boiling bandages in the willow bark tea. All of these things were readily available in the ancient world. But cobwebs? Who knew? Actually, there is documentation of the properties of blood coagulation by spider webs on Penn State University's website.

The injuries ascribed to the prophet are consistent with the type of injuries received from lightning strikes. Cataracts can be formed over the eyes, and blood vessels bursting from the discharge of electricity and heat can form a Lichtenberg figure on the skin; a pattern of scars that can look like the limbs of a tree.

In the Cimbrian War series I have presented the northern Germanic tribes' religion as an early version of the Norse religion of a thousand years later. What most people might be familiar with thru contemporary media, was a well-developed religion by the time of the Vikings, who came from the same region. All religions change and develop over time, and it was my intention to represent the religion of Borr's time as an early version.

During the second and first centuries BC there was much westward movement across the Rhine. Eastern Celts were pushing against the Germanic tribes of the forest lands, who were in turn invading across the Rhine into Gaul. The Suebi War fought by Borr and his allies is fictional, but this was a time of great conflict and change.

Ice skating has been a part of the human story for at least 5000 years. A pair of bone skates, as described in the story, pulled from the bottom of a lake in Switzerland dated back to about 3000 BC. They are considered to be one of the oldest skates ever found.

In 1878 a sandstone marker was discovered in the forest near the Greinberg Hill at Miltenberg, Germany. Historians still have not deciphered the inscriptions, but it may have served as a historical marker of some sort. Some believe it commemorates the presence of the Teutones. In Rise of the Red Wolf, the marker is placed by Borr's ally Teutobod, chieftain of the Teutones, to commemorate a battle that occurred at this site.

The Rhine Falls is the largest waterfall in Europe, located on the Rhine River several miles past the head of Lake Constance. Formed about 15,000 years ago the falls roar over limestone boulders and around two large sentinels located in the center of the falls as millions of gallons of water a year makes its way from the Alps to the North Sea. In "Rise of the Red Wolf", Borr and the Cimbri cross the Rhine River just above the falls and enter the territory of the Helvetii, a Celtic tribe living at the edge of Gaul in today's Switzerland, as they continue their epic journey in search of a new homeland.

The legend of the Lorelei became widely known with the nineteenth century poems and songs by German composers, but like many folk tales the original story is much older and has been part of the lore of the Rhine River and surrounding area for much longer.

In his "Epitome of Roman History", Florus wrote that the Cimbri sent envoys to Silanus requesting, "The people of Mars should give them some land by way of pay and use their hands and weapons for any purpose they wished." Silanus replied that, "Rome has no lands to give and desires no services."

Florus and Strabo write of the monument erected by Domitius Ahenobarbus and Fabius Maximus on the battle site where they defeated the Arverni and Allobroges at the confluence of the Isar and Rhone rivers. It consisted of white marble stones topped with trophies made of the enemies arms.

In 104 BC, five years after his devastating defeat by the Cimbri and allied tribes, Marcus Junius Silanus was put on trial for his military failure by the people's tribune Gnaeus Domitius Ahenobarbus, the son of the Ahenobarbus who conquered the Arverni and Allobroges at the confluence of the Isere and Rhone rivers near present day Valence, France.

Greek historian Strabo wrote about Silanus' defeat in Gaul, but it is not clear where that defeat took place. Silanus lost an entire consular army, but escaped with his own life, and was acquitted of responsibility at his trial.

Posca was a mixture of vinegar and water seasoned with salt and other herbs. Wine was reserved for the more senior soldiers, but as unused wine aged it turned into vinegar that found its use in the hospital tent for cleaning and wound treatment and in the popular energy giving drink of the common soldiers. It was a cheap alternative and often safer than local water sources.

Sugarcane was cultivated in India by the 5th century BCE. The sugar extracted from the cane was primarily used as medicine in that time and became a valuable trade good to the west via Arab and Roman traders.

Gaius Marius was famed for his stoic courage. The incidence of surgery on his leg is documented in the "Life of Marius" by Greek historian and philosopher Plutarch.

GLOSSARY

MAJOR TRIBES/NATIONS

ADUATUCI – A Gallic/Germanic tribe living in what is today Belgium during the late Iron Age. Fifty years after the Cimbrian War Caesar wrote: "The tribe was descended from the Cimbri and Teutoni, who, upon their march into our Province and Italy, set down such of their stock and stuff as they could not drive or carry with them on the near side of the Rhine, and left six thousand men of their company therewith as guard and garrison." Roman historian and senator Cassius Dio also mentioned that the Aduatuci belonged to the Cimbri race.

AEDUI – A Gallic tribe living in what is today's Burgundy region in France.

ALCIMOENNIS – A Celtic oppidum located on a rocky promontory above the town of Kelheim, Germany.

ALLOBROGES – A Gallic tribe dwelling in the area today known as France defeated by Domitius Ahenobarbus and Fabius Maximus in 121 BC.

AMBRONES – A Germanic tribe whose homeland is unknown but suspected to have been south and west of Jutland. They joined the Cimbri and Teutones years after their journey began.

AMBISONTES – A Gallic tribe centered on the oppidum that was then located at present day Salzburg, Austria

ANGLES – A Germanic people living along the Elbe River at the time of the Cimbri. They would eventually invade the island of Britain, and the later nation of England would be named after them.

ARVERNI – A Gallic tribe dwelling in the area today known as France defeated by Domitius Ahenobarbus and Fabius Maximus in 121 BC.

BOII – A Gallic tribe in Cisalpine Gaul centered around modern-day Czech Republic, Bavaria, and Bohemia. Shortly after the time of this story they moved northward as far as Poland.

CELTS (Kelts) – The Celts migrated into the areas of central and western Europe in pre-Roman times. The term is generally interchangeable with Gauls.

CIMBRI (Kimbri) – An ancient Germanic tribe originating in Jutland, today's Denmark. They were possibly of Celtic descent and combined traits of both cultures. For unknown reasons, the Cimbri nation migrated throughout Europe coming into contact with Rome in the second century BC.

EBRONES – A Gallic/Germanic tribe living in northeast Gaul before the Roman conquest; today's eastern Belgium and German Rhineland.

GAULS – In the second century BC, the area today known as France was known as Gaul and the tribes from that area generally referred to as Gauls, though they referred to themselves as Celts.

GERMANS – The area north of the Danube River and east of the Rhine River was referred to by the Romans as Germania and the tribes from that area as Germans.

HELVETII – A loose confederation of Gaulish/Celtic tribes living on the Swiss plateau during the second century BC.

JUTES – Their origin is unknown, but there is some evidence to support that at the time they invaded England, they came from the Denmark peninsula. They may have been a combination of the remnants of earlier tribes that originated in the area such as the Cimbri and Teutones, and migrating tribes like the Gutones and Charudes.

LINGONES – Another Gallic tribe located in today's northern France.

MARCOMANNI – A Germanic people east of the Rhine and part of the large Suebi confederation.

NEMETES – A Germanic tribe living along the upper Rhine River.

NORICI – A Celtic tribe located in what is today's Austria. Probably the same people as the Taurisci.

RAETIANS – A confederation of Alpine tribes who lived in present-day Tyrol in Austria, eastern Switzerland, as well as northern Italy on the south side of the Alps.

RAURICI – A small Gallic tribe living around today's Basel, Germany during the pre-Roman Iron-Age.

SAXONES – A Germanic tribe living to the north of the lower Rhine. The name may be derived from the seax, the short sword favored by the northern tribes during this time period.

SCORDISCI – A Celtic tribe living in what is now Serbia, Croatia, Bulgaria, and Romania. They successfully resisted Roman incursions for decades.

SEQUANI – A Gallic tribe located in the Doubs River valley and the Jura Mountains during the pre-Roman Iron-Age.

SUEBI – A large confederation of Germanic peoples from what is now Germany and the Czech Republic along the Elbe River. Their members included the Marcomanni, Quadi, Hermunduri, Semnones and Lombards.

TAURISCI – A Celtic tribe that came down from the Alps mountains. They warred with Rome for several years which ended in their status of "Friend and ally of the Roman people".

TEUTONES – A Germanic tribe living south and east of Jutland among the sea islands and rocky shores of the Baltic Sea. They joined the Cimbri on their epic journey throughout the known world.

TIGURINI – A Gaulish tribe, part of the Helvetii alliance, living in what is today southern Germany and Switzerland. Allied with the Cimbri, Teutones and Ambrones to invade Gaul and fight Rome.

TOUGENI – A subtribe of the Celtic Helvetii.

TREVERI – A Celtic tribe living in today's Belgium inhabiting the valley of the Moselle River.

TRIBOCI – A Germanic people living in eastern Gaul, what is now Alsace.

VINDELICI – A Gaulish tribe that controlled the lands west of the Inn River to Lake Constance and Lake Geneva, and south of the Danube River to the peaks of the Alps. They shared a border on their west with the Helvetii.

IMPORTANT PLACE NAMES

ADUATUCA – Fortress of the Aduatuci. Caesar wrote that "Their stronghold was fortified by stones of great weight, sharpened beams, and walls built with manned stations. It was large enough to shelter at least 57,000 people."

ALCIMOENNIS – A Celtic oppidum located above the modern town of Kelheim, along the Danube River in Bavaria, Germany. Settlement of the Vindelici people, a Celtic tribe of Gaul.

AQUILEIA – An ancient Roman frontier city founded in the early second century BC. North of today's Venice.

BOIODURUM – Oppidum of a sub-tribe of the Boii, located at what is today Passau, Germany.

BORREMOSE – Iron age fortress located in present day Denmark near the village of Aars.

CARTHAGE – Ancient capital of the Carthaginians. One of the most important trading hubs in the ancient world and hereditary enemy of Rome.

DONARSBERG – (Donnersberg) The highest point in the Palatinate region of Germany. The name is thought to refer to the Germanic thunder god Donar (the later Thor). A large oppidum was built on the Donnersberg around 150 BC. A part of the settlement's wall has been reconstructed.

GALLIA NARBONENSIS – Roman province in Gaul north and west of the Alps mountains. Today's Switzerland and southern France.

GERMANIA – The geographical area north of the Danube River and from the Rhine River to the Vistula River in the east.

HERCYNIAN FOREST – An ancient forest that stretched from the Rhine River across southern Germany into the Carpathian Mountains and north of the Danube. It formed the northern boundary of the area known to Rome at the time.

HISPANIA – Today's Spain and Portugal.

JUTLAND/CIMBERLAND/CIMBRIAN CHERSONESE – Present day Denmark and the German state of Schleswig-Holstein.

LUGUDUNON – Gaulish name for the fortress at what is now Lyon, France. The Romans renamed it Lugdunum in 43 BC.

LUVAVUM – Oppidum of the Ambisontes tribe located at today's Salzburg, Austria.

MANCHING – A large Celtic oppidum near today's Ingolstadt in Bavaria, Germany. Capital of the Vindelici, a Celtic tribe in Gaul. It was destroyed sometime in the second century BC.

MASSALIA – Greek trading port on the coast of the Mediterranean Sea. Modern day Marseilles.

NOREIA – The capital city of Noricum and the Taurisci people near Klagenfurt in today's Austrian Alps.

NORICUM – Celtic kingdom located in modern-day Austria and Slovenia.

NUMANTIA – An ancient Celtiberian town in Spain near the modern city of Soria.

NUMIDIA – An ancient kingdom located across much of North Africa.

PANNONIA – An area encompassing parts of modern-day Hungary, Austria, Slovenia, Croatia, and Serbia.

POSONIUM – Modern day Bratislava, Hungary. A Celtic oppidum on a hill high above the Danube River.

PYRENE – (Heuneburg) A Celtic fortress city located on the north bank of the Danube in what is now Baden Wurttemberg, Germany. The oldest city north of the Alps, it is enthroned directly above the Danube in a dreamlike landscape. In the Hallstatt period of the 6th century BC, it experienced its heyday as a Celtic trading center with about 5000 inhabitants and is mentioned by the Greek author Herodotus as Polis Pyrene.

SINGIDUNUM – Fortress of the Scordisci that is now the city of Belgrade, Serbia, near the confluence of the Sava and Danube rivers.

TEUTOBERGIUM – An ancient settlement at modern-day Dalj, Croatia where the Drava River meets the Danube. Believed to be founded by the Teutones.

VIENNE – A Celtic settlement at the confluence of the Rhone and Gere rivers occupied for hundreds of years before the Cimbri arrived. Its location was ideal for trade and travel between the Greek colony of Massalia on the Mediterranean coast and northern Gaul. The port was protected by two oppida on nearby hills. It was the only place in the region where the Rhone could be crossed on foot.

WODANWALD – (Odenwald) A low mountain range and forested area east of the Rhine River and along the Neckar River in today's Germany.

ROADS, RIVERS, and SEAS

VIA AURELIA – The Roman coastal road that led from Rome to Pisa. In 109 BC the road was extended to Genoa and then to Placentia by the Princeps Senatus Marcus Aemilius Scaurus.

ALBIS RIVER – The Elbe River rises in today's Czech Republic and flows northward seven hundred miles to the North Sea near present day Hamburg, Germany.

ALCIMONA RIVER – Altmuhl River in lower Bavaria.

DANUBIUS RIVER – The Danube River is the second longest river in all of Europe rising in the Black Forest of Germany and traveling to the Black Sea. It stood as the frontier of Rome for centuries.

DRAVUS RIVER – A tributary of the Danube, the Drava River flows from its headwaters in Austria to Dalj, Croatia.

EN RIVER – The Inn River is also a tributary of the Danube and empties into the great river at Passau in southern Germany.

FLAVUS RIVER – The Tiber River is where Rome sits today.

ISARA RIVER – Located in north central France.

ISAR RIVER – Located in the Tyrolean alps and flows into the Danube.

MAAS RIVER – The Meuse, flowing from Rotterdam in Belgium through France.

ODRA RIVER – The Oder River is the longest river in today's Poland and served as the eastern boundary of the Teutones.

RHENUS RIVER – The Rhine River flows from the Swiss Alps to the North Sea and is one of the major rivers in Europe, second only to the Danube in length.

RHODANUS RIVER – The Rhone River of Switzerland and France.

SAONE RIVER – (Son) The name is taken from the Gallic river goddess Souconna and carries to this day similar to its original pronunciation.

MARE SUEBICUM – Roman name for the Baltic Sea.

MARE NOSTRUM – Today's Mediterranean Sea.

OCEANUS GERMANICUS – The North Sea.

SWABIAN SEA – Lake Constance/Bodensee in Switzerland. The second largest lake in western Europe, after Lake Geneva.

LACUS LEMANUS – Latin name for Lake Geneva, shared by Switzerland and France.

LACUS VENETUS – Latin name for Lake Constance, bordered by Austria, Germany, and Switzerland.

GODS/RELIGION/MYTHS/LEGENDS

Much of what we know of the Norse and Scandinavian religion is found in the Icelandic Poetic and Prose Eddas of the 13th century. At that time this was an advanced, developed religion that had its origins in Germanic paganism. In the Cimbrian War series, set about one thousand years prior to the Viking age, you will see references to the early Germanic beliefs that later developed into the better known Viking age religion.

AESIR – The principal clan of gods in the Scandinavian pantheon, led by Wodan/Odin.

ASGARD – The city of the Aesir.

AUDHUMLA – The primeval cow that provided life-sustaining milk to Ymir, the first frost giant and revealed the first Aesir god, Buri, from the primordial salt block.

BESTLA – Wife of Borr and mother of Odin.

BORR – Mentioned in both the Poetic Edda and the Prose Edda, the Norse legends of gods and creation, Borr is the son of Buri, husband of Bestla, and father of Odin, Vili and Ve.

BURI – The father of all Norse gods and first of the Aesir. Created when Audhumla licked him free of the primordial block of salt.

DONAR – The Germanic thunder god, later known as Thor.

DRAUGAR – An undead creature, usually the soul of a long dead king or great warrior.

FENRIR – The giant wolf-god who would bring about the end of the world by devouring Wodan/Odin and usher in Ragnarok.

GERI & FREKI – A pair of wolves according to legend created by Odin as his companions.

HEL – Goddess who rules the land of the dead. Also name of the realm she rules.

HELHEIM – (Hel) The Norse realm of the dead, presided over by the goddess Hel, daughter of Loki.

JORMUNGANDR – In Norse mythology the serpent who lives in the sea that encircles Midgard and bites his own tail. When it releases its tail, Ragnarök will begin.

JOTUNHEIM – The mythical home of giants and other creatures of Norse mythology.

JUPITER – King of the Roman gods, god of the sky and thunder. Equivalent to Zeus in Greek mythology.

LOKKE – Early Germanic version of the Norse god Loki.

MIMIR – Known as the wisest of the Aesir gods. In one legend Mimir was the keeper of the well of knowledge. Odin sought to drink from Mimir's well to gain supreme wisdom and when Mimir asked him what he would sacrifice for this knowledge, Odin offered his eye.

MUSPELHEIM – The Realm of Fire in Norse mythology. Presided over by Surtr the fire giant, who is destined to burn the fabled city of Asgard during the final battle of Ragnarök.

NJOROR – God of the sea and father of Freya

RAGNAROK – The final battle before the end of the world of gods and men.

RHENUS PATER – Father Rhine, the god of the Rhine River.

SAMHAIN – Pagan festival to mark the end of the harvest season and to usher in the dark half of the year.

SHIP SACRIFICE – Iron age sacrifice to the gods. Weapons and armor were thrown into a ship which was then buried in a bog or sunk into a lake or river.

SKADI – Germanic goddess/giantess associated with hunting, winter, and mountains. Married the sea god Njoror who she later left to marry the sky god Wodan.

SKOL – Borr named his wolf Skol after the warg Skol that chases the sun through the sky each day.

VALHOLL – Wodan's mead hall where he receives the souls of his warriors. Later known as Valhalla.

VILI & VE – Siblings of Odin/Wodan.

WICKER MAN – Ancient Roman historian and author Florus documented human sacrifice of prisoners of war by the Scordisci by burning. Strabo and Julius Caesar document the wicker man as a Druidic sacrifice.

WILD HUNT – A north European myth of the god Wodan and other gods conducting a hunt across the winter sky.

WODAN – An ancient Germanic god of war and king of the gods. Later known as Woden, Wotan and Odin.

YGGDRASIL – The tree of life. The giant ash tree that supports the universe. When Yggdrasil dies, the world of gods dies with it.

YMIR – The first of the frost giants and father to all Jotun who follow.

YULE – Pagan Germanic holiday of the winter solstice, marking the beginning of the new year.

GENERAL

ADHERABAL – Son of Micipsa and grandson of Masinissa. He was a king of Numidia between 118 and 112 BC.

ALE – A type of beer brewed in ancient Europe.

ALPES MOUNTAINS – The Alps Mountains in central Europe.

ARMILLA – A gold, silver, or bronze armband awarded to Roman soldiers for bravery. Often shaped in the likeness of a serpent coiled around the upper arm.

AUXILLIARY – Non-Roman citizens attached to the army as cavalry and other special troops.

BARRITUS – Battle cry of the ancient Germans and Celts.

BATTLE OF NOREIA – Battle between the Cimbri and Roman Consul Gnaeus Papirius Carbo in 113 BC, near modern day Klagenfurt, Austria.

BOAR'S HEAD – A wedge shaped military formation used by the Germanic and Celtic people.

BUCCINA HORNS – A bronze horn used by the Roman army.

BURIAL MOUNDS – Ancient European cultures buried their heroes, kings and other important people in large tombs of rock covered with earth called tumulus mounds.

CALIGAE – The leather shoes/sandals worn by Roman legionaries.

CALTROPS – Iron spikes used to deter infantry and cavalry troops by injuring their feet.

CARNYX – A bronze trumpet used by the Iron Age Celts and Germans. The bell was usually styled as an open-mouthed boar or other animal.

CASTRUM – Roman military camp/fort.

CENTURION – Roman officer. Commander of a century, about 100 men.

CIRTA – Capitol city of Numidia, known today as Constantine, Algeria.

CONSUL – The highest elected official of the Roman Republic.

CORNU/CORNICEN – The brass signal horns used by Roman legions to issue orders and communicate between units.

CURIA HOSTILIA – The Senate house of ancient Rome.

CURSUS HONORUM – The succession of political offices required for a Roman of senatorial rank seeking advancement.

CURULE CHAIR – The official chair used by Rome's highest magistrates.

CURULE MAGISTRATE – Executive officer of the Roman state.

DECIMATION – The practice of punishing severe crimes, particularly cowardice, by having every ten men beat one of the ten to death.

DELPHI – The ancient site of the oracle of Delphi. Located near modern day Greece.

EQUESTRIAN – The equestrian order of ancient Rome was a middle class of citizens who ranked just below the senatorial class. Often served as the Roman cavalry during the late Roman republic.

FRIEND AND ALLY OF THE ROMAN PEOPLE – A status that Rome used to incorporate former enemies or belligerent tribes into the republic, and later the empire, by recognizing their sovereignty and providing defense, while requiring them to pay taxes and be subservient to the Roman senate.

GLADIUS – Sword of the Roman legions.

GRAECIA – The ancient area of, as opposed to the modern nation of, Greece.

HASTAE VELITARES – A thirty-inch wooden throwing dart employed by Velites, the front-line skirmishers used in the republican Roman legions.

HASTATI – Roman legionaries who made up the front rank of the republican manipular legions once the Velites had launched their darts. Usually fought as spearmen.

HELLENES – Name for the Greek people of ancient history.

HIEMPSAL – Son of Micipsa the king of Numidia. He was assassinated by his adoptive brother Jugurtha in his efforts to consolidate power.

HUNNO – The leader of a Germanic clan or tribe that lived in a village or series of villages that made up a district. Also, the military leader of his district, responsible for raising his "hundred" in times of war. The "hundred" was a term used to denote the military unit formed from the Hunno's clan and stems from the fact that it was generally around one hundred warriors that made up the "hundred".

IMPERIUM – A form of authority granted by the Roman Senate that provided the scope of a general's power as well as his military mission, such as removing the German tribes from Noricum.

JUGURTHA – Adopted son of Micipsa, the king of Numidia. Jugurtha killed both of his adopted brothers to seize the throne, and in the process became an enemy of Rome. Jugurtha was defeated by Gaius Marius and eventually killed. He was familiar with Marius from having served together under Scipio Africanus in Numantia.

LEAGUE – A unit of length originating with the ancient Celts and adopted by the Roman world. Generally, about the distance a person could walk in one hour, roughly three and a half miles.

LEGATUS – A high-ranking Roman officer equivalent to a general officer today. During the Republic a Legatus was usually second in command of a Roman Army. In later years a Legatus was in command of a legion.

LEGION – In the Roman republic the legion consisted of 4,200 infantrymen broken down into ten cohorts and 300 cavalrymen broken down into ten turma. Each infantry cohort consisted of four maniples which were further broken down into two centuries, each divided into ten contubernia. At this time the four maniples were organized one as Velites, one as Hastatii, one as Principes, and one as Triarii.

LORICA HAMATA – The Roman mail coat used during the late Republic.

MACEDONIA – Became a Roman province in 146 BC. Rome fought with the Celtic Scordisci and other tribes in the area for control of the mountainous interior for centuries. Corresponds roughly to modern day Macedonia.

MANIPLE – A Roman military unit of 120 men during the late republic. There were four maniples in a legion.

MEAD – An alcoholic drink made by fermenting honey with water, and sometimes adding various flavors by using spices, fruits, or other.

MEDICUS – A physician or combat medic in the Roman army.

MILITARY TRIBUNE – An officer in the Roman army who ranked between the centurion and the legate. Usually the first step on the cursus honorem.

MISSIO CAUSARIA – Medical discharge out of the Roman army.

NOVUS HOMO – Latin for "new man". The term used for the first in a family to serve as a senator or elected consul. Sometimes used by the patricians and old families as a derogatory term for someone up and coming.

NUBIA – A region along the Nile River in Africa, the former kingdom of Kush.

OPPIDUM – A fortified settlement in central Europe during the Iron Age. They were built as far apart as Spain and the Hungarian plain. Hundreds were built during the second and first centuries BC.

PANNONIA – An undefined area north and east of the Danube. Roughly corresponds to parts of present-day Hungary, Austria, Croatia, Serbia, Slovenia, and Bosnia/Herzegovina.

PATRICIAN – A member of the aristocracy of ancient Rome.

PILUM/PILA – A javelin used by Roman soldiers.

PLEBIANS – Free Roman citizens that were not part of the aristocracy. The commoner.

PLEBIAN TRIBUNE – The tribune of the people was an election of a common citizen, who provided a check on the power of the Roman Senate and magistrates.

POPULARES – A political faction led by the Gracchi brothers during the late Roman Republic. They supported the agendas of reforming Rome's policies in favor of the plebeians, or common citizens.

POSCA - A mixture of vinegar and water seasoned with salt and other herbs, drunk by Roman legionaries.

PRAETOR – The commander of an army, or an elected magistrate.

PRAETORIUM – The legion commander's personal tent and headquarters in a castrum.

PRIMUS PILUS – The senior centurion of the first cohort in a Roman legion.

PRINCIPES – Spearmen in the late republican army. Men in their late twenties and thirties. They were in their prime both physically and financially, and could afford better equipment. They fought in the second battle line between the Hastati and the Triarri.

PRINCIPIA – The legion headquarters in a Roman military camp.

PRINCIPS SENATUS – A prestigious office that was awarded to the most respected and capable of Roman senators.

PRO-PRAETOR/PRO-CONSUL – A Roman of senatorial rank who had served as Praetor or Consul the previous year. Usually assigned as governor of a province, or military general. The position was used to extend an individual's authority past the one year they were elected to office.

PTERUGES – A defensive skirt of leather or linen strips suspended from the waists of Roman soldiers to protect the hips and thighs.

SCANDIA – Ancient name for the Scandinavian peninsula that includes present day Sweden and Norway.

SCORPION – A Roman field artillery piece that functioned like a large bow and arrow. It fired bolts as long as a man at high velocity.

SEAX – Usually associated with later centuries, the seax was a small sword, or large knife, also used by the Germanic peoples of the Migration Period.

SIGNIFERS – A standard bearer in a Roman legion.

SPQR STANDARD – An abbreviation for the "Senate and People of Rome". A symbol of not only the legion, or cohort that carried it, but also the citizens of Rome and its policies.

TESTUDO – A Roman military formation where soldiers used their shields to form a tortoise-shell-like protection against the enemy. Especially effective against thrown weapons.

TEUTONENSTEIN – A sandstone marker found in 1878 near the Greinberg, an ancient hillfort near Miltenberg, Germany on the Main River. The inscriptions continue to puzzle historians to this day, but it may commemorate the presence of the Teutones and served as a border marker.

TOGA PRAETEXTA – A white toga with a broad purple stripe on the border. This toga indicated that the wearer was a senator, magistrate or had a special ritual status, for example, they were a priest, or someone charged with tending a shrine. The stripe of the *toga praetexta* was known as the *latus clavus*. The Tyrian purple die was extracted from the murex shellfish.

TOGA VIRILIS – A plain white toga, worn on formal occasions by adult male citizens.

TORQUE – A large neck ring made of rigid metal. Symbolizes the strength and virility of the wearer. Usually awarded for bravery or special action.

TRIARII – The third line of troops in the manipular legions of the Roman republic. They were the veterans, the oldest and wealthiest men in the army and could afford the best equipment.

UTISETA – An ancient Germanic pagan vision quest.

VELITES – The skirmishers in the Roman legions of the republic. They were light infantry and spearmen who carried thirty-inch wooden darts, a gladius, and a small shield. They rarely wore armor as they were the youngest and the poorest soldiers in the legion.

VELLUM – A prepared animal skin that was used for writing in the ancient world. It is scraped thin and manipulated until it is very pliable, then rolled and stored carefully to prevent rot.

VITIS – A centurion's staff made from a grape vine about three feet long. Used for discipline in the Roman army.

A WORD FROM THE AUTHOR

DEAR READERS:

I invite you to join the tribe, and I am asking you for your help.

Thank you for reading book two of the Cimbrian War series, "Rise of the Red Wolf".

A word about creating a self-published book. Unlike being published in the traditional manner by a publishing company, the entire process is on the shoulders of the self-published author. All the costs of publishing are paid up front. Editing, formatting, cover and other art, website, advertising, social media and many other costs are the responsibility of the author. In traditional publishing, the author typically is paid an advance, and these costs are picked up by the publisher. A self-published author receives no payment until the book begins to sell and must cover all costs long before they see any profit.

So again, thank you for buying this book. If you enjoyed it, please help me by taking a few moments to leave a review on Amazon and Goodreads (see below) whether you bought the book on-line or in a store. Reviews on both will help if you have the time. Reviews are the way all books, self-published or traditional, gain momentum for more sales. Many readers buy books based on reader reviews, and the algorithms used by book sellers compound the sales and reviews to sell more books. Comments are always welcome, but you don't have to write anything if you don't want, you can just rate it using the five-star system. A few moments of your time will help me immensely. Thank you for your help!

HOW TO LEAVE A REVIEW

Amazon

- Go to your order detail page

- In the US – Amazon.com/orders

- In the UK – Amazon.co.uk/orders

- Click the "Write a product review" button next to your book order

- Rate the item and write your review and click "Submit"

Goodreads

- Go to Goodreads.com

- Search for the author or book title

- Click on the star rating under the book cover and leave a review

CONTACTS PAGE:

LET'S STAY IN TOUCH!

Click the +Follow button on my Amazon author page.

Follow me at:

Facebook: https://www.facebook.com/JeffHeinAuthor

Twitter: https://www.twitter.com/JeffHeinAuthor

Instagram: https://www.instagram.com/JeffHeinAuthor

LinkedIn: https://www.linkedin.com/in/JeffHeinAuthor

Webpage: https://www.jeffhein.net

Jeff Hein was born and raised in Wisconsin and served in the U.S. Army for twenty years, then returned home to Wisconsin. He is now retired and lives with his wife Dawn and their two lab/shepherd mixes Daisy and Annie, aka Mischief and The Tank.

Jeff writes historical fiction based on ancient writings and modern archeological discoveries. He loves to weave the story together with known facts and plausible fiction that fills in the blanks and could very well have been how things happened, keeping the reader engaged, while staying as true as possible to actual history.

Watch for book three of the Cimbrian War series

"Terror Cimbricus"

coming in 2024.

Made in the USA
Middletown, DE
03 December 2023

43885549R00175